CN00408192

THE TRADI

By

Craig Duncan

This book is a work of fiction. Although some of the objects, places and characters in The Trader exist in real life, the events they are depicted in and the dialogue attributed to the characters are entirely fictional.

No part of this novel may be reproduced, stored, or transmitted in any form or by any means, electronic, mechanical, photocopying, recording or otherwise, without the prior written permission of the author.

First Edition

Copyright © 2018 Craig Duncan

ISBN No.: 9781980494775

For Fiona, Laura & Alex

INTRODUCTION

My name is Bronson Larkin. I'm fifty-four years old and I live in Scotland. I'm a trader. Not a financial trader though. Equities and bonds have never appealed to me. Too abstract. I could never spend my days following the fortunes and misfortunes of companies, speculate on the future value of commodities or track financial indices on a computer screen.

I trade real things. Things you can see, touch and feel. Rare and beautiful objects. Everything from antique jewellery to million-dollar artworks. I've traded classic cars, rare watches, vintage wines and scarce whiskies. I've even traded rare coins and antique furniture.

I've enjoyed a long career buying and selling unique, one of a kind items of very high value. Scarcity, provenance and authenticity are key. I love the chase. Scouring the globe for such items, finding and acquiring them from all types of people. Everyone from crooks and thieves to millionaires and famous celebrities.

I've sold items to a similarly wide and varied clientele. Mostly wealthy individuals who genuinely appreciate rare and beautiful things, though sometimes to rich people who just want to flaunt their wealth. I've sourced items for museums and art galleries that want to draw in crowds to admire their collections and I've even obtained precious items for royalty.

I mostly work on commission, taking a percentage of the sale price as my fee. Sometimes I operate on my own, buying and selling individual items for profit. I'm not an avid collector myself, but I do experience the best of both worlds. I get to see some of the world's most beautiful artworks and hold some of the rarest, most prominent items from history in my hands. I get to touch and feel objects of unimaginable beauty and I get very well paid for doing so.

I was born in 1963, in Aberdeen, North East Scotland, around the time that oil and gas discoveries were first being made under the North Sea waters between the United Kingdom and Scandinavia. Once a provincial seaside town known for farming and fishing, Aberdeen's geographical position made it perfect as a base for companies aiming to get rich from the black gold just off Scotland's shores.

The city enjoyed four decades of rapid growth with the oil boom, which helped create dozens of local millionaires by the end of the 20th century. But not everyone in the area earned an oil inflated income.

I grew up in a tough, working-class neighbourhood. My parents struggled to make ends meet and every penny was a prisoner. I envied the kids I went to school with who regularly went on fancy holidays and always had brand new clothes.

I think this modest early life sparked a fierce desire in me to become rich one day. From as far back as I can remember, I always wanted to build a life of abundance for myself that meant I didn't have to toil the way my parents had. I dreamt of living the good life, having the means to see the world, to drive nice cars and live in a big house.

I left school at seventeen and started work in the oil industry as a structural designer. At school, I'd been pretty good at technical drawing and I flirted with the idea of becoming an architect, but that profession required six or seven years of further education, which I couldn't afford, so when the designer opportunity came along, I signed up and started earning.

My first foray into trading came when my grandfather passed away, leaving his collection of rare coins and some war medals to me in his will. He kept scores of different coins from various countries he'd been in during the second world war and by the early 1980s, collectors throughout the United Kingdom were paying big money for some of the rarer coins.

Through studying books from my local library and by browsing collector magazines, I became an expert on what was selling for the highest prices. I made numerous calls to dealers around the country, using their contact details from adverts in magazines.

I learned I could make a lot more money selling one rare coin at a time than selling many similar coins in one go. I managed to convince dealer after dealer that I only had one example of a certain coin when I really had several and managed to drive up prices by implying scarcity.

I made £800 selling around fifty of my grandfather's rare coins and I learned my first lesson in trading: always create real or perceived scarcity for an item to drive up its price.

My grandfather's war medals were somewhat trickier though. Nobody in my family attached any real sentiment to his medals so there were no issues with my intention to sell them. But, finding a buyer proved difficult. I telephoned museums around the country and struggled to find anyone interested.

Then I caught a lucky break. Some locals were thinking of setting up a new war museum in Aberdeen and they placed adverts in the local newspapers asking for people with any interesting objects to contact them. I figured there might be plenty of folk offering war medals so I wanted to make my grandfather's ones stand out.

I went to a local jeweller where one of my older brother's ex-girlfriends worked and asked her if they had any spare display boxes. She showed me four small velvet lined trays that had previously been used for displaying rings and necklaces. She said that her boss had recently bought larger trays for a new window display and didn't need the four, so she offered them to me for free, just so long as I took her out on a date.

The trays were perfect so I took them and said I'd call her over the next few days, but I never did and haven't seen her since, luckily for me. I then made a display card for each tray and using a calligraphy pen, wrote my grandfather's name along with a description of when, where and why each medal had been awarded, onto each card. I cut out some black and white headshot photos of him and glued them in place, then arranged the medals and cards neatly on the velvet jewellery trays. They looked fantastic.

The museum paid me £200 for the four trays with six medals. A week earlier I couldn't give them away and now I'd cashed in big. I had also learned my second lesson in trading: items that have a prominent history, a famous previous owner or an interesting story, are more desirable than those that don't. I'd made my first £1,000 trading and I was hooked.

I spent the next couple of years buying and selling desirable objects in my spare time, mostly vintage pieces of jewellery, making more money on the side than I did as a full-time designer. Finally, in 1987, at the age of twenty-four, I quit my day job and started trading full time.

Since then, I've spent the last thirty years on a roller coaster adventure, chasing precious collectables. I've travelled all around the world to find some of the rarest pieces. I've hunted down some of the most reclusive and inaccessible people on the planet. I've been in countless scrapes along the way too. I've been attacked, punched, kicked and even shot at. All in the pursuit of the world's most sought-after treasures.

Now that I'm in my early fifties, perhaps I should be slowing down, but this business I'm in is like a drug. The rush of finding a missing Stradivarius or stumbling upon a rare artefact in a random antique shop is exhilarating, and I can't stop.

When I look in the mirror, my grey hair reminds me of my advancing years and that I'm not as physically capable as I used to be, yet I can still find myself in dangerous situations. Like haggling with a New York gangster over the price of a Rolex watch or evading thugs trying to rob me of a valuable painting.

In such situations, I need some back-up. That's where my man Winston comes in. He's my oldest friend, colleague and confidant.

He's a couple of years younger than I am, but he's as scary as hell. A giant of a man with hands the size of shovels. He looks out for me in confrontational situations and I provide him with a good income and a roof over both our heads.

I consider myself to be a very fortunate person. I love my life. Trading has allowed me to travel around the world and has brought me a great deal of wealth, which means I can enjoy a privileged lifestyle, live in a big house and own nice things. But chasing the next trade is what puts a spring in my step every morning. I never know where my next pursuit will take me or who I'll meet along the way.

Sometimes you find the most wonderful people in the most unexpected places. Sometimes you meet a person who will be a friend of yours for life. Then again, sometimes you meet someone who will claim to be your friend, but who will betray you without a second thought. In fact, one such person was about to show up at my house. Someone I'd not seen for a very long time.

ONE

Aberdeenshire, North East Scotland
November 2017

A 1960 Rolls Royce Silver Cloud appeared just outside the entry gates to the driveway of my country house in North East Scotland. The car was one of only three thousand Silver Clouds ever made. It was painted silver and black with whitewall tyres, and it exuded a truly old-world elegance, as its engine idled softly on the road outside my property. Of all the Silver Clouds in the world, only one was ever owned by Marilyn Monroe: this one.

Marilyn had bought it as a birthday present for her third husband, the American Playwright, Arthur Miller. When Miller died in 2005, the car was found in one of the outbuildings on his property in Roxbury, Connecticut, where it had been for over forty years, ignored and forgotten.

The executors of his estate sold it to a classic car collector, who had it carefully restored. Four years later, it was sold at auction for $2,000,000 to a classic car museum in Detroit.

In 2012, a fire at the museum destroyed ninety percent of its car collection. The 'Marilyn' Rolls was presumed to have been lost in the fire, since the owner claimed an insurance pay out for it. The car had never been seen since, until the day it appeared outside my property.

From inside the main house, Winston pushed the button to open the entry gates remotely and the car slowly made its way along the tarmac driveway towards the house. I was in the garage cleaning my own vehicle when I spotted the Silver Cloud gliding along majestically. I quickly buffed off the last of the wax from my SUV and headed over towards the car to greet my guest.

Through the windscreen, I could see the beaming smile of the very rotund Max Van Aanholt, as he brought the car to a stop at the steps in front of the house.

"Bronson, my boy. Has it really been ten years?", he said as he got out of the car.

"It's good to see you, Max", I responded as we shook hands.

"You look amazing, Bronson. Botox?"

"No", I said, laughing, "Not yct anyway. Moisturiscr. You should try it, it really does work."

Max looked at the house behind me.

"Wow, that's some pile of bricks. A trade?", he asked.

"No, I had it built from scratch. This is what I've been working for my whole life. I love this place."

Another car arrived and parked behind the Rolls. A black, late model Mercedes. Max's man, Archie, got out and waved to us. Max's ride home. He too looked at the house, then nodded his head towards me. Archie approved.

"Ready for the trade of a lifetime?", Max asked me.

"Yeah, let's go inside", I replied, then asked, "Is he coming?", motioning towards Archie in the Mercedes.

"Does he need to?", asked Max, raising an inquisitive eyebrow.

Trust is a precarious thing in our business. I smiled to put him at ease.

"Come on, I'll give you the tour."

We entered the house through a pair of ten feet tall oak double doors and Max's mouth gaped open when he saw the grand staircase ahead. The steps were made from Italian marble, the balustrade was polished nickel and the handrails were a dark, brushed steel.

The self-supporting staircase was the centrepiece of the foyer, with a wide base that curved gently upward and narrowed at the top where it joined the first floor. The surrounding walls were oak panelled with period mouldings and ornate cornicing.

Each wall was adorned with portraits of my family and ancestors in swept antique frames, illuminated by steel wall lights. Oak columns were evenly spaced around the sides of the foyer to support the galleried landing on the floor above. The tiled floor was white and grey, with the inlaid gold Larkin family crest incorporated into the floor tiles near the front doors, which is where Max and I stood at that moment.

"It's beautiful, Bronson."

"Thanks", I replied.

I showed him into the drawing room, where Winston was waiting. He offered Max a hot towel, which he took and freshened up his face and neck. He'd been on the road for many hours.

"Winston, you still look fighting fit", said Max.

"Thank you, sir", he replied and left the room.

I led Max through to the dining room, a large rectangular room with a high ceiling and a long mahogany table in the centre.

"Where did you get that?", asked Max pointing at the table.

I explained how I first saw it at Hugh Heffner's Playboy mansion in 2014. Hugh gave me the dining table in exchange for a vintage Porsche I had at the time. That may sound like an unbalanced trade, in Hugh's favour. A classic sports car in exchange for a table? But this table was special.

It was a one of a kind commission, designed and built by Thomas Chippendale in 1776. His client was John Hancock, the president of the Continental Congress, who took delivery of the table, along with sixteen matching chairs, shortly before America gained its independence from Great Britain. Hugh only had the table though. The matching chairs disappeared many years ago.

Max and I walked through the kitchen and family room, then I showed him the bedroom suites upstairs. We took the elevator down to the lower floor where I showed him my gym, movie theatre and swimming pool. We chose a Cuban cigar each from my humidor then went back upstairs to the library.

I could sense Max's excitement as he anticipated finally laying eyes on what he'd spent the last quarter of a century searching for and the reason he had come to see me today.

Winston had lit the open fire in the library. The temperature outside was only a couple of degrees above freezing so the heat from the fire and the sweet smell of burning wood was very welcoming.

I designed this house myself, the main reason for which, was so I could build several hidden rooms into it, one of which was accessible from my library through a secret door, disguised as a bookcase. I walked over to it and Max stood behind me as I gently pressed the front of the bookcase. The secret door sprung out slightly towards us then I pulled the door fully open to reveal a dark space beyond.

I stepped forward into the room and a light came on automatically. I heard Max draw in a sharp breath as he saw what was inside. The small room was only about ten feet long by eight feet wide with a low ceiling height. There was a round table in the middle of the room and on it sat half a dozen very old bottles of wine.

Included in the six, was the world's last remaining bottle of Chateau Laffite 1787. This very bottle of red wine had last sold at auction in 1985 for $156,450, yet it remained unopened. It's been said that, for drinking, even the finest Bordeaux only lasts for around fifty years. So why would anyone pay such a high price for a wine that was bottled two centuries ago?

The reason was that this bottle of red wine had a very famous previous owner. It formed part of one of the greatest wine collections in history and belonged to America's third President, Thomas Jefferson.

Before becoming President, Jefferson had served as the American Minister to France and as a dedicated oenophile, he made frequent trips to Bordeaux in search of fine wines to add to his collection back home. The Laffite's bottle was made of a handblown dark-green glass capped with a seal of thick black wax. It had no label, but etched into the glass was the year 1787, the word 'Lafitte' and the letters 'Th.J.'

Alongside the Laffite, was a bottle of 1787 Chateau d'Yquem, the most expensive bottle of white wine ever sold, which had fetched $56,588 at auction. The others were a Mouton, a Margaux, a 1784 Yquem and a 1775 sherry that had previously changed hands for $43,500. All six bottles had the unmistakeable 'Th.J.' etched markings.

Since their disappearance in the late 1980s, these six bottles of wine had been known as 'The Lost Jefferson Collection' and although valued individually at between $25,000 and $400,000 per bottle, together as a collection this half dozen would be worth over $2,000,000.

Max was dumb struck. He'd been looking for these wines since they disappeared and he had almost given up hope of ever seeing them. He picked up the Laffite and gently rubbed some dust from the bottle in his fingers. He then turned to me and smiled.

"Deal?", I asked.

"Absolutely", he replied, "but first, you have to tell me how the hell you got your hands on these. Then you can have the keys to the Silver Cloud."

"Okay", I said, "let's take a seat back through in the library and I'll tell you all about it."

We left the small anteroom, then lit our cigars and settled into a pair of armchairs facing one another next to the fire. Winston brought through a bottle of whisky on a silver tray, along with two crystal glasses and a small jug of water. He removed the cork and poured two fingers in each glass then left us alone. I poured a small amount of water in mine. Max left his neat.

"Cheers", we said, clinking our glasses together.

"Here's to the fun we've had over the years, playing our unique game of hide and seek", said Max, "The Italian Mafia has an appropriate phrase, you know? 'La Cosa Nostra', literally meaning, 'our thing'."

"Indeed", I replied raising my glass, "Here's to our own thing."

Then I began my tale.

TWO

Berlin, Germany
November 1989

I first met Winston Murchison in the centre of Berlin, on the West German side, in the late Autumn of 1989. He was working as a security guard, sometimes bodyguard and occasional out and out thug, for the owner of an art gallery called Thomas Richter.

Richter's family had come to prominence in the mid 1950's when his father, a retired judge and recently exonerated former Nazi officer, along with Thomas's older brother Gert, bought an old church in a village on the outskirts of Berlin.

They were converting it into apartments to sell on for a profit and when breaking through a wall one day, discovered dozens of priceless works of art, including a Vincent van Gogh and several by the renowned Spanish painter, Bartolome Esteban Murillo.

The paintings had been stolen by the Nazis during World War II and hidden away in the church's basement for over a decade. In all, the Richter family returned twenty-four stolen masterpieces to their rightful owners with help from one of several Monument Men organisations set up after the war to recover valuable works of art and national monuments that had disappeared during the hostilities.

Although the Richter family was praised publicly, art world insiders long suspected that not all the paintings discovered in the church had been handed over by the family.

In 1981, Thomas Richter opened an art gallery in the centre of Berlin, selling works by up and coming German artists, his profits from which were bolstered from time to time by the mysterious re-appearance and sale of numerous valuable artworks previously thought to have been lost in the war.

Unfortunately for Thomas, one of the more famous paintings that he sold to a private collector was outed as being a forgery when the original was put up for auction at Christie's by another seller in London. The auction house had art experts authenticate its painting as the original, which made the buyer of Richter's copy furious.

However, not wanting to admit publicly to the rest of the art world that he had been duped by Richter, the buyer decided to inflict his own measure of justice on the art dealer. One night, after Thomas had closed his premises for the day, he was attacked in the street outside his gallery by two men who beat him with metal bars.

He suffered serious injuries to his face and legs, but his body recovered in time. The Police never arrested anyone, but there's little doubt who was behind it, since the forged painting was smashed over Richter's head during the attack.

In response, Thomas decided to hire someone to keep him and his gallery safe from similar attacks, as he had no intention of converting his business to a wholly legitimate enterprise. He was making too much money.

Richter's younger brother, Bernt, had studied at a University in England, where he took up the game of rugby. Among his team mates was a ferocious and powerful flanker named Winston Murchison. Winston was a six-feet, eight-inch colossus of a man. He seemed to be as wide as he was tall, yet he was deceptively quick for someone his size.

After failing to graduate in political studies, Winston joined the British Army and became a highly successful and decorated soldier. In the summer of 1986, whilst on holiday in the South of France, and as a complete coincidence, Thomas and Bernt bumped into Winston in a bar and the former rugby teammates enjoyed a beer fuelled evening of catching up.

Winston had recently left the army and was on a career break. He had no plans and no ties, and when Thomas offered him a job as his personal security consultant, he accepted without hesitation and moved to Berlin a few weeks later.

Winston, the only son of an English farmer, had been an honest and hardworking young man, but very naïve. His time at University changed all that. His rugby team mates taught him how to drink and, through drinking, he also learned how to fight. Then the army taught him how to drink more and fight better. Soon after joining him at the gallery in Berlin, he guessed that Thomas Richter's business was not totally legitimate. After all, how many art dealers have a need for a bodyguard?

Initially, Winston enjoyed working for Thomas. The money was good and the work was mostly easy, but after seeing how dishonest his employer was with clients, he became wary of Thomas and did not think their working relationship would last forever.

In early 1989, I first encountered Thomas Richter for myself. He was rumoured to be in possession of the 'Dolorosa Madonna, 1665', painted by Bartolome Esteban Murillo. An artworld contact of mine said he'd heard that Thomas's father and brother may have found and kept the Murillo as part of their church discovery as it hadn't been seen since before the war.

I telephoned Richter from my apartment in London and he confirmed to me that he had the painting. I then spent the next few months trying to acquire it from him on behalf of my client, the curator of the Museum of Fine Arts of Seville in Spain.

I made numerous offers for the painting by phone, but Thomas wanted more money than the museum was willing to pay and he wouldn't budge on price. I changed tact with him and moved away from offering cash for the painting until we finally agreed on an alternative. The museum offered Richter three very rare coins in exchange for the painting and he accepted.

The Liberty Head nickel is an American five cent coin, issued in 1913. It was produced in very limited numbers and without the official authorization of the United States Mint. The existence of the coins only became public knowledge in

1920 and were all owned by a former employee of the Mint, named Samuel Brown.

One Liberty Head nickel sold for $100,000 in 1972. No others had surfaced since and I'd never even heard of them until the curator in Seville told me his museum had three of the remaining five coins still believed to be in existence and that it was willing to trade them for Richter's Murillo.

So, at the beginning of November 1989, I flew from London to Berlin with the three Liberty Head nickels in a small velvet pouch safely tucked inside my jacket pocket.

Throughout my twenties, I had frequently been mistaken for David McCallum, the Scottish-American actor who played Illya Kuryakin in the 1960's hit TV show, 'The Man from U.N.C.L.E.'. Like McCallum, I had blond hair with dark brown eyes, a light skin tone with sharp facial features and a firm jaw line.

Based on the number of second looks I got from people in the airport when I arrived in Berlin, I thought either the zip on my jeans was open or 'The Man from U.N.C.L.E.' was enjoying a revival on German TV. I quickly checked my zip as some German students went past me in the arrivals hall. One of the boys stared at me and pointed, but before he could say "Kuryakin", I shot him an annoyed glance and he looked away.

After exiting the airport building, I hailed a cab and settled into the back seat for the ride to my hotel. I'd never been to Berlin before and was looking forward to it. Some friends had told me how liberal the West side of the city was, compared with the Soviet occupied socialist state of East Berlin.

As the taxi stopped at a set of traffic lights, I looked out of the window and saw a tall, bushy haired, bearded man, with bare feet and wearing a woman's summer dress, run across the junction straight towards us. His bizarre appearance startled me and I felt instantly alarmed when he opened the front passenger door of my taxi and climbed in.

The driver shouted at him angrily, but was ignored as the bearded man closed the door and yelled back at the driver in German. The lights turned green and we moved forward.

As we travelled along the road, the bearded man turned to me, smiled, said something in German that I couldn't understand and raised his hands in a kind of apology.

After a couple of blocks, when the taxi stopped at another set of red lights, the strange man jumped out of the cab and ran off down the street. The driver didn't say anything. He just shrugged and shook his head, then we continued onward to my hotel.

Ten minutes later, we arrived at the Hotel Savoy on Fasanenstrasse, West Berlin, just as daylight was starting to fade. I paid the driver, grabbed my bag and got out of the taxi in front of the hotel.

It was a grand old building with an impressive marble frontage surrounding a set of big glass entry doors and a large opaque glass canopy with shiny brass signage.

I stepped onto a welcoming red carpet and went inside to check in. The lobby area was very luxurious with a marble floor, deep red walls and a large crystal chandelier.

I'd read in a brochure that the Hotel Savoy was built in 1929 by the architect, Heinrich Straumer, and was the first hotel in Berlin where each room had its own private bathroom. It had a simple, elegant décor and was one of only a few hotels in Central Berlin that survived World War II intact.

The hotel had quite a history. In wartime, the Japanese embassy in Berlin suffered severe bomb damage and staff were moved into some rooms at the Savoy Hotel, using it as a replacement embassy until 1945. At the end of the war, because the hotel was in good shape, it was used as the British operational headquarters until 1946.

At the beginning of the 1950s it was returned to hotel use and in 1957 its capacity was expanded to thirty rooms. A bar was added as part of the expansion, which in 1984 was named 'Times Bar', and became a classic of the Berlin bar scene. It had its own library and a wide range of Cuban cigars, which made it popular with poets and artists.

My room was on the sixth floor and was very elegant, with a plush grey carpet, cream coloured walls with grey painted panel mouldings and a large comfortable looking bed. The bathroom had pristine white tiling and brass fittings throughout.

My room also had a glass access door that led out to a private roof terrace with views over the city. In all, it was a very stylish and classy base from which to conduct my dealings with Thomas Richter.

I'd eaten on the plane so I wasn't hungry, but felt like having a drink so after a quick freshen up and a change of clothes, I headed down to the bar.

In keeping with the classical décor throughout the hotel, Times Bar was supremely elegant, with wooden parquet flooring and dark walnut panelled walls. Still too early for the pre-dinner crowd, it was quiet when I entered.

I ordered a whisky from a miserable looking barman and settled into a big brown leather armchair next to the library wall full of books. I didn't read or speak German so I didn't bother with a book, but I did check out the wide selection of cigars available on a menu at my table. As I perused the list, I felt some eyes on me from the direction of the bar.

Female eyes.

I looked over and she turned away. She had long blonde hair and a light skin tone. She was wearing a plain white t-shirt, blue jeans and a pair of black, biker style boots. She glanced back in my direction again without looking straight at me.

She had a slightly rounded face and didn't seem to be wearing much makeup. She was cute. I thought she looked younger than me, early twenties maybe and was sitting alone on a bar stool. She then looked straight at me and our eyes met. I smiled politely before breaking eye contact. I looked back down at the cigar menu for a moment or two, then when I looked up she was standing right next to me.

"American?", she asked, smiling.

"British. Well, Scottish actually."

Up close she was beautiful. She had big blue eyes and was taller than she had seemed sitting down. Almost the same height as me: around five feet, ten inches. I could see the barman behind her staring at both of us, he still looked grumpy.

I wondered to myself, when did porn star moustaches and mullet hair styles become such a big hit with the Germans?

"Thinking of home?", she asked.

"I'm sorry?", I replied, then seeing that she was pointing at my scotch, I said "Oh, the whisky. No, I've just arrived here on a plane from London. The drink is to help me unwind. Do you like whisky?"

"It depends. Which one is that?", she asked pointing at my glass.

"Glenmorangie", I replied.

"I've never tried that one."

"Would you like to join me?"

"Yes, okay. I'm Anna."

"Bronson. Good to meet you."

She sat down on the chair next to me and we shook hands, then I looked over towards the barman, who was still staring at us and I motioned for him bring us two Glenmorangie.

His moustache cracked me up.

She spoke English very well, but I didn't think her accent was German, so I asked where she was from.

"Norway. I'm studying here at the University. Art History."

"Really? I'm in the Art business myself. Occasionally".

"You don't look like an artist", she said.

The barman arrived with our drinks, along with some ice and water. I thanked him and he returned to the bar.

"No, I'm not an artist. Sometimes I'm a buyer, other times I'm a seller. It depends on who wants what, who it's by, who has it now and how much it can be bought or sold for. Usually Old Masters, but I find myself becoming more and more involved with contemporary pieces."

"Do you have a favourite?", she asked.

"Yes, I've always loved the work of Henri Matisse. I think his use of colour was sensational. So bold and intense. His 'Woman with a Hat, 1905' is probably one of my all-time favourite paintings. How about you?"

"Auguste Renoir. His artworks are very different from Matisse. I love his nudes and his portraits are so life-like. Have you ever seen Renoir's 'Girls at the Piano, 1892'?"

"No, I haven't."

"It's wonderful. The colours are unusual, almost pastel shades. The outlines of the two girls are so soft, giving the painting a dream-like quality", she said.

"I'll have to check it out some time."

We made eye contact again. She was very attractive.

"How long have you been in Berlin?", I asked.

"Just over a year. I'm about to start the second year of my degree. What about you? Are you here for business or pleasure?"

"Business."

"That's a shame. Berlin's a great city to have fun in", she said, smiling.

"And, I bet you would be a fun person to explore Berlin with?"

"I could be, if I had the right companion", she said coyly.

"Okay, let's say, hypothetically, that I was to be your companion for the evening, where would we go?"

"That's easy, the casino", she replied.

"Which one? Aren't there several in this city?", I asked.

"Yes, but there's a private one at the back of this hotel. That's the one I meant. I think if you're a guest at the hotel you're allowed to go there. It doesn't open until ten o'clock though, so we'd have to find something else to do until then, hypothetically."

"Did you know there's a roof terrace upstairs? My room has access to it. We could go up and take in the view, hypothetically. Maybe you could point out the sights?", I suggested.

"Why not", said Anna, "let's get our hypothetical selves upstairs."

We finished our drinks and walked towards the bar. I asked the guy with the mullet to charge the drinks to my room. 612. Larkin. He nodded and wrote something on a notepad. Anna grabbed her coat, which she'd left on one of the bar stools and we left.

In the lobby, I pressed the elevator call button then we stepped inside when the doors opened.

"Did you try any of the cigars?", she asked.

"No. I couldn't make up my mind between a Montecristo and a Partagas. Do you smoke?"

"Not cigars. I smoke cigarettes sometimes. I know I shouldn't, but when I'm out with my friends, they all smoke so it's difficult not to."

The two drinks I'd had made me feel slightly buzzed when we stepped off the elevator on the sixth floor.

"How long will you be in the city for?", she asked, as we walked towards my room.

"A couple of days, maybe longer, depending on how business goes."

We stopped outside room 612, I unlocked the door and we went inside.

"This is very nice", she said, admiring the surroundings.

"Thanks. Do you like champagne?", I asked.

"Yes, I love champagne."

I walked over to one of the bedside tables and picked up the phone.

"You can get to the roof terrace through that door", I said, pointing to a glass door at the other side of the room.

I watched Anna go out to the terrace as I dialled zero for the hotel reception. A man answered and I asked about drinks so he transferred me through to the bar. I ordered some chilled champagne then took off my jacket and laid it on the bed before going out to join Anna on the terrace.

The evening air was cool with a slight breeze. She'd put on her coat and stood at the edge of the terrace looking out over the city. The sky was dark now and the street lights stretched out before us. Anna pointed out a few landmarks and we could make out a large crowd gathering a few streets away in the distance. I asked her what was going on.

"The wall", she said, "there's going to be another rally tonight. I've heard a rumour the politicians have agreed to bring it down."

I thought about that for a moment. Demolishing the Berlin Wall would be momentous.

"Do you think that will be good or bad for Berliners?", I asked.

"I think it will be good for everyone", she replied and I supposed she was right.

I excused myself and went back inside to go to the bathroom and when I came out, I heard a knock on the door. I opened it up to find mullet mustachio from Times Bar standing there with our champagne on a tray along with two glasses. He still seemed humourless. I invited him in, then he set down the tray on a table and poured.

I thanked him and handed him a couple of Deutsche marks then he left the room. I went back out to the terrace with the champagne and handed a glass to Anna.

"Cheers", we said, raising our glasses.

"This is my first visit to...", I started, then stopped suddenly when something caught my eye.

I saw a reflection in her glass. A glimpse of something moving behind me. I turned quickly and saw through the glass door that the barman had come back into my room. He had his hand inside the pocket of my jacket on the bed.

"Shit!", he was trying to rob me.

I threw down my drink and dashed back inside the room, hearing the crash of glass behind me. The barman threw my jacket towards my face and bolted out of the room, slamming the door behind him.

"Idiot", I said, angry with myself for being so careless, as I opened the door and chased after him.

He was clutching something while he ran, which I figured meant he'd stolen the pouch with the coins from my jacket. He headed straight for the emergency exit at the end of the corridor. The bang of the stairwell door echoed loudly off the walls as he sped through it.

I gained on him slightly as I shot down the stairs after him, leaping one flight at a time, adrenaline and outrage spurring me on.

I reached the bottom of the stairs only a few paces after him, but as he exited the stairwell and ran into the street behind the hotel, he stopped, turned and faced me as I came out of the building.

Then I felt a searing sharp pain on the side of my head as someone punched me from behind. The blow caught me above the temple and I fell to the ground, face down. I felt numb and disorientated.

I blinked my eyes a couple of times and lifted my head. I saw the barman throw the velvet pouch behind me, then he fled down the street and around the corner out of sight.

I made it back up onto my feet and turned to where he'd thrown the pouch.

Oh bollocks, I thought.

There was an enormous, scary looking bloke standing opposite me and I could see he had the pouch in his hand. His back was to the hotel and I stood between him and his escape route to the street.

We looked each other in the eye. It was fight or flight time and I didn't like my chances, but I had to get the coins back somehow.

I'd been in a couple of fights as a teenager, all part of growing up I suppose, but I was no Bruce Lee and this guy was gigantic. He looked alert and ready, but not nervous. I must have been shaking with fear and my head was buzzing from his sucker punch.

His eyes were fixed on me as he moved to put the pouch into his front jeans pocket, but his massive hands seemed to struggle with it. Just as he glanced down to see what the problem was, I reacted.

In a split-second window of opportunity, I aimed a kick at his groin. He was too slow to block or evade my foot and he took a full kick right in the nuts. Then, as his body contorted in pain, I cracked my fist into the side of his head and he fell to the ground. The fight was over.

He was down and hurt, but still conscious, so I didn't hang about. I quickly ripped the pouch from his hand then ran off down the street and around the corner towards the front of the hotel.

I was breathing hard and felt a continued rush of both adrenaline and fear as I ran back inside the hotel and rode the elevator up to my room.

Anna was gone, unsurprisingly. I'd been marked by someone who knew I would be staying at this hotel, on this day and would have the coins in my possession. Anna had been the bait and my stupid male ego bought it.

I stuffed my things into my bag, then went back down to the lobby and walked out of the hotel without looking at, or talking to, anyone.

The street was dark and I scanned left and right, checking to see if the giant was hanging around, but saw no sign of him. I crossed to the other side of the road and jogged down the street until I was well clear of the Hotel Savoy. My head was pounding and so was my heartrate.

I needed to find somewhere else to spend the night, so I hailed a passing taxi, jumped in and asked the driver to take me to any hotel nearby he thought might have a room.

We'd only travelled a few blocks when he slowed to a stop outside a place called Hotel Tiergarten, on Alt-Moabit, in the centre of West Berlin. I paid the fare and got out, quickly checking my surroundings to make sure I wasn't being watched or followed, before disappearing inside the hotel.

It was a small, family run place. I managed to get a room on the top floor and hunkered down for the night. I stayed in my room and took a shower. I checked that the door and window were both locked securely and went to bed, flinching nervously at every slight sound. It took a while before I eventually nodded off and I didn't sleep well.

In the morning, I went out to the street and walked around for a couple of blocks to get my bearings. The sky was cloudy, but it was dry and it felt good to be out in the fresh air. I bought coffee and a pastry from a street vendor then walked on until I found a nearby park.

I took a seat on a wooden bench and thought carefully about whether I should still go ahead with the trade for the painting or cut my losses and run, considering the events of the previous evening.

I'd feared for my life when I was face to face with the huge guy behind the hotel and felt extremely lucky to have made my escape with the coins, unharmed.

Thomas Richter was the only person I could think of that knew which hotel I had planned to stay at, and that I would have the coins with me. I figured he wanted to steal the coins from me and keep the painting too. How devious and deceitful, I thought, as my apprehension turned to indignation and anger.

I decided I needed to meet him, at the very least to let him know I'd figured out he was behind the attempted theft of the coins. I checked my street map then walked the half mile to Richter's gallery, but got the surprise of my life when I saw through the window who was inside with him.

I opened the door and stepped into the small gallery. At the back of the room, there were two men seated at a long rectangular table.

"Good morning", I said.

They both looked up towards me. One of them was short and wiry with receding grey hair. I assumed this was Thomas Richter, whom I'd never met before, since the other person was someone I recognised instantly. It was the giant I'd kicked in the balls the previous night.

The big man stared, but said nothing as Richter acknowledged me.

"Good morning to you, Mr. Larkin."

He stood up and walked around the table towards me, offering a handshake.

"I must apologise for your encounter last night with Winston here."

I ignored Richter's offer of a handshake and looked over at the giant.

"Sorry about kicking you in the nuts, but you shouldn't have tried to steal from me. I hope you're not planning to try again?", I asked.

He held up his hands defensively.

"No hard feelings here", he said, "you beat me fair and square. A bit of a lucky kick maybe. Mr Richter tells me the coins you have are worth a fortune. Maybe it was naïve of you to come to Berlin on your own."

"Yeah, I'm beginning to think that myself."

I looked at Richter.

"So, what now?", I asked.

"Can I see the coins?"

"Where's the Murillo?"

"Come and see", said Richter, motioning that I should follow him toward another room at the back that was in darkness.

"No, I don't think I will. Why don't you bring it out here so I can look at it in natural light?"

He went into the other room alone. I looked back towards the beast.

"Winston, eh? You sound English. What brings you here?", I asked.

"I was in the army, but I'm out now. I met Mr. Richter on holiday and he offered me a job."

"Do you like working for him?"

"It has its good days and bad, just like any job."

"I don't think yesterday was a good day, for either of us", I said.

He nodded in agreement.

Richter returned with the painting, wearing white gloves and making a show of handling it carefully. The canvas was in a wide edged wooden frame that looked brand new.

"Where's the original frame?", I asked.

"These things get damaged, broken from time to time. This is a very old painting, you know?" he said, as if I was an idiot.

I asked him to take the painting out of its frame, which he did then laid it out flat on the table. I looked at it in silence for a long time. The Dolorosa Madonna. The image was beautiful.

A seated woman was dressed in pink and blue robes, wearing a golden headscarf with her arms outstretched, looking towards the heavens. The background was dark, except for a faint hint of light surrounding her head that gave the impression of a halo.

I looked closely at the brush strokes and scanned the whole front surface of the painting. I asked Richter to turn the painting over so I could look at the back and he seemed to hesitate momentarily, before turning it over slowly.

I checked the back, focussing on the corners and my heart sank when I noticed something was missing. The museum curator from Seville had told me that Murillo always scratched his initials in a corner, on the back of all his paintings. There were no such markings on this canvas. With anger rising inside me again, I looked up at Richter.

"This is the second time in less than twenty-four hours you've tried to screw me over."

Winston's head dropped slightly and he looked at the floor, as Richter pursed his lips and thought about a reply.

"You have me at a disadvantage. Please explain what you mean", said Richter.

I did, telling him what I knew about Murillo having marked a back corner of all his paintings. He feigned surprise and looked at the back of the painting himself.

This really pissed me off.

"First you have the Incredible Hulk here try to steal the nickels from me, then you try to pass this forgery off as the Murillo", I berated him.

"Do you think I'm an amateur?" I asked through clenched teeth, pointing at him threateningly.

"Take it easy, Mr. Lark…", he started.

"I don't want to hear it", I snapped, then took a breath, trying to think what to say or do next.

I wanted to pummel him, but figured his paid man-beast would stop me. The room was silent as I fought to regain my composure.

"Let me tell you what I think", I started, "Your forger, clearly has talent. The brush work and colours are perfect and the aging process used has made this copy very authentic looking.

"However, the absence of Murillo's markings leads me to believe that, although your forger was in the presence of the original when he or she made this copy, the original was never taken out of its frame during the process. Hence, the forger missed Murillo's initials on the back corner."

Richter was silent and pensive, which made me think I must have hit the nail on the head.

"Do you have the coins?", he asked quietly.

"Where's the real painting?"

"I know where it is. Please, may I see the coins?"

I paused briefly, then slowly took the velvet pouch out of my jacket pocket, loosened the drawstring and felt for one of the Liberty Head nickels inside. I pulled one out and handed it to Richter.

He took it in his gloved hand and his eyes narrowed as he inspected it. After a moment, he looked up at me.

"Okay. I apologise. I was testing you, Mr. Larkin. I needed to know you were a serious trader."

"That sounds very much like bullshit to me. Do you think I would fly all the way to Berlin if I wasn't serious?"

I snatched the coin back from him.

"Screw you and screw your giant. I'm going back to London."

I turned around and made for the door.

"Wait Mr. Larkin, please", said Richter.

I ignored him, kept walking and nearly had my fingers on the door handle when he called out again.

"Two", he blurted out.

"I beg your pardon?"

"I'll take two coins for the painting."

"Two Liberty Head nickels in exchange for the real painting?", I asked, my eyebrows raised.

We stared at one another for a moment as he and I both did the arithmetic. The last cash offer I'd made over the phone for the painting was $350,000, which he'd declined. Nobody really knew what the remaining Liberty Head nickels were worth, as there were so few left in existence and they'd been out of circulation since the early 1970s.

Two nickels could still be worth anywhere from $250,000 to $500,000, maybe even more. If Richter was willing to take two coins instead of three for the painting, then maybe he had already agreed a price for them with an eager buyer and had a better idea of their current value than I did.

Either way, it sounded like a good enough deal for me, provided I really did get the original Murillo in exchange.

"Yes. Two coins for the painting", he said, "However, the exchange must happen today. My forger has the original, but he is leaving Berlin tomorrow. I will telephone him and arrange for him to meet you. You and he can then exchange the coins for the painting."

"Where and when?", I asked.

"I will arrange it. You will meet him in a bar near the wall. It's called Prost. He will be there at four o'clock this afternoon."

"You won't be there?"

"No", he didn't offer any explanation.

"You're crazy. Do you think I'd make the exchange in a bar, on my own, after you've already made two attempts to try and cheat me? No chance."

Richter thought for a moment.

"Winston will go with you. He will make sure the deal goes ahead as agreed", he offered.

Winston and I both raised our eyebrows.

"He punched me in the head last night. How do I know he won't take another shot?"

"Mr. Larkin, you and I may have gotten off to a bad start, but I am a business man. This deal is very lucrative for both of us. I promise you, Winston will do nothing except make sure the trade is completed properly."

This was Richter's final attempt to persuade me. I looked at Winston, who nodded.

"Okay, deal. But he comes with me right now. I'm not spending another minute in this city without someone having my back."

"As you wish", said Richter, then Winston picked up a jacket from the back of one of the chairs.

"Four o'clock at Prost, near the wall. What does your forger look like?", I asked.

"Don't worry about that, Mr. Larkin, my forger will find you inside the bar. You and Winston will not be hard to spot."

"What does that mean?", I looked at Richter inquisitively.

"You'll see. Goodbye Mr. Larkin. I doubt we shall ever see each other again."

I certainly hope not, I thought. Winston nodded at Richter then the two of us left the gallery together.

THREE

As soon as we entered Prost, I realised exactly what Richter had meant. I thought for a moment that we'd stepped back in time to the late 1970s. The bar was packed full of braces wearing, bomber jacketed, bovver booted skinheads. Scores of young hooligans, male and female, some with tattoos of Nazi slogans and Swastikas.

They were all watching a football match on television and roaring furiously. Winston pointed towards a table in the corner away from the TV.

"Take a seat over there and I'll get us a couple of beers", he said.

I went to the table and sat down with my back to a wall so I had a view of the whole place. There were blue and white striped football shirts, flags and other sporting memorabilia on the walls.

A couple of guys were playing pool at a scruffy looking table off to one side and there was a well-used dart board in another corner of the bar. It wasn't the classiest of establishments.

Winston came back with two huge jugs of lager. I drank half of mine in one go, which made him smirk.

"Nervous?", he asked.

"Yup. I feel uncomfortable in here. I hope you'll do as Richter promised and look after me if there's any trouble."

"We'll be fine", he said, looking unconcerned.

The football team the skinheads were supporting scored a goal and they all went bonkers. People were bouncing up and down, screaming in triumph as their team went ahead. I felt a little intimidated being surrounded by this group of drunken lunatics, especially if the game turned in the other team's favour. I hoped we wouldn't be there for very long and said so to Winston.

We made small talk for a while and he seemed like a nice enough bloke. He said he had done some things he wasn't proud of under instruction from Richter and that maybe, after our altercation the night before, the time had come for him to move on.

I apologised again for kicking him in the balls and punching him in the head. He waved off my apology, saying it was his own fault. He felt he'd carelessly underestimated me and had paid the price.

I excused myself to go to the toilet and felt self-conscious as I walked through the bar. It was half time in the football match and the skinheads had diverted their attention away from the TV.

I went into the men's room and saw someone bent over throwing up in one of the cubicles. It was gross. I took a leak and finished up quickly, wishing the forger would show up so we could get the hell out of this place.

I washed my hands, but there were no paper towels so I dried them on my jeans and left. However, when I opened the door, a skinhead girl was right in my face at the threshold.

She looked about eighteen. She had very pale skin with tattoos on her neck and down her arms.

"Hello, English. What are you doing in here?", she asked in a stern, almost combative tone of voice.

Here we go, I thought.

"I'm having a beer. And I'm not English, I'm Scottish", I replied.

"What's the difference?", she asked.

"Well, we Scots are content not to overstate our importance in the world. Whereas, the English think they rule the world."

"Buy me a drink", she demanded, but with a smile that had replaced the sternness.

"Sorry, no. I have to get back to my friend."

"The big man? He has someone else with him now, sitting in your seat."

I looked over her shoulder towards Winston and could see what looked like a teenager sitting beside him.

"I have to go", I said calmly and stepped past her.

"Your handsome, you look like Kuryakin", she called after me.

"Oh, for God's sake", I sighed and walked back over to our table.

"This is Rob", said Winston. "He says he's the forger's cousin. He's English, from Bristol and says he's over here with his parents, visiting his dad's family."

I looked at the boy. He looked very young, maybe sixteen.

"Good to meet you. Where's your cousin?", I asked.

"He's close by. Come on, I'll take you to him."

Rob led us out of Prost and we followed him down the street for a bit, then crossed the road. We walked on for about another hundred yards, then turned a corner into a large expanse of scrub ground, at the far end of which, was the iconic Berlin Wall.

I'd seen the wall before on television, but I felt awestruck seeing it in person. The guarded concrete barrier had physically and ideologically divided East and West Germany since its construction in the 1960s. It was about fifteen feet high and covered in colourful graffiti.

The whole area was filled with groups of tourists and protesters. There were some small bonfires and it looked like some people had been drinking. A lot. There was some singing too and there was a kind of party atmosphere, which made me think of Anna's comment from the previous night about its possible demolition.

Rob led us towards a less crowded area next to the wall and I spotted a guy who I assumed was the forger, standing with his back against the wall, looking in our direction.

He seemed about my age, mid-twenties. He was skinny with short dark hair and was holding a cardboard tube about two feet long, just the right size for a rolled-up painting. I guessed the original frame wasn't going to be part of the deal.

As we got closer, I noticed he was standing awkwardly. The way he'd positioned his body seemed like he was trying to cover up something behind him. When we arrived next to him, his teenage cousin shoved him aside and pointed at the wall behind.

"What do you think of my handiwork?", he asked.

Rob had an exuberant confidence about him that teenage boys often have. A sort of naïve belief that he was invincible.

Winston and I were stunned by what we saw. The teenage Rob had painted a graffiti image onto the Berlin Wall that would surely outrage those who saw it.

The image was of a young boy wearing a striped t-shirt and a pair of shorts, who was depicted urinating on the unmistakable, uniformed figure of Adolf Hitler lying on the ground below him. It was a perverse and shocking picture.

"Are you insane?", I asked Rob.

He just smiled proudly and introduced us to his cousin, seemingly oblivious to how provocative and inflammatory his graffiti image was.

I wanted to get the deal done and get the hell out of there. I looked at the forger.

"Let's see it then", I said to him.

He looked around furtively then pulled the rolled-up painting out of its cardboard sleeve and handed it to me. I unfurled it and inspected it closely, holding the painting at several different angles in the fading daylight.

After a moment, I turned it over and checked each of the corners on the back. I spotted a tiny set of Murillo's initials on the top left corner and breathed a sigh of relief.

Then suddenly, there were raised voices coming from somewhere in the distance and the four of us looked back toward the street we'd just come from. I quickly rolled up the painting and held it in one hand, then reached inside my jacket pocket with the other.

The forger turned to me and was about to ask me for the coins when I tossed the velvet pouch up in the air for him to catch. He grabbed it out of the air, then loosened the drawstring to check what was inside. He took out both coins and inspected them, then returned them to the pouch. I'd already put the third coin in my jeans pocket earlier.

Winston nudged me.

"We've got trouble", he warned, but looked calm.

I looked beyond him and saw the skinhead girl from the bar coming straight towards us. It looked like she'd brought all the other skinheads along with her. She raised her finger, pointed towards me and shouted something in German.

The others quickened their step beside her and were within ten feet of us when the biggest skinhead, now at the front of the mob, eyeballed me.

"Give me the fucking painting, English", he demanded.

"I'm not Engli…", I started, then looked at the forger, who had moved back to the wall in front of his cousin's mural to try and hide it from the Nazi skinheads.

"Give him the tube", I instructed him.

The forger threw the tube over to the big skinhead who caught it.

"The coins too, where are they?", grunted the skinhead.

Upon hearing this, I realised immediately that Thomas Richter had set me up yet again.

"Time to go, Richter has screwed us all", said the forger who must have reached the same conclusion.

Both he and his cousin then sprinted off, revealing the image on the wall of the boy pissing on Hitler.

Winston looked at me, suddenly alarmed.

"Run" he said.

Then he smashed his oversized fist into the big skinhead's face. The guy's nose exploded with blood and he yelped like a wounded dog as he crumpled onto the ground. Winston and I darted off at full speed before any of the other skinheads could react.

After a couple of hundred yards, we slowed a little and looked back in the direction of Rob's mural to see that a large crowd of onlookers had gathered around it.

Thankfully for us, the crowd was impeding the skinheads trying to pursue us. They didn't seem to know who to chase after. Me and Winston, or the forger and his cousin.

We'd fled in different directions and they couldn't know which of us had the coins. They would assume the painting was inside the tube, which the big guy writhing on the ground in agony had in his possession. However, I'd slipped the rolled-up Murillo inside my jacket when we heard the shouting from the street. I now had the painting tucked under my arm as we ran.

With a healthy gap between us and the mob, Winston and I lost sight of them as we turned a corner and within a minute we felt well clear of them, so we slowed down to a walk.

After a few more streets, we seemed to be back in a more commercial part of the city. Winston spotted a cab and hailed it for us. We jumped in and he told the driver a destination in German. I sat down as the taxi set off and glanced toward Winston beside me.

"That was close. Your boss is some piece of work. Still thinking about finding a new employer?", I asked.

"That seems more likely now", he responded.

"Why don't you join up with me for a while?"

"Let's get out of here and we can talk about it."

We sat in silence as the cab ride put more distance between us and the mayhem at the wall.

I replayed the past twenty-four hours in my wind. It was my first and thus far only visit to Germany and I'd just about managed to get out of there with both the painting and my head intact, but it had been close.

Who would have thought that a simple exchange of a painting for a couple of rare coins could turn out to be so dangerous? Was this still the right business for me to be in? I wasn't sure.

After spending a second nervous night at the Tiergarten, I met Winston for breakfast in the hotel's restaurant and we discussed what to do next.

Winston told me he'd decided to ditch Thomas Richter and asked me about what I did, where I lived, where he could live in London and what work I would want him to do.

I told him he could rent my spare room if he liked and that I could use his help with odd jobs and errands here and there, maybe occasionally he could join me for a trade to watch my back and look menacing to intimidate the other party. Nothing too heavy.

He said it sounded okay to him and he accepted. We flew back to London together later that day and Winston has been my friend, bodyguard and trusted companion ever since.

FOUR

From my recollections of the teenage Rob's crazy mural on the Berlin Wall and those of many similar provocative images that have appeared on buildings throughout the world since, there's no doubt in my mind, that he later became the political graffiti artist or part of the group known as Banksy.

I often mused that if more of his unique artwork had been transportable, saleable to the highest bidder, perhaps our paths would have crossed again. I think I would have done well trading Banksy's art over the years. A missed opportunity.

Still, I had returned from Berlin with one of the three Liberty Head nickels still in my possession, which was a hell of a bonus considering its worth.

Within a few days of our return to England, Winston and I met the museum curator from Seville in the cocktail bar at Claridge's hotel in London's Mayfair. He was accompanied by two colleagues who quickly verified the authenticity of the Murillo painting and then the curator handed me a cheque for my £35,000 fee.

We all enjoyed a boozy lunch as Winston and I took turns telling them all about our Berlin adventure. Then I told the curator I had a surprise for him. I pulled out the one remaining nickel from my jacket pocket and laid it on the table in front of me. The Spaniards fell silent and looked puzzled.

"It turns out, these must be worth much more than we originally thought", I said and slid the coin over to the curator who picked it up.

Winston and I watched his reaction.

"He took only two coins for the painting?", asked the curator.

"Yes."

"Incredible."

"Well, he'd been kind of an asshole to me, so I threatened to abort the deal and we came to an alternative arrangement. In fact, I also ended up poaching Winston from him, so I think I've had a successful trip", I smiled.

"Why didn't you keep the coin and sell it yourself?", asked the curator.

"I think that would have been dishonest of me and I wouldn't want to ruin the relationship I have with you. Maybe you'll need my help again in the future."

"Very admirable, Mr. Larkin. You're a gentleman."

"My reputation is an important factor in my business."

He looked at me and seemed to be contemplating something.

"I have an idea", he said, "My sister owns a specialist business right here in London. Please allow me to arrange a gift for you."

"What kind of business?", I asked.

"She's a perfumer. She blends the world's rarest and most extraordinary natural ingredients to make bespoke fragrances for men and women."

"My own fragrance?"

"Yes, why not? Go and see her. I will tell her to expect you and I will ask her to send the bill to me."

"That's very generous. Thank you. Where will I find her?", I asked.

"Her store is named 'Ylang Ylang'. It's on Oxford Street", he replied.

"Ylang Ylang?"

"It's the name of a Madagascan plant used in perfume making. My sister's name is Lydia. Go and see her, I think you will like it. Please accept this gift with my complements", he said.

"Thank you, I will."

"Oh, and this lunch today is on us. Our museum and I thank you very much for the Murillo, Mr. Larkin. And for the nickel", he said.

Winston and I then stood, said farewell to the Spaniards and left.

FIVE

A few days after the lunch at Claridge's, I found the perfumer's phone number in London's yellow pages, then called and made an appointment to go and see her. I chose a weekday so I wouldn't have to battle the Saturday crowds on Oxford Street.

I took a black cab from my Kensington apartment. Winston stayed behind. He still had some unpacking to do. I didn't know what to expect. The only bottles of cologne I'd ever owned were brand names bought from department stores, usually by my mother or a girlfriend, then given to me as a birthday or Christmas gift.

The cab driver had never heard of the place, so I had him drop me in the middle of Oxford Street and I took a leisurely walk around, window shopping on that most famous of streets, until I found it.

It looked a very unassuming building from the outside. No big, colourful signage. No ostentatious window displays. A plain exterior, with a number on the door and the store name, Ylang Ylang, in subtle black lettering on its main window. I opened the door and went inside.

I entered a beautiful wainscoted reception room of about twenty feet square with a hardwood floor. The lower half of the walls were panelled in a very dark stained wood, with the upper half painted a light grey colour. There were some commercial artworks hung up around the room, a few framed Pablo Picasso and Salvador Dali prints, as well as silver antique wall sconces that gave the room a gentle ambiance.

A dark wooden counter was located at the far side of the room flanked by a door at either side. I spotted a scented candle burning on the countertop, which filled the room with a wonderfully sweet aroma. A good first impression for a perfumery.

Behind the counter, stood a woman of about forty with dark, pulled back hair wearing a black dress and spectacles. She looked up and smiled at me, welcomingly.

"Good morning. You must be Mr. Larkin", she said, with a very soft Spanish accent.

"Yes, Bronson. I think we spoke on the phone."

"We did. I'm Lydia. It's nice to meet you Mr. Larkin. My brother has told me so much about you. Welcome to Ylang Ylang."

"I had no idea this place was here. I must have walked past your perfumery countless times, without ever realising it."

"We like to maintain a low profile. I've never liked gaudy advertising and so far, thankfully, it hasn't been necessary. Most of our new business comes by way of recommendations from existing clients. Are you ready for your consultation?", she asked.

"Sure."

"Please follow me, then", she said and led me through the door to the left of the counter.

It was like entering another world. We stepped into a large room around fifty feet long, filled with natural light streaming in from above through a pitched roof with metal framing that held big rectangular glass panes.

The vast room was filled with rows of wooden glass fronted cabinets, which themselves contained bottles of all shapes and sizes, containing liquids in many different colours. There were two other women in the room busying themselves with bottles and clipboards.

"Would you like some tea, Mr. Larkin? I'm afraid we prefer not to offer our clients coffee. Such a powerful aroma can affect the senses. We wouldn't want to create the wrong fragrance for you", said Lydia.

"No tea for me, thank you."

"Let's get started then, shall we?"

She led me to the far end of the room, past all the cabinets and through a further door into a small office. She sat down behind a large desk and offered me the chair opposite. There were about a dozen small bottles of liquid on the desk in front of her, separated into four groups. A pile of fragrance tester strips was placed neatly next to each group.

"First, we must find your preferred fragrance family", she said, "Please put this on."

She handed me a blindfold, which I placed over my eyes and tied round at the back of my head.

"We have four fragrance families that we use for men: fresh, floral, oriental and woody. A person is usually drawn to one of these as a predominant preference. You may have several different bottles of cologne at home, but it's likely that they all come from the same family."

I heard her come around to my side of the desk and a few seconds later she offered me the first scent to smell on a tester strip. She didn't say which family she had started with, which I suppose is the purpose of a blind test.

She had me try samples of all four families in turn, including different scents from the same family, while stating a number from one to four for each sample, then we repeated this twice before she asked me to take off the blindfold.

"Now then. One, two, three or four. Which one did you like the most?", she asked.

"Three", I replied without hesitation.

"That's woody. A very masculine fragrance base. Now let's have some fun with blending", she said and we went back through to the large room with all the cabinets.

The next four hours went by in a total blur. I must have tried over a hundred different ingredient blends and by the end my head was spinning. Several times I had to take a break to give my senses a rest until I finally settled on a scent with a sandalwood base, blended with lemon, vanilla, bergamot and cinnamon.

Lydia then asked me how I wanted my fragrance packaged. She offered several different bottle sizes, colours and shapes. There were countless labelling options too and I even had to choose between an atomiser spray or a screw top. Everything was customised.

She also said my package would include a refillable, travel size atomiser spray and various sizes of scented candle for use in my home. Lydia also explained that my bespoke cologne would be made in a large batch and I would receive fifty bottles that should last around twenty-five years.

"How much does all this cost?", I asked.

"My brother gave me a budget of £10,000 for you."

"£10,000?"

I was stunned and didn't quite know what to say.

Lydia smiled knowingly at my shock, as if she'd seen this reaction many times before.

"We use some of the rarest ingredients in the world, many of which are very labour intensive and therefore, expensive to obtain. Hence, the cost", she said, by way of an explanation.

"Would you like to give your fragrance a name?", she asked.

"I've no idea. How about you just put my name on the bottle."

"Very well."

Lydia told me my fragrance would be ready in around ten weeks. She promised to deliver it to my home when it was ready, so I wrote down my address for her.

I thanked her, we said goodbye and I left, making a mental note to send her brother, the museum curator, the mother of all 'thank you' letters.

I couldn't believe he'd gifted me a bonus worth £10,000 for returning one of the coins. It was truly incredible and I felt very grateful.

Back out on Oxford Street, with my senses starting to recover in the fresh air, I'd only walked ten paces or so when a man in a dark suit stepped right in front of me, blocking my way.

"Mr. Larkin?", he asked.

"Who wants to know?"

"Our employer would like to ask for your help with something", he said, nodding his head behind me to another man in a similar suit who was blocking my retreat.

Right at that moment, a long dark Audi, possibly an A8 model, pulled up alongside us at the kerbside and the first man motioned for me to get in. I hesitated and stood where I was, then he tried to persuade me.

"If we were going to hurt you in some way, we'd have done it by now. Please join us in the car. My employer has a job offer for you. I think it will be worth your while."

If only I'd had Winston with me, I thought. I glanced beyond the man facing me, looking for any kind of help from a member of the public or an escape route, but both men were too close and I knew I wouldn't be able to evade them.

Without much of a choice, I gave in and moved towards the car, the man behind me opened the rear door and I got inside. I sat in the middle of the back seat and the two suits joined me, one on either side. Only a driver was in the front. He put the car in gear and we eased away from the kerb joining the rest of the busy Oxford Street traffic.

"Where are we going?", I asked.

"To meet our employer", came the reply and I thought for a moment I was in a James Bond movie.

I didn't bother asking anything else and stayed silent as we travelled slowly through the heavy London traffic. The car headed west onto Regent Street, then south for a block or two, before turning west again onto Hanover Street. We seemed to be heading back towards my apartment.

Sure enough, the car turned left at Hanover Square going south onto St. George Street, then right on Maddox

Street and onward to Grosvenor Street. We continued west through Park Lane and Knightsbridge and I gazed out of the window as we drove past Hyde Park on our right.

We were within a few streets of my home, which puzzled me, but then at the end of Kensington Road, the car made a right turn onto Palace Avenue and I felt my heartrate quicken as I realised where they were taking me.

The car made a final right turn and slowed as it approached a pair of gilded metal entry gates. The gates were open and a guard waved us through. We travelled straight ahead for several hundred yards, then passed a white statue of a seated Queen Victoria, before coming to a stop in front of an enormous red brick baronial mansion.

It was Kensington Palace. The home of the Prince and Princess of Wales.

I felt immediately nauseous with nerves. I had no idea why I was there or who I was there to meet. The three of us exited the car and the vehicle drove off in the direction we had come from. I took a deep breath.

I was led inside through a main door into a large reception area at the front of the building by one of the suited guys, with the other following closely behind me. We walked through several red carpeted hallways with high frescoed ceilings. Oil paintings and royal family portraits in large gilded frames adorned the walls. My eyes darted everywhere at once as I tried to take in my opulent surroundings.

Finally, we went into a large stateroom where a man sat at an antique desk by an open fire and raised his head as we entered.

"Good afternoon, Mr. Larkin", he said.

"How do you know my name? Who the hell are you?",
I asked, utterly bewildered.

He nodded at the two suits who disappeared back
through the door and I was left alone with the man at the
desk.

"My name is Sir Philip Rathbone. I am the Principal
Private Secretary to their Royal Highnesses, the Prince and
Princess of Wales", he replied.

My mouth suddenly felt dry.

"And, what do you want with me?", I asked.

"His Royal Highness, the Prince of Wales, would like
your help."

"With what?"

"He'd like you to acquire something for him. A rare
item that he would like to give as a birthday present to a very
close friend of his."

"Why me? Don't you have the resources to just go out
and buy whatever the Prince wants?" I asked, confused.

"Ah, were this a simple errand, Mr. Larkin, that would
be so."

"But?", I enquired, eyebrows raised.

"A request such as this, requires a professional who
operates with the utmost discretion. There are people we've
used in the past for similar services, but I'm afraid not all of
them have been able to keep from bragging to their friends,
family members or the odd tabloid newspaper. You were
recently of some service to the Museum of Fine Arts in
Seville were you not?"

"Yes."

"I've been informed that the museum's curator was
very impressed by your integrity, your sense of honesty.

Something about you returning a rare coin when you could have kept it for yourself? His Royal Highness would be very grateful for your help in this matter and I can assure you, sir, you will be very well compensated", said Rathbone.

"What does he want me to get for him?", I asked nervously.

"A very old, one of a kind piece of jewellery. A white gold diamond brooch made by Van Cleef & Arpels in 1908. A bespoke piece, commissioned by a man called Arthur Edward Capel, which he gave to the love of his life. The woman he was having an affair with behind the back of his friend, a young French ex-cavalry officer by the name of Étienne Balsan.

"The woman had been Balsan's own mistress, but she and Capel fell in love soon after Balsan himself introduced them to one another. Her name was Gabrielle Bonheur Chanel. Otherwise known as...."

"Coco Chanel", I muttered.

"That's right, Coco Chanel.", said Rathbone.

"Why does the Prince want that specific brooch and who does he want to give it to?"

"I'm afraid, I can't tell you that, Mr. Larkin. I can tell you that it is made of twenty-four carat white gold in the shape of a butterfly with over fifty, small, round one carat diamonds on the wings and body."

"Value?", I asked.

"Today, it's thought to be worth about $500,000", he replied.

I reeled slightly at the amount.

"Who has it, and where?"

"That's part of our problem, Mr. Larkin. We have absolutely no idea."

Great, I thought, then he continued.

"One of Chanel's unofficial biographies includes a lot of detail about her affair with Capel. It mentions the brooch and that it was one of the first gifts he gave her early in their relationship. In the book, the author describes it as 'a token of love in an illicit affair'. Very romantic."

"Who wrote the biography? Do you have a copy of it?"

"Yes, we have a copy. The author's name is Eleonore Chevalier, but we think that's a pseudonym. The book's introduction mentions something about the author being a seamstress friend of Chanel's and that the pair socialised together around the time Chanel met Balsan and Capel."

"How long do I have to find the brooch?"

"The Prince needs it by early July", replied Rathbone.

It was January 1990, so that gave me about six months to find it.

"I'd need an expenses budget for tracking it down, then sufficient funds for acquiring it from its current owner. Then there's my fee on top of that, of course", I said.

"Of course," repeated Rathbone. "His Highness is willing to pay you a retainer of £20,000 up front, to cover all your investigative expenses. We can discuss a purchase price once you've found it. The Prince is willing to pay you a fee of £50,000 for your services. Would that be acceptable, Mr. Larkin?"

"Yes. That's very generous", I said, smiling, "When do I start?"

"I think you just have", he replied.

He wrote me a cheque for £20,000 and the suits reappeared at the door to collect me. I shook Rathbone's hand and he gave me a card with his contact details. He then reached into a desk drawer and withdrew a copy of the biography, which he handed to me.

"Good luck, Mr. Larkin. The Prince is counting on you. Please keep me appraised of your progress. I would appreciate a regular phone call from you to keep me updated and, of course, your discretion is of the utmost importance", he said, raising an index finger to his lips in a 'keep it quiet' gesture.

"Understood", I said then left the room and the two suited guys escorted me back out to the front of the palace.

The same Audi that took me there was waiting outside the building when we came out. One of the suits opened the rear door and invited me to go inside, but I declined, saying I'd rather walk back to my apartment on foot to take in the fresh air. This was fine with them and we parted company.

When I arrived back at my apartment on Phillimore Gardens, Winston was sitting on the couch in the lounge, drinking a cup of tea.

"How did it go?", he asked, meaning my visit to the perfumer on Oxford Street.

"I've had an interesting day", I replied slumping into an armchair opposite him.

"Kettle's just boiled if you fancy a cup?"

"No thanks. Go and get your jacket Winston, we're going to the pub. We'll both need something stronger than tea when I tell you what our next gig is."

We left the apartment and went down the stairs.

"What do you know about Coco Chanel?", I asked, on our way out.

"I know she was a French fashion designer. I think she's dead now though", he replied.

Then after a brief pause.

"Are we going to Paris, boss?", he asked.

"It looks very much like it", I replied and off we went to our local pub.

SIX

A month later, Winston and I flew from London to Paris. I'd booked us a single room each at the Ritz Hotel, a stone's throw away from the Van Cleef and Arpels flagship store on Place Vendôme.

After bringing Winston up to speed about my being accosted on Oxford Street and taken to Kensington Palace, then my meeting with Sir Philip Rathbone about acquiring the brooch for the Prince of Wales, I waited for the £20,000 cheque to clear, then went to work.

Winston and I took turns reading Chevalier's book from cover to cover, as well as what felt like every other book on Chanel in existence, after which we had assimilated little more information about the brooch than what Rathbone had already told me.

The first plan I came up with was to find the author, Chevalier, and see what he or she could tell us about the brooch. I called the book's publisher and asked about the author, but got nowhere. Over the phone, they confirmed that Eleonore Chevalier was an alias, but wouldn't reveal the author's real name.

The person I spoke to said they'd only ever published one book by Chevalier, the unofficial Chanel biography, back in 1954, more than thirty years ago. They did, at least, tell me the author was a woman, but that they had stopped paying royalties long ago. They said the book had been out of production for many years and that they didn't even have current contact details for its author, their client, on file.

They figured that to have been a teenage friend of Chanel around 1908, the author could be nearly a hundred years old and was most probably deceased. Truth or not, this route seemed to be leading us nowhere.

Our plan B was to see if Van Cleef & Arpels had any information about the brooch. When I called the company's headquarters in Paris, they told me they kept all kinds of historical information in their archives and that I was welcome to view them in person. I made an appointment with them and booked our flight right away.

We took an airport taxi to the Ritz Hotel and checked in. I'd never been to France before and recalled very little from my French classes at school. Whatever French Winston had learnt during his time in the army was also a bit rusty.

As a result, the hotel receptionist seemed to think Winston and I were a same sex couple and that we only needed one room, but after displaying some exaggerated looks of offence and a lot of communication by hand gestures, we managed to sort things out and went up to our rooms, which were next door to one another.

I made a dinner reservation for us in the hotel's fine dining restaurant and was looking forward to trying some high-end French cuisine, along with some good wine. I arrived at the restaurant first and the maître d' led me to a table at the back of the dining room. I ordered a whisky and admired my surroundings.

I felt like I'd been transported back to the 1700s to one of King Louis XVI's royal palaces. Everywhere I looked around the room was luxurious. Gilded cornicing with cherubs, damask printed period fabrics on the walls and antique crystal chandeliers suspended from the ceiling. There were flamboyant curvaceous dining chairs with plush seats, pristine white table linens and beautiful silver cutlery.

The restaurant staff were all dressed formally in vintage style livery, bowties and all. My drink arrived and I took a sip, then almost spat it out in shock as I saw Winston enter the dining room.

He was wearing a jacket several sizes too small. He looked ridiculous and drew veiled sniggers from around the restaurant as he made his way to our table.

"Sorry I'm late. No hot water in my room. I had to take a cold shower", he complained.

"Ah, the French", I joked.

The jacket creaked at the seams as he sat down.

"So, ten-year-old Winston called. He said he wants his jacket back."

"It's the hotel's. I didn't bring a sports jacket with me. The maître d' said there's a dress code here and wouldn't let me in unless I was properly dressed."

"Properly dressed?"

A waiter arrived to take Winton's drink order.

"Un verre de Chateauneuf du Pape s'il vous plaît", said Winston to the waiter, who nodded and went off to fetch it.

"Well, at least your French has improved since we checked-in. Nice wine choice, by the way", I said.

"When in Rome…", he replied.

"You mean Paris."

"Eh?"

"Never mind", I said shaking my head.

We scanned our menus silently for a moment, then both chose the Chateaubriand steak. I joined Winston with the red wine once I'd finished my whisky and we enjoyed an exquisite dinner before going upstairs to our beds.

I never seem to sleep well the first night in a strange bed and despite enjoying the most comfortable and luxurious bed I'd ever laid down on, I tossed and turned for most of the night.

Maybe it was the wine, or perhaps I was nervous about our search for the brooch. No matter, though. In the morning, despite not hearing a peep from the room next door, I would tell Winston his loud snoring had kept me awake all night. I always found that bullshitting him into a guilt trip first thing in the morning made him more earnest in whatever we were up to.

We enjoyed a quick breakfast of croissants and strong coffee in the Ritz's brasserie, then went outside into the bright Parisian sunshine to begin our search. Despite the sun, it was a cool morning, but we didn't have far to walk. The Van Cleef & Arpels headquarters was only a couple of hundred yards away, around the corner from our hotel.

The jeweller occupied a large double aspect building in a corner of Place Vendôme. It had a light-coloured stone facade and large black framed window, each topped with a white branded awning above. We entered the building and were greeted warmly by a well-dressed young woman. I told her we had an appointment to view the archives and she went off in search of our host.

She returned a moment later accompanied by an older woman in a knee length black dress who approached us. She looked about fifty years old and had olive coloured skin, bobbed black hair and green eyes. She smiled and we shook hands.

"Good morning. I'm Doriane."

"Bronson. This is Winston", I said motioning behind me.

"Please follow me", she said.

She led us through a door at the rear of the ground floor, then down a flight of stairs and through several narrow hallways until we arrived at a set of double doors displaying the word 'Enregistrements" in black lettering on frosted glass door panels.

We walked through the doors and entered a long rectangular room containing rows of tall library style shelved cabinets on the left. On the right side of the room there was a long table with a dozen chairs round it. The walls had old black and white framed photographs and the room had no widows.

There was a sign in/sign out register on a small table next to the doors, which I guessed was for logging any borrowed items removed and returned from the shelves.

Doriane invited us to sit at one end of the long table, on top of which lay a thick folder.

"This is our catalogue", she said, "It's arranged chronologically rather than alphabetically and contains a descriptive list of all the one-off pieces we've made here since as far back as the early 1900s when the company was first founded.

"Alongside each description, there's a code letter and some numbers that correspond to a location on the shelves over there", she pointed to the rows of tall cabinets.

"The letter is for the row and the first three numbers relate to the cabinet in that row. The last four numbers identify the shelf and box file that contains the information listed in the respective catalogue entry.

"I think you said you were interested in one of our earliest commissions so you should start at the beginning of the catalogue", she said helpfully, then offered, "if you tell me what you're looking for, perhaps I could direct you more easily."

"That's alright", I replied, remembering Rathbone's insistence about discretion, "we're rather looking forward to doing the search ourselves, but thank you."

"Well, I'll leave you to it then. Please don't remove anything from the room. You don't have to put things back on the shelves once you're finished. Just leave them on the table and I'll return them later. If you need any help at all, please ask for me upstairs. Good luck", she said, then walked out of the room.

I opened the hefty catalogue and flipped over a few pages until I found where the archive list began. I placed my finger under the first line of text as both Winston and I began reading, but we stopped almost immediately and looked at each other in realisation.

The descriptions were written in French.

I sent Winston outside in search of a bookshop with an Anglo-French dictionary, which in hindsight, I should have brought with me anyway. He left and I went for a wander around the room looking at some of the photos on the walls distractedly.

I wasn't really taking anything in, though. I was looking, but not seeing, as my mind was elsewhere. Which key words should we be searching for? Chanel? Brooch? Maybe Capel, he'd been the customer, after all.

I walked over to the door and leafed through the first few pages of the in/out register. There were lots of signatures in columns alongside dates, but the register began too recently, 1989 onwards, so I didn't think anything in there would help us.

I returned to the catalogue on the main table and scanned the first few pages for year entries. The archive list seemed to have been started in 1906, so I turned over a few pages to where the 1908 entries began.

Winston returned with a dictionary and I asked him to find the French words for 'brooch', 'white', 'gold' and 'diamond'. After a few minutes, he'd made a list on a sheet of note paper that read: 'broche', 'blanc', 'or' and 'diamant'. I added 'Capel' to the list, then we both started carefully scanning the pages of text in front of us.

Half an hour later, Doriane brought in some coffee, allowing us a welcome break, which had thus far yielded nothing. Winston rose from his chair and stretched his legs, strolling around the room with cup in hand, glancing at the photos on the wall, as I had done earlier.

I made small talk with Doriane about the jewellery business, without giving much away about what we did for a living. She asked again if she could help us search, but I declined her offer as politely as I could. I finished my coffee and resumed my search in the catalogue as she took Winston's empty cup from him and left the room.

Around midday, we finally found something. An entry for 1908 that contained two of our key words within some faded, but neatly written script: 'Capel' and 'broche'. I traced my finger across the page and found a location code, 'D-145-0106'.

I shot a triumphant look at Winston who, without speaking, made for row 'D' in the cabinets on the other side of the room. I followed and we soon found cabinet '145', then the top shelf marked '01' and finally, our scanning eyes settled on a cardboard archive box with '06' marked on the side.

Winston pulled the box down from the shelf and brought it over to the main table, then lifted off its lid. He peered inside, then lifted out its contents and laid them on the table. We glanced over about ten sheets of paper, in different shapes and sizes, laid out before us.

The first sheet I picked up was what I took to be an order form, containing Capel's name, maybe his address, some descriptive text and some numbers, one of which at the bottom was underlined. The price, I figured. 3,870 francs.

Winston found a few small sheets that contained part sketches drawn in charcoal that could have been initial design thoughts for different parts of the brooch. There were also a couple of sheets with hand written notes that could have been to do with materials of construction.

I found a page that contained fractional numbers that seemed to be dimensional measurements and another sheet with some calculations. However, there were no photographs and there was no overview drawing showing the piece in its entirety. We both stared at the paper in front of us.

I felt deflated. I wasn't sure what I should have expected, but I was disappointed nonetheless. I spent another hour looking in the catalogue again for any more entries that could have been commissioned by Capel, but found none as the list moved onto entries from 1909 onwards.

I concluded that what we'd found probably was associated with the Chanel butterfly brooch, but it hadn't given us any clues as to where to look next. Another dead end.

"Let's go and get something to eat", I suggested to Winston, who nodded.

We gathered up the sheets and put them back in the archive box. Winston replaced the lid just as Doriane arrived back in the room.

"Success?", she asked.

"I'm afraid not", I replied with a sigh of disappointment.

"I'm sorry to hear that."

"We're going to find somewhere to have lunch and regroup, then figure out what to do next. Are there any cafes or restaurants nearby you would recommend?", I asked.

"Well, there's…", she started, but Winston interrupted her.

"Wait", he said.

I turned towards him. He was staring at one of the photos on the far wall and pointing.

"Who's that?", he asked.

Doriane and I joined him at the photo. He was pointing at a young woman. She had dark short hair and was wearing a long flowing black dress, standing between two pairs of men, all four of whom were dressed in dark suits.

"You probably don't recognise her. This was taken before she was famous. That's Coco Chanel", said Doriane.

The young Coco in the photo was wearing a butterfly shaped brooch.

"Winston, you've found it", I said and patted him on the shoulder.

"Is that what you were looking for?", asked Doriane, "the brooch?"

She looked closely at the photo.

"I had no idea it was one of ours, Van Cleef and Arpels I mean."

"Who are the others in the photo?", I asked.

"The men to her left are Alfred Van Cleef and his uncle Salomon Arpels, the founders of our company. The man closest to her on the right is Arthur Capel and next to him is Alain Rousseau, a close friend of Alfred's who was our company's lawyer.

"In fact, if I remember correctly, Monsieur Rousseau's son took over his father's law practice and was the executor of Coco Chanel's estate when she died."

The executor of her estate, I repeated inside my head. I wondered if the contents of Chanel's last will and testament had included the brooch, assuming she still owned it at the time of her death.

My heart rate quickened with excitement, whilst Winston looked at me, puzzled by the look on my face. If we could find a copy of Chanel's will, perhaps it would mention the brooch being passed on to someone.

"Do you know if the law firm still exists?", I asked Doriane.

"Yes, Rousseau's firm is still our company's lawyer today."

I could have kissed her, and nearly did. Instead, I asked for the lawyer's contact details, which she gave me. I thanked her several times, then Winston and I leapt up the stairs and left the building with a surge of optimism. I felt like we were finally getting somewhere.

We grabbed sandwiches and coffee from a nearby delicatessen and found a local park, where we sat on a patch of grass and ate our lunch. I relayed all my thoughts about finding Chanel's will to Winston and a lightbulb went on as he grasped how that might lead us to the brooch. I then made two calls from a payphone.

The first was to Rathbone back in London to let him know that we'd finally had a breakthrough of sorts. We didn't yet know the brooch's current whereabouts, but at least we'd seen a photograph of it being worn by Chanel herself. He agreed with my thinking about the will and wished me luck tracking down the lawyer.

The next call I made was to Rousseau's law firm. I told them we were searching for an old piece of jewellery that we thought could have featured in Chanel's will back in 1971. After being put on hold for about ten whole minutes, during which I nearly ran out of coins for the phone, they agreed for one of their lawyers to meet with us that afternoon, but said it was unlikely we would be allowed to see the actual will itself.

I filled in Winston about the phone calls and we walked from the park area back to the city centre to find a taxi. Thirty minutes later we arrived at the grand law offices of Rousseau, Lefevre & Dubois in the heart of Paris's business district.

Inside, we were met by a young suited lawyer who introduced himself to us as Marc Dubois. He led us to a meeting room on the second floor with a large oval conference table surrounded by plush leather chairs and windows along a far wall. He offered coffee, which we declined.

During some initial pleasantries, Dubois told us that he was the nephew of the firm's senior partner that bore his surname and that his uncle had long since retired. He said the firm's original founder, Alain Rousseau died many years ago and Rousseau's son, Pierre, was also now retired. Marcel Lefevre was now the firm's senior managing partner and was close to retirement himself.

"How can I help you?", Dubois asked.

"We're looking for a piece of jewellery made by Van Cleef and Arpels in the early 1900s that we think could have been mentioned in Coco Chanel's last will and testament back in 1971. We visited the jeweller's archives this morning and were informed that Rousseau's son was the executor of Chanel's estate", I told him.

"I see", said Dubois and he thought for a moment.

"We probably have a copy of her will here somewhere. I may not be allowed to let you see it, but I will check. Let me see what I can find out. Please make yourselves as comfortable as possible. I will return as soon as I can, excuse me", he said, then rose from his seat and left the meeting room.

Winston and I placed a wager with each other. I reckoned the will would mention the brooch and who it was left to. Winston was less optimistic and said this would be yet another dead end. I paced the room as we waited. Winston remained seated, gazing out of the windows.

Dubois returned about twenty minutes later and he was joined by an older man.

"This is Marcel Lefevre, our senior managing partner", he said, introducing his boss.

"Good to meet you", I said and rose from my seat to shake hands with Lefevre.

We all sat down and Lefevre unfolded some papers he had brought with him. A copy of the will?

"Marc has told me why you are here. I've brought a copy of Madame Chanel's will. Can you describe the item you are looking for please, so I know what to look for?", asked Lefevre, "The will lists many pieces of jewellery".

"It's a Van Cleef and Arpels diamond encrusted white gold brooch in the shape of a butterfly that was given to Coco Chanel by Arthur Capel in 1908. We have a client that wishes to purchase the brooch", I replied.

Lefevre unfolded the document in his hands then both he and Dubois scanned it in silence as Winston and I held our breath. After several minutes, Lefevre raised his head from the paper and looked at me.

"I cannot let you see this document, but I can tell you that it does mention a brooch like the one you described. It says here that it was Madame Chanel's wish for the brooch to be given to a long-time friend, named Estelle Chastain. There's an address for her here too. It's a chateau in the countryside about a hundred kilometres from Paris", said Lefevre.

Estelle Chastain. A name with the same initials as the biography author's alias, Eleonore Chevalier, the seamstress friend of Chanel. I thought there was a better than even chance that Estelle Chastain was the real name of the author.

I began to feel confident as Winston and I shared a hopeful glance at one another. Winston scribbled down the name and address, then I thanked the lawyers very much for their time and help.

As Dubois led us back to the main reception area we passed another conference room that had its door wide open. Winston and I caught a fleeting glimpse of two men seated at a table, one of whom was silent while the other was berating an unseen person at the other side of the table. The complainant drew my attention because he was speaking in English with a very posh London accent.

He seemed very angry about something and was giving it both barrels to some poor soul at the other side of the room we couldn't see. After we passed the door to the meeting room, Dubois turned back to me slightly and our eyes met. He shrugged his shoulders light heartedly, motioning to the complaining Englishman.

"Another satisfied client", he joked.

Winston and I left the law offices, brimming with confidence as we re-joined the foot traffic out on the street. I sent Winston off to rent us a car for a couple of days so we could head out to the countryside in search of the chateaux, which I reckoned had been the author's house.

I, meanwhile, bought a road map so I could plan our route from the hotel. We arranged to meet back at the Ritz for dinner and decided on the brasserie instead of the restaurant so that King Kong wouldn't have to borrow an undersized jacket like the night before.

Dinner was a hoot as we basked in the day's success and I chastised Winston for his pessimism regarding the will. His forfeit for losing our wager was that he had to pay the evening's drinks bill, which I took full advantage of.

Winston had the boeuf bourguignon; beef stewed in red wine, while I enjoyed the poulet à la bretonne; chicken simmered in apple cider, which was delicious.

We shared a bottle of house red wine with the food, then I coerced Winston into some whisky tasting, much to his chagrin. I couldn't be sure if it was the whisky he didn't like or having to pay the drinks bill that irked him, but in truth, we had a great evening. We then went up to bed early, to get some rest before resuming our search in the morning.

We ate breakfast in the brasserie again the next morning, then Winston went off to fetch the rental car while I grabbed the road map from my room. I headed out of the front door to wait for him in the sunshine. The air was crisp and cool, like the day before, which I welcomed after the previous night's alcohol.

After waiting for a few minutes sat on the steps outside the hotel, a small white Renault Five appeared and came to a stop alongside me. There was an elephant inside it, sitting in the driver's seat. Winston wound down the car's window and beckoned me to hop in.

"Couldn't find a smaller car?", I teased.

"I thought Renault would be a good choice in France. I've never driven one of these before. Come on, you'll love it", he said.

I shrugged, got in the car and we began our drive to the country.

SEVEN

We spent a couple of hours driving and made a few wrong turns before we finally spotted a sign at the entranceway to the address given to us by the lawyer. Winston drove slowly on the uneven surface of a long narrow tree lined driveway for a mile or so before we could make out a large house in the distance beyond the end of the trees.

As we approached, my first impression of Chateau Broussard was that of a grand period mansion, but as we drew closer, it became obvious that this seemingly impressive building had seen better days. The stonework was in a poor state of repair, it was discoloured and flaking. Paint was peeling from timberwork around the windows and the gardens surrounding the house were overgrown.

Winston stopped the Renault in front of the house. I climbed out and knocked on the front door. Fingers crossed.

After a moment, I heard the door being unlocked from inside and the door opened. I came face to face with a woman who looked around sixty. I did some number crunching in my head and thought that she could well be the author's daughter.

"Oui, puis-je t'aider?", she enquired.

"Bonjour, parles-vous Anglais?", I asked.

"Yes", she said.

"We're very sorry to bother you. My friend and I have travelled all the way from London. We're looking for a woman named Estelle Chastain who we believe used to live here twenty years ago. Do you know her?", I asked tentatively.

I felt this was make or break for us. She nodded in recognition immediately.

"Yes. Estelle Chastain was my mother. I'm Ginette. Please come in."

She pulled the door wide open, then Winston and I entered the house and introduced ourselves to Ginette. It was mid-morning and she offered us coffee, but we declined and she led us into a drawing room.

Everything around us seemed very old and dilapidated, just like my impression of the outside. We all took a seat and she started with some bad news.

"I'm afraid my mother, Estelle Chastain, died ten years ago. Why are you looking for her?"

"I'm very sorry to hear that", I said, deflated, "We think Coco Chanel left your mother an item of jewellery in her will. A brooch. We met with lawyers from the firm who handled Chanel's estate who told us this yesterday. We're trying to find the brooch for a client of ours who wants to buy it."

Ginette looked puzzled. She sat back for a moment with her head tilted slightly upwards and looked at the ceiling. Thinking.

"My mother didn't have much jewellery, I don't remember ever seeing a brooch or my mother ever mentioning a brooch. I certainly don't recall her ever talking about being left a brooch by Coco Chanel. I'm afraid this must be a mistake."

"This house, Chateau Broussard, was listed in Chanel's will as your mother's address. That's how we came to be here", I said.

"Yes, my father's last name was Broussard. When he and my mother got married, she kept the Chastain name", explained Ginette.

She sat silently for a moment. Processing.

"When my mother died, she left all her jewellery to me. I'm sure there is no brooch, but in case I am making a mistake, come with me and we can look at what I have."

We stood and followed her through a series of hallways to another part of the house, still on the ground floor, and into a bedroom. She pulled open a drawer from a large wooden chest, lifting it out completely and laid it on the bed.

We all peered inside scanning the drawer's contents in search of a butterfly shaped brooch. There were plenty of bracelets, rings, necklaces and ear rings, in yellow and white gold, some in silver and some fashion jewellery. But no brooches.

"Could she have given it to someone else, a sister or a friend perhaps?", I asked.

"I have no idea. As I said, I don't remember my mother ever mentioning such a thing. I'm very sorry."

Winston and I were out of ideas. We shrugged at one another silently and the three of us left the bedroom. Another dead end.

As we made our way back toward the drawing room, a small bell sounded from somewhere upstairs. Winston and I looked at one another inquisitively. Someone else in the house? Ginette gave us an explanation.

"My grandmother", she said, "she's upstairs and must be needing something", she explained, then stopped suddenly.

"What?", I asked.

"My grandmother, my mother's mother, lives with me. I take care of her. I've known her as grand-mère Justine all my life, but I've just remembered that Justine is her middle name. Her first name is Estelle, but no one ever called her that."

She led us past the drawing room and up a grand staircase, then around a corner and into a sitting room on the first floor. It was a large, but shabby looking room with wallpaper peeling back slightly along one or two edges. A rug in the middle was heavily worn and a musty smell filled the air.

Over by an open fire sat a very old looking woman, her knees blanketed and wearing fingerless gloves. She had thin grey hair and a tired pale face, but had intelligent eyes that looked up toward the three of us as we entered the room.

The old woman said something to Ginette in French. Ginette replied, then there followed some discussion between them, back and forth, which I assumed was Ginette telling her grandmother who we were and why we were there.

"Approchez-vous", said the old woman, beckoning us closer so Winston and I stepped forward and I gave her a friendly smile.

She studied each of our faces in turn before speaking.

"Broche papillon?", she asked in French.

Winston and I looked at Ginette for help.

"Butterfly brooch", she translated.

I felt the hairs on the back of my neck stand up.

"Yes", I said, "the brooch is shaped like a butterfly. White gold with diamonds."

Some more talk in French followed between grandmother and granddaughter, then Ginette left the room. Madame Chastain motioned for us to sit down, so Winston and I took an armchair each and waited.

After a minute or two, Ginette returned to the sitting room with a beaming smile on her face. She handed something to her grandmother who then opened her hands for us to see. It was the Chanel butterfly brooch.

We'd found it.

It seemed smaller than it had looked in the old photograph at Van Cleef and Arpels, but there was no mistaking how beautiful it was. The white gold was slightly dull, as were the diamonds, but there appeared to be no damage and the pin at the rear looked to be in pretty good condition too considering its age.

Now what?

"Do you think she would sell it?", I asked Ginette.

She relayed my question in French to her grandmother, who was now looking down fondly at the brooch in her fragile old hands.

A moment passed, then the old woman responded to Ginette, in French, who led Winston and I back downstairs to the drawing room, leaving her grandmother upstairs with the brooch. We took our seats again and I felt apprehensive as Ginette looked at me calmly.

"You two have travelled all the way from England, searching for a vintage diamond encrusted gold brooch that was once owned by Coco Chanel. Therefore, having gone to such trouble to find it and with it previously belonging to one of France's most famous daughters, I assume it is very valuable and worth a lot of money, should my grandmother wish to sell. Why should she sell it to your client instead of auctioning it to the highest bidder?"

It was a fair question. I asked if I could make a quick call to London from her house phone and offered her five francs, which she accepted and said okay.

I then called Rathbone and told him the good news. He was thrilled. I spoke to him for several minutes about price before hanging up, then returned to the drawing room and made my pitch to Ginette.

"You may or may not know that your grandmother and Coco Chanel were close friends a long time ago. In the mid-1950s your grandmother wrote an unofficial biography about Chanel's life, or at least the part of it your grandmother was privy to.

"Her book mentions the brooch being given to Chanel by her lover, Arthur Capel. In the biography, she referred to it as, 'a token of love in an illicit affair'.

"My client is a very famous and important person. I cannot tell you who he is, but I can tell you that by selling this brooch to him, it will not end up being stuck in some museum or paraded and boasted about at dinner parties.

"He wants to give this brooch as a birthday present to a very valued friend. Wouldn't it please your grandmother to know that by selling it to my client instead of auctioning it to the highest bidder, it would become a 'token' of friendship between two people?"

I then fell silent to let that sink in before adding an incentive.

"I can also assure you, Ginette, that our client is prepared to pay your grandmother a lot of money for the brooch."

I looked around the tired looking room.

"He would be offering a more than fair price. Perhaps a life-changing amount that could be used to return your home to its former glory", I added.

Ginette seemed to take in everything I said, then she left the drawing room and we heard her go back upstairs. Winston and I waited anxiously in silence for what seemed like a very long time, but which may only have been five minutes or so, before Ginette returned with the brooch in her hand.

"My grandmother is sentimental and she likes what you said about the brooch being a special 'token' between two people. You are correct, Bronson. Our family was once very wealthy, but through death and divorce, our circumstances are somewhat different these days. If, as you said, your client is willing to offer my grandmother a more than fair price for the brooch, then she says she will sell it to him."

I breathed for the first time in a moment or two, then thought carefully about the conversation I'd just had with Rathbone and what we'd agreed regarding price. I hoped my next words wouldn't screw everything up. Winston stood by expectantly.

"Winston and I visited the archives of Van Cleef and Arpels in Paris yesterday, the jeweller that made the brooch for Arthur Capel back in 1908. They still have the original purchase invoice, which we saw. Capel paid 3,870 francs for the brooch. That sum would equate to around $15,000 today."

I then paused, watching her reaction, but she gave nothing away.

"My client is willing to make your grandmother a one-time only, non-negotiable offer for the brooch, of $500,000. That's just over 2,700,000 French francs at today's exchange rate", I said slowly.

Ginette's reaction was priceless. She gasped slightly when I mentioned the amount and her legs seemed to wobble, then she sat down waving her hand in front of her face like a fan. She started laughing and laughing, then before long Winston and I were also laughing, nervously, before Ginette finally regained her composure, took a deep breath and then there was silence.

She stood and went up to tell her grandmother. We heard a shriek and more laughter coming from upstairs, then a moment later, Ginette returned to the drawing room and her big smile was back.

"Will the money be paid in US dollars or French francs?", she asked.

"In any currency you and your grandmother desire", I replied.

She started laughing again and came towards me, arms outstretched and hugged me tightly.

"Deal", she said and I almost collapsed with relief.

EIGHT

Once we had all calmed down, Winston went out to start the car while I arranged some details with Ginette for the exchange to take place the next day. I made a final call to Rathbone from the house to tell him we'd struck a deal and so he could contact His Royal Highness to get the money wired to the Chastain bank account first thing in the morning.

We agreed that Winston and I would return to Chateau Broussard at two o'clock the following afternoon, then we said our goodbyes and I left the house to join Winston at the Renault.

His head was under the bonnet.

"Problems?", I asked.

"I think there's a radiator issue", said a voice from the engine bay.

"Ah, the French", I joked, again.

He dropped the bonnet to close it then shoe horned his massive frame into the driver's seat.

"I've topped up the level with some water. If she starts, we should manage to get back to Paris alright. Here goes", said Winston.

The engine started up successfully and I hopped in. We set off back down the long driveway, then onward in the direction of Paris.

The drive back was a very enjoyable one. We were buzzing with the excitement of not only finding the brooch, but also agreeing a deal for the Prince to buy it. We laughed at how our faces must have looked when we went from despair at Ginette's late mother having left her no brooch, which we assumed meant another dead end, to pure elation when her grandmother held the brooch in her hands and we saw it for the first time. It really was beautiful and we could understand why the Prince of Wales wanted it so badly.

Back at the Ritz, I took a long shower and dressed in some fresh clothes while Winston took the car back to the rental company so they could check out the radiator. I had some time to kill before he returned, so I went out for a walk and came upon some clothes shops. I popped into one and bought a present for Winston, then walked back to the hotel.

I heard him return to his room around six-thirty so I knocked on his door and, when he answered, told him I'd booked us a table in the hotel's formal restaurant for dinner at seven-thirty. He frowned at this, since it meant he would have to search through the hotel's collection of spare jackets again to see if he could find one large enough to fit him.

I arrived at the dining room first and was shown to a table in the centre. The restaurant was nearly full, which made me smirk wryly at the thought of a bigger audience for Winston's imminent wardrobe debacle. As expected, he ambled into the dining room sulkily, wearing the same jacket he'd been given the other night and looked just as ridiculous.

He did well to ignore the glances from other diners. I waited until he had crossed the entire dining room and sat down beside me before I passed him a carrier bag.

"What's this?", he asked.

"Something to remember our trip by."

He opened the bag and pulled out a brand new grey sports jacket with the tag still attached. He stood and held it up, then took off the undersized one, with some difficulty, which was just as amusing as seeing him wearing it. He tried on the new one, which fit like a glove, then pulled the tag off and smiled proudly.

"How do I look?" he asked, hamming it up with a twirl, which drew some smiles from nearby tables.

"Fabulous", I replied, "like a gorilla dressed for a wedding."

"Thanks Bronson", he said appreciatively.

A waiter arrived and we ordered water, then he departed with the discarded, stretched out of shape loan jacket and we perused the menu. We both decided on fillet steaks and Winston chose a bottle of red from the wine list.

"Petrus 1988 s'il vous plait", said Winston showing off his very limited French again.

"Ah, I'm very sorry monsieur, we do not have any of the '88 Petrus left. The gentleman at that table has just ordered the last bottle", replied the waiter, motioning to a table near the back of the restaurant.

Winston and I both turned slightly towards the table the waiter was referring to. Two gentlemen were sitting there, in conversation. There was something very familiar about them, but my mind drew a blank.

"How about the '85 Claret instead?", offered the waiter.

"Oui, merci", replied Winston.

I tried to place where I'd seen the two men before, then Winston remembered.

"Were those two not sitting in a conference room as we left the lawyer's office yesterday? The fat guy was giving somebody a right rollicking, remember?"

He was right. I tilted my head slightly towards them and eaves dropped for a moment, listening for the fat one's accent. It was the posh London chap alright. The man next to him had a slim build and although sitting down, he looked taller than the other man. He had been sitting next to the chubby man at the table in the lawyer's conference room.

I watched Winston for a moment as he looked at the slim guy, while wearing a flat expression. He was processing something. I waited.

"Bronson, do you think there are other people out there, who have a similar relationship to the one you and I have?"

"There's bound to be."

Then I realised that Winston had seen a kind of familiarity in the slim man at the other table. Perhaps he'd seen something of himself in the other man. Not in his appearance, but how he sat listening to the fat man next to him, whilst constantly surveying the room at the same time. On guard, cautious of their surroundings. Just like Winston himself. A peer maybe.

We paid them no further mind as our meals arrived, along with the wine and we enjoyed another first-class dinner, followed by a couple of whiskies. Afterwards, our route out of the restaurant led us past the hotel's cocktail bar.

It was a stunning antique French themed lounge with huge glitzy mirrors, walnut panelled walls and intimate booths with brown leather seats along one wall. The wall itself was filled with signed photographs of A-list celebrities and movie stars.

It was busy too, with a pianist in a corner playing classical music. I spotted 'fat boy and slim' sitting at a booth together near the bar, the chubby guy was still doing all the talking.

I walked over to their booth, perhaps emboldened by the whisky I'd had, with Winston following dutifully behind me.

"Good evening gentlemen. How was the Petrus?", I asked the fat one.

"I'm sorry?", he replied.

"The wine you had at dinner. We tried to order it, but the waiter told us you got the last bottle. Did you enjoy it?"

"Yes, it was delicious, Mr…?"

"Larkin. Bronson Larkin", I replied, "This is my friend, Winston", I added, pointing to the Hulk next to me.

"Max Van Aanholt", he replied and we shook hands.

The slim guy stood up and he and Winston towered over me.

"Archie Munro", said Winston's fellow giant, but in an unmistakable Scottish accent.

"Good to meet you Archie. Where are you from?", I asked.

"Glasgow", he replied, "You?"

"Aberdeen", I said.

"Ah, a sheep-shagger", he kidded me and we all laughed.

"And how about you Max, where are you from?" I asked.

"The London Borough of Richmond upon Thames", he replied, theatrically. "Sorry about the Petrus my boy, what did you have instead?"

"A very nice '85 Claret", Winston replied.

"A great wine. As good as the Petrus in my book", said Max.

"You sound like you know your wines", I said.

"I know about drinking them", he joked, "Please, join us."

Max slid along the leather seat in the horseshoe shaped booth to make room for us and a waiter appeared as Winston and I sat down.

"Four double whiskies", barked Max towards the waiter, "Macallan, eighteen-year-old. Bring some water and ice too."

I was impressed with Max's choice of dram and thought to myself that he must know his whiskies as well.

"What brings you to Paris?", I asked him.

"Wine, as a matter of fact", he replied, "I'm a collector. I've been on the hunt for some very rare wines that have been out of circulation since the mid-1980s. A collection of six very old bottles that were once owned by the late American President, Thomas Jefferson, a couple of hundred years ago."

"It sounds like you're on quite an adventure", I said.

Max continued.

"Indeed, it is. I read about them in the Sotheby's auction lot archives in New York a few years ago. They were profiled in a brochure alongside some American artworks that were about to be auctioned. The article described the collection's origins in France and about them being discovered on Jefferson's property after he died.

"It then charted their various auction appearances over the next hundred or so years, as they changed hands from collector to collector, then the piece concluded with their mysterious disappearance."

I was intrigued. Our drinks arrived and Max took a sip, then carried on.

"I asked around, but none of the major auction houses knew where they were. All my collector contacts were dumbfounded. It's like they just disappeared. Archie and I finally thought we were onto something a couple of weeks ago that led us to a law firm here in the centre of Paris.

"We travelled all the way here from London to meet with some lawyers yesterday, but it was a waste of time. They were supposed to be the legal representatives of a reclusive French collector who was rumoured to have mentioned the Jefferson collection in a drunken boast at a bar in Prague last August. A friend of mine overheard him. We then did some digging to try and find out who he was.

"Anyway, to cut a long story short, that search led us here, but as it turns out, the lawyers have never even heard of him. I wish they'd told me that when I telephoned them last week. Arseholes", he ranted.

"Ah, the French", I said with sarcasm then asked, "what would the Jefferson wines be worth today?"

"An absolute fortune, my boy", said Max, "probably over a million dollars."

"Bloody hell", said Winston.

"For six bottles of wine? What would you do with them if you found them?", I asked.

"Buy them, take them home and drink the fucking lot", he said.

I loved the way it sounded when posh people say the F word. It sounded like 'facking'.

"Anyway, I'll probably never find them, so that's that. How about you two, what brings you to the Ritz, a romantic holiday?", Max joked.

"Anything but", I responded, "we were searching for something too, but fortunately for us, we've found it. We'll collect it tomorrow, then head back to London."

"Well, here's to you then", said Max raising his glass, "success", he said, then we all clinked glasses and finished our scotch.

We enjoyed one another's company for another couple of hours or so. I bought a round of drinks, then Max bought a round and so it went on all evening. He had some hilarious stories and he told them very well, a born entertainer and probably a great dinner party host too. Eventually, the barman started putting chairs upside down on tables and we got the hint that it was time for us to go.

"Bedtime for me, gentlemen", said Max, "I've had a bloody good evening with you chaps. I wish you the very best of luck in your endeavours, Bronson, Winston."

"You too", I replied, "Thanks for inviting us to join you and good luck finding your Jefferson wine collection."

We all stood up and said goodnight, then Max and I shared a kind of older brother, younger brother, man hug that didn't feel at all awkward, probably due the amount of alcohol we'd consumed. Archie and Winston did not follow our lead, then we all retired upstairs.

NINE

In the morning, I met Winston downstairs in the brasserie for breakfast and we planned our day. I asked him about the car and he said the rental company had given him a replacement. Jolly good.

We checked out of our rooms and he left to bring the new car round to the front while I put in another call to Rathbone back in London. He told me the money had been transferred as requested, so we were good to go for collecting the brooch. I told him I'd see him the next day at Kensington Palace, then hung up and went outside to wait for Winston.

Another crisp but dry and sunny day in Paris. I inhaled deeply and made small talk with the hotel doorman as I waited. A few minutes later, a red Peugeot 205 approached the hotel and stopped alongside me. I couldn't believe it. This car looked even smaller than the Renault, but Winston seemed triumphant when he lowered the passenger side window.

"Electric windows", he said, "better leg room too", then he gave me a 'thumbs up'. I put my bag in the boot, got in the car and away we went, back out to the French countryside.

The drive seemed longer than it had the day before, maybe I was just apprehensive, anxious to have the brooch in my possession. Ginette was standing at the open front doorway when we arrived at the end of the Chateau Broussard driveway. She waved as we approached and was smiling broadly. This was a big day for the Chastain family, I supposed. Half a million dollars would be life changing for anyone.

"Bonjour", I called out as I exited the car. Winston unfolded his body and squeezed himself out of the driver's side.

"Good morning Bronson, Winston", said Ginette and she opened her arms to give both of us a hug.

"Did you sleep well?", I asked.

"Not a wink", she replied, "I was too excited, thinking about the money. My grandmother and I stayed up most of the night talking about Coco Chanel and the friendship they had together. This doesn't seem real."

"Have you called the bank?", I asked.

"Yes, everything is in order. They seem desperate to get their hands on our money already. They tried to set up an appointment with me tomorrow to discuss their range of investment products, but I declined."

"Smart move", I said, "I think the best person to decide what to do with your money is you, and your grandmother, of course."

We went inside, Ginette led us upstairs and served coffee. It was a dark rich blend, Columbian, I think, with a wonderfully strong aroma. Her grandmother was in good spirits and we enjoyed an hour of her storytelling about the old days. Ginette handed me the brooch inside a small black jewellery box, which I opened and gazed once more on this most beautiful and enchanting of pieces.

I hugged and kissed Ginette's grandmother in gratitude, then Winston, Ginette and I went back downstairs. At the front door, Ginette and I said our final goodbyes as Winston headed for the car. She was tearful as we hugged again and thanked me for finding them.

"Thank you for getting your grandmother to sell the brooch. Otherwise, this would have been a wasted trip. Good luck, Ginette. Spend the money wisely", I said.

"Merci. Bonne chance, Bronson", she replied and we left.

Winston and I drove in silence for a while. I thought about how lucky we'd been over the past few days. If Winston hadn't spotted the brooch on the young Chanel in the photo at Van Cleef and Arpels, we could be nowhere right now. Instead, we'd be £50,000 better off in a day or two once we were back in London. What an incredible trip.

We returned the rental car and took a cab to Charles De Gaulle airport. As usual, the airport was overcrowded, with nowhere available to eat. Ah well, maybe that's what comes with the tenth busiest airport in the world.

Our flight home was uneventful and Winston dosed for much of it. I nudged him awake as the plane taxied towards the terminal upon our arrival at Heathrow. Once inside the building and through passport control, we collected our bags from the luggage carousel and took a black cab back to our apartment in Kensington. Home sweet home.

Winston immediately put the kettle on and I went for a long hot shower to unwind. I slept soundly that night with the brooch safely tucked away in my safe. Half a million dollars' worth.

In the morning, Winston and I set off on our journey to Kensington Palace on foot, stopping at a nearby café to pick up some takeaway coffee and a bacon roll each, with brown sauce. The French have nothing on us Brits for a classy breakfast.

A small crowd of tourists was gathered outside the entry gates to Kensington Palace when we arrived. The gates themselves were closed this time and it took a few conversations with a guard, then his superior, before Winston and I were allowed into the Palace grounds.

A flag on top of the main building was at full mast, which meant at least one member of the royal family was in residence, and explained why on this day at least, the grounds were closed to tourists.

I recognised one of the suits from my first visit standing at the front door of the main building as we arrived and he escorted us inside. He led us along a couple of long hallways filled with gilded statues and marble pillars, before we arrived at the grand King's staircase.

We walked through a majestic and opulent archway before climbing the steps that led up to the Prince of Wales' apartments on the second floor. Designed in 1727 by William Kent, the walls around the staircase were lavishly painted with frescoes depicting an 18th century royal court scene, full of characters from the time of Great Britain's King George I, including the King's mistress, Melusine von der Schulenburg, the Duchess of Kendal.

The ceiling was spectacular too, with dentil moulded cornicing and ornate mouldings, all finished in gold leaf.

When we reached the second floor, we were led through a short passageway into the King's Gallery, a long rectangular stateroom filled with grand paintings in lavish gold frames and beautiful red patterned walls. Sir Philip Rathbone was there, standing by a beautiful white marble fireplace.

"Good morning Mr. Larkin", he said and we shook hands.

"Good morning. This is my associate, Winston", I said.

"Yes, Mr. Murchison, ex-British army I believe", said Rathbone, shaking Winston by the hand.

"Yes sir", replied Winston.

"His Royal Highness will join us momentarily. Can I offer you some coffee, gentlemen?", Rathbone asked.

"No, thank you Sir Philip, we've just had some on our way over here", I replied.

"Well, it sounds like you two had quite an adventure in Paris. Well done for finding the brooch. May I see it?", he asked.

I produced the black jewellery box from my jacket pocket and opened it, then handed it to him. He put on a pair of spectacles and inspected the brooch closely, then took it out of the box and looked at it from back to front and all around in his hands.

"Magnificent, isn't it?", he said.

"Yes, it's beautiful", I agreed, "The Prince has very good taste. I'm sure his friend will be thrilled with her birthday present".

Then a door opened at the far end of the gallery and in walked the Prince of Wales, himself.

He was accompanied by an aide who walked a step or two behind him. I was completely star struck.

The Prince was dressed casually in a light blue shirt with a dark blue tie, a mid-grey suit and polished black shoes. Although this was his own residence, he carried himself with a kind of regal presence, graceful and deliberate, the sort of practiced confidence of a man who is always on show, even in his own home.

"Good morning, gentlemen", said the Prince, with a pleasant, but firm air of authority, immediately establishing himself as the one taking charge of our meeting.

"Good morning, Your Highness", we all replied, almost in unison.

Rathbone introduced us to the Prince and I felt goose bumps all over. Royalty. This was totally surreal.

Rathbone handed the brooch to His Highness who studied it for a moment, looking carefully all over the brooch, handling it very gently.

"You have my utmost gratitude Mr. Larkin. This is a truly wonderful piece of jewellery. It has such history too. Its recipient is a big fan of the late Coco Chanel and will appreciate this immensely", said the Prince.

"I'm glad I was able to be of service, Your Highness", I replied, nervously blurting the words out.

"Thank you" said the Prince, then he smiled at me, shook my hand, nodded to Rathbone and left the room, his aide following dutifully behind.

A moment of silence followed the Prince's departure and I finally felt my nervousness subside, then Rathbone handed me a cheque for £50,000. I took it and thanked him, then our suited escorts reappeared at the door.

"You remember what I said about discretion, Mr. Larkin?", said Rathbone.

"Of course.", I said, then we said goodbye and Winston and I left the building.

Once we were back outside, I took a deep breath and looked at Winston.

"Yeah", he said, "I didn't think we'd actually meet him."

"Let's go and put this cheque in the bank", I said, then we strode off back towards the Palace gates.

TEN

A few days later, the cheque had cleared and I gave Winston a cash bonus of £5,000, which he was very pleased with. He deserved it for spotting the brooch in the photo, as well as for putting up with all my teasing about his snoring and his size.

We enjoyed some fun times that Spring. With plenty of money and no ties, we spoilt ourselves on fine dining, drinking, casinos and gallery events to which we were constantly invited.

After a very late Friday night out in SoHo in mid-April, I awoke in the morning with a start as the entry buzzer to our building was ringing continuously in the hallway. When I answered the door entry phone, a delivery guy said there was a package for me, so I let him in.

I felt badly hungover as I cracked open the door to the apartment and watched as he came up the stairs carrying a large carboard box with 'Ylang Ylang' branded stickers all over.

My fragrance had arrived.

I signed for the parcel, closed the door, then took the box through to the kitchen and opened it. Inside were stacks of small boxes containing cologne, scented candles and some oils, all of which were labelled with my name, the bottles' contents and the maker's logo. I opened one of the bottles of cologne and took a sniff.

I loved it instantly. I recognised the beautiful masculine aroma of sandalwood and the citrusy freshness of lemon. I noted just a hint of vanilla and some spice, which I assumed was the cinnamon. I didn't quite detect any bergamot, but overall, the smell was amazing, unique, distinctive and right up my street.

Lydia had nailed it.

I was really excited about it and took another deep sniff. It was beautiful. I then put the kettle on to make some coffee and took a couple of painkillers to try and ward off my hangover.

For the next few weeks, Winston and I took things a bit easier and I mulled over what to do with the growing funds in my bank account. I didn't want to blow it all on living the high life and needed to firm up an investment strategy.

After attending a stream of recent gallery events, I felt a burgeoning passion for art and decided to invest in a painting. I'd always been fascinated by 19th century impressionist painters, like Henri Matisse (1869-1954) and Henry Moret (1856-1913). I found Moret's landscapes captivating and I admired Matisse's ability to make an image leap from the canvas through his wonderful use of colour. Coastlines, forests, valleys, in every season Matisse seemed to observe his subjects with all his senses, reproducing them with great passion, spirit and sincerity.

I made enquiries with the big auction houses in London and New York, but it took several weeks to finally track down details of an upcoming sale at Christie's, in London, that would include a few lots by Henri Matisse.

The auction house's sale catalogue for Friday, 12 October 1990, listed Matisse's La devideuse picarde (La mère massé dans son intérieur à Bohain) as lot sixty-four, with a price estimate of £25,000 to £30,000. It showed a small printed image of the painting, depicting an old woman sat at a spinning wheel in a room with bare surroundings and a few framed pictures on the walls.

It also included provenance information for the painting, stating that it was believed to have been first owned by Auguste Matisse, the artist's brother. He sold it in July 1971 at a Sotheby's auction in London to one of the city's art galleries. Later in the 1970s, the painting changed hands again when it was bought by a private collector in the United Kingdom, who was now putting it up for auction at Christie's.

I'd seen photographs of La devideuse picarde before, in art books, but never dreamed I'd ever have the means to acquire the real thing for myself. I called Christie's and registered my interest. I asked how many others had done the same, but the person I spoke to was tight lipped, saying only that my enquiry was not the first they'd had.

On the morning of 12 October, Winston and I left the apartment just after nine o'clock and took a leisurely stroll through Kensington Gardens, then Hyde Park, heading east with some strong takeaway coffee. The scenery as we walked through the park was stunning.

The myriad colours of the leaves at varying stages of fading from bright green to yellow, red and brown reminded me of how much I loved Autumn in London. Leaves from some of the park's deciduous trees had already fallen and a gentle breeze made the crisp brown leaves swirl around our feet as we walked on the path.

I started feeling nervous when we left the park and began our approach through Piccadilly towards Christie's auction house on King Street in St. James's.

We were welcomed inside by a suited young man standing at the building's open door who asked if we were there for the Impressionist auction. I said 'yes' and he invited us into a reception area. I gave him my name and handed him my driving license as proof of my identity. Winston also had to provide him with proof of his identity to attend the auction, even though he wasn't there to participate.

The young man checked a list, crossed my name off with a pen, then handed me a glossy sale catalogue and a small plastic bidder paddle. The number eighteen was stamped in black on both sides of the circular white paddle. He instructed a suited woman in the reception area to escort Winston and I upstairs while he returned to his post by the door.

When we reached the first floor, the woman led us down a long hallway and into a large sale room about sixty feet long by forty feet wide. It was a very grand setting with crystal chandeliers, brass wall sconces all around and a high ceiling.

At the opposite end of the room from the door was a raised platform with a lectern in the centre. In front of the stage, a dozen or so rows of chairs were laid out, about half of them already occupied. Some members of Christies' staff were sat at tables with telephones along the left-hand wall, presumably for remote bids from buyers who wouldn't be there in person.

The sale was due to start at eleven-thirty, so we had ten minutes to wait. I scanned the assembled attendees, wondering if I would spot someone I knew, but didn't recognise anyone. I found myself trying to pick out who among them might be a rival when it came to the Matisse. Would it be the handsomely dressed country gent in the second row, who was scribbling notes on his catalogue, or perhaps the mature, nervous looking woman seated at the back, who was sipping champagne while her eyes darted around the room taking in the scene.

We were offered a glass of champagne, which I accepted. Winston declined, since he was there primarily to look after me. I drained the champagne immediately, returned the empty glass and picked up another, trying to ease the knots in my stomach.

"Take it easy, boss", Winston warned, "I've heard people can get carried away at these things. We don't want you freaking out and giving up our home to pay for the painting."

"I'm fine. Just thirsty from the walk", I lied, continuing to survey the room.

As well as those seated, there were several other people milling about in a group near the door, sipping champagne and laughing loudly at one another's jokes. I got the impression they were seasoned auction goers, who weren't all together, but who perhaps had met before at previous auctions.

"Let's take a seat", I said to Winston and led him to the fourth row which had a couple of empty seats at one end.

We sat and waited. Winston browsed the sale catalogue and I went through my bidding strategy in my head for the hundredth time. A few minutes later, I heard the door being closed and the auctioneer made her way up to the lectern. She switched on a microphone and the room fell silent.

"Good morning everyone", she started, in an Italian accent, "I'm Allegra Colarusso and, on behalf of Christie's, I'm delighted to welcome you to today's sale of 19th century Impressionist artworks."

She looked around thirty years old and was dressed impeccably in a navy pinstripe suit with a cream blouse. Her skin was tanned, she had long flowing dark hair and bright blue eyes. She oozed class and sex appeal with a slightly raspy voice that I immediately found captivating. A very attractive woman. Winston stared at her longingly, his mouth slightly open and I had to nudge him out of his reverie before others noticed.

I would have sixty-three lots to sit through before La devideuse picarde would come up, but I was more than happy to sit back and watch this stunningly beautiful auctioneer take charge up on the stage.

"At this time, I invite bids for lot number one. May I present to you The Night Café, painted in 1888 by Vincent van Gogh. This is an oil on canvas, measuring approximately 28.5 inches by 36.3 inches. Showing here, ladies and gentlemen", she gestured towards a young man in a white laboratory style coat who paraded across the room in front of the lectern, holding the painting high above his head, for all to see.

Van Gogh's painting showed the interior of a café or bar, with a half-curtained doorway in the background and various people sat at tables along the walls. A billiard table was in the middle of the room with a waiter in a light-coloured coat standing next to it, facing the front. The soft glowing ceiling lights in the painting bore the unmistakable Van Gogh swirly brush strokes. In all, a beautiful painting, which I expected was about to go for some serious money.

"I would like to start the bidding at £200,000", she announced.

A buzz started around the room as the first bidder number was held up from amongst the seated crowd and all eyes scanned the room to see who had kicked things off. Counter bidders joined in and the price quickly rose to £250,000, before things slowed down a little.

"I have £250,000 in the room, here to my left. Do I hear £260,000?", Colarusso called out.

The room paused silent just for a moment, but then, as if a starter's gun had sounded, things took off again, as three bidders in the room and one telephone bidder battled it out for the Van Gogh, which within minutes reached a staggering £670,000. Way over the £500,000 upper estimate.

My stomach was in knots and I wasn't even bidding. Winston beside me seemed to be having the time of his life. His head swivelled from side to side, like he was watching a tennis match, as bids were heralded from around the room, all the while looking completely enchanted by the sexy Italian auctioneer at the front. Eventually, Colarusso's gavel knocked loudly at £695,000, as the first lot was sold and a small round applause echoed around the room.

A casually dressed chap in the middle of the crowd held his bidder number aloft to identify himself as the winner to the auction house staff. He seemed about forty, with an unshaven face and unkempt scruffy looking hair. I wouldn't have guessed from his appearance that he had just bought a precious artwork for nearly three quarters of a million pounds. I suppose it just proved the adage: 'never judge a book by its cover'.

A minute or so later, Colarusso had regained her composure after the dramatic intensity of the first lot, and with a sip of water, then a brief check of her notes, she was ready to go again. The room fell silent as she announced lot number two, a Monet.

Over the next hour and a half, bids came from everywhere and Colarusso's gavel cracked loudly, as lot after lot sold at a breath-taking pace. She was masterful and controlled each sale with a well-practiced professionalism. We saw scores of fantastic works from some of the greatest painters of the 19th century, including Renoir, Pissarro, Sisley, Degas and others. Several of Moret's paintings also featured, all of which were snapped up for more that their pre-sale estimates.

As a buyer, this didn't bode well for me. During a coffee break, Winston and I remarked to each other that most of the lots sold thus far had reached prices higher than estimated, which presumably meant I would have competition for the Matisse.

The auction resumed with lot sixty-three, another Pissarro, which sold near the upper limit of its estimate, after which I sat up in readiness for the Matisse that was up next. I took a deep breath and focussed my concentration on sticking to my strategy, so as not to screw up over the next few minutes. I looked at Winston who wished me luck with a double 'thumbs up'.

Finally, Colarusso announced lot number sixty-four and completed her preamble describing the Matisse. I tried hard to focus on what she was saying, but I felt distracted by the auctioneer's startling good looks.

"May I start the bidding at £20,000?", she called out.

I sat motionless and listened, in line with my strategy.

"Thank you, sir. I have £20,000 bid, in the room, the gentleman at the back. Do I hear £22,000?", said the auctioneer and we were off and running.

Several bids then followed from within the sale room, with Winston surveying the crowd to see who I was up against. He reckoned there were two other bidders in play, both men and no telephone bidders, yet. Bids went up to £28,000 before slowing down. I still sat in silence, waiting.

"Ladies and gentlemen, £28,000 I am bid. Do I hear more?", Colarusso called out, then she started closing, "Going once at £28,000. Fair warning to you all. Do I hear £28,500? No? Are we all done at £28,000?", then she raised her gavel, suspending it above her head, as if she were about to crack a whip.

I gulped and shot my bidder number in the air.

"£29,000", I shouted, sweat instantly beading up on my forehead.

"Thank you, sir. New bidder, in the room, near the front. £29,000 I am bid. Do I here £30,000?", then she paused, surveying the room. Her eyes met mine briefly and she smiled ever so slightly. She was so sexually attractive I found myself being more fixated on her than the auction.

There was a moment of silence in the room, the tension was palpable. Our eyes met again, before she continued.

"No? Alright, do I here £29,500 then?", she asked, her raspy voice echoing around the room through the microphone.

"£29,500", a man's voice called out from the back of the room and I immediately wanted to punch him. I'd been daydreaming for a fleeting moment that there were only the two of us in the room: me and the stunning Italian beauty on stage. This other bidder had broken into my fantasy and was trying to ruin everything.

Winston turned to see who had bid against me, as I raised my bidder paddle again.

"£30,000, sir?", Colarusso asked me. I nodded and she continued.

"Thank you, sir. I have £30,000 bid, the gentleman here on my left", she pointed in my direction, "Do I hear £31,000?", she announced and I wanted to scream out 'No! The Matisse is mine, you bastards', but managed to keep this thought to myself.

We were now at the upper limit of the pre-sale estimate and it looked like we were down to two bidders. Me and the guy at the back of the room. I wondered which one of us would blink first.

"£30,500", the guy at the back shouted.

"Thank you, sir. £30,500 I am bid. Do I hear £31,000?", she was looking right at me, along with every other person in the room, and with so much pressure bearing down on me, I now wanted to punch everyone in the face.

I paused a beat, partly for effect, to make the other guy think I was past my limit and partly to calm myself down.

Then Winston did something crazy. Colarusso's eyes met his and Winston winked at her with a smile, which the auctioneer took as a signal that he was making a bid for my painting.

"Yes, sir. Are you making a bid at £31,000?", she asked him.

"No, no. Sorry", he replied, shaking his head vigorously and some of the onlookers broke into laughter.

"For Christ's sake, Winston. Stay still, will you?", I hissed and thumped him in the arm.

I took a deep breath, then held up my paddle, nodding at Colarusso.

"£31,000, sir?" she checked and I nodded to confirm my bid.

"£31,000 I am bid, ladies and gentlemen. Do I hear £31,500?", then she paused, "No? I have £31,000 bid, here in the room, from the gentleman on my left. Do I hear more?", she was really good at her job and, despite how beautiful and sexy her voice was, at that moment I desperately wanted the Italian goddess to be silent and stop asking for more bids.

"You, sir, at the back. Are you all done?" she asked.

The guy at the back said nothing.

"Going once then, at £31,000. Fair warning to you all. Are we all done?", she called out.

Every sinew in my body tensed up as I prayed internally to any God in the Universe who might be listening to somehow make Colarusso slam her gavel down and release me from this torture.

"Fair warning, then", she repeated, and raised the hammer.

"I am selling now, at £31,000", she said, then paused again.

The hammer was aloft in her hand and I sat there willing it with all my might to come down.

Next to me, Winston was on the edge of his seat, his fists clenched tight with tension.

Time stood still. I couldn't breathe and was now sweating profusely all over.

"Sold."

I closed my eyes and breathed as the relief washed over me. Winston slapped me on the shoulder amid a few claps of applause from the room.

"Don't ever let me do this again", I said to him with a set jaw, reeling from the strain.

He laughed and grabbed my hand, thrusting it up in the air to show my bidder number to the auctioneer. I was drained and slumped down in my chair. A moment later Colarusso was away again, announcing lot number sixty-five and Winston could tell I'd had enough.

"Let's go and get some air", he said.

"That's the best advice I've ever heard", I replied and we eased out of the room quietly, then went downstairs and walked out onto the street.

I enjoyed the fresh air for a good five minutes, with Winston congratulating me excitedly as I struggled to take in what had just happened. I'd bought my first ever Matisse. True, having a winning bid at an auction accepted was exhilarating, but based on the stress I'd just experienced, I thought that this may well be my first and last visit to an auction house as a bidder.

And what was up with that auctioneer? Talk about an added distraction. Couldn't they find a stuffy old dinosaur to run the sale?

After another twenty minutes or so, I had calmed down, so we went back upstairs to watch the final lots, and to continue lusting over the gorgeous auctioneer. Eventually, at around three-thirty in the afternoon, the auction was over.

Colarusso announced, on behalf of Christie's, that the day's auction had seen seventy-two paintings change hands for a total of more than £2,000,000, which heralded a final, more pronounced round of applause from those present. Only four lots listed in the catalogue had not been sold. Perhaps their reserves had been set too high, by overly ambitious sellers.

Winston and I went back downstairs and I signed some paperwork to complete the purchase. I had opened an account with Christie's a week before the auction, into which I'd deposited £40,000, in anticipation of being the winning bidder for the Matisse.

We waited for another hour, while the auction house carefully packaged up my painting along with all the others being collected on the day. I was then handed a refund cheque for £2,800, the difference between the amount I had deposited and the £31,000 purchase price, minus the buyer's premium, Christies' own commission, which was twenty percent of the hammer price.

Winston carried the packaged-up painting for me as we left the auction house. When we were outside, I hailed a cab to take us back to the apartment in Kensington. Despite

Winston's menacing appearance, neither of us thought it would be a good idea to walk back through Hyde Park with an original Matisse in our possession.

Ten minutes later we were back home and I unpackaged the painting carefully on the kitchen countertop. I felt a wave of satisfaction come over me when I removed it from its wooden crate and held it up in front of me.

Even its ornate, antique frame was a sight to behold. I carried it through to the lounge, standing it upright on the sofa, the top of the frame resting on the back of the couch. Winston brought tea through from the kitchen and we sat down opposite the painting.

I sat there, gazing at it for what seemed like hours, with a warm feeling of pleasure and appreciation. I also felt more than a little proud of myself, for having acquired something so beautiful and for having most likely invested my money in an appreciating asset, rather than pissing it all away.

Then we went out to the pub and got blind drunk.

TEN

Rimini, North East Italy
April 1994

Over the next four years, Winston and I worked harder than ever, trading everything from antique furniture to vintage cars. We travelled all over Europe, buying great pieces at bargain prices and selling them back home in London, making excellent profits. The rich were getting richer every day and our business was booming.

The early 1990s had seen a boom in the global financial industry, with London seeing its fair share of new millionaires. As a result, the city saw a growing number of classic car collectors, with rare vintage sportscars achieving record prices at auctions in and around Southern England.

I had an uncle in the motor trade, who told me about a barn find he'd stumbled upon inadvertently, when negotiating a deal to buy a Ford Escort from a farmer in East Sussex. The farmer had a 1960 Jaguar Mark II saloon hidden away in an old farm building. It hadn't been roadworthy for many years and needed a full restoration, which my uncle had no interest in, but he called me about it to see if I wanted to have a look. So, me and Winston ventured out to see it.

The car was totally original, in black, with an automatic gearbox, a 3.8 Litre engine and a full dossier of documentation, including maintenance history and original receipts. We decided to take a gamble on it, paying just £2,400 for the car in the Spring of 1991. Then, after two years of painstaking work by a Jaguar re-build specialist, which cost a further £9,500, we sold the fully restored car for £22,000, making a profit of £10,000, which equated to around $15,000 based on the respective pound Sterling to US dollar exchange rate in mid-1993.

While the Jaguar was undergoing its restoration, we happened on another bargain find in the summer of 1992. We stumbled upon a genuine pine and brass 'Zig Zag' chair by the world renowned Dutch furniture designer, Gerrit Thomas Rietveld, at an antique shop on a quiet back street in the centre of Amsterdam.

Widely regarded as one of the most ingenious contemporary designs of the 20th century, the chair had no legs and was made up of only four flat wooden tiles, formed into a Z-shape with a back on the top, using dovetail joints.

The example we found was made by Rietveld in 1934, but had some damage: the pine back tile had a split up its middle and one of the joints in the Z needed to be re-glued. As a result, we paid just under 7,000 Dutch Guilders for it, around $3,900 at the time, which was well below market value even in its damaged condition.

After having the piece repaired by a master craftsman back in England for around £2,000, we sold the fully restored

'Zig Zag' chair a year later, for a staggering £24,450 at a contemporary furniture auction in London, yielding a profit of just over $30,000.

We were equally surprised later that year, when we found a First Edition copy of Harper Lee's 'To Kill a Mockingbird', signed by the author, hidden away on a back shelf inside a second-hand book store in Madrid, Spain.

I managed to haggle the store owner down from 150,000 to 140,000 Spanish Pesetas, thereby acquiring it for the equivalent of just under $1,100. I sold it at a Books & Manuscripts auction in London two months later for £12,750, making a profit of around $18,000.

I made a lot of money and invested in two more Impressionist artworks: a Monet and a Degas, as well as a nice watch: a Rolex GMT Master in stainless steel with a black dial. I also rewarded Winston generously, giving him fifteen percent of all the profits on top of his annual salary.

By the Spring of 1994, I was exhausted and figured it was time for a break, so I had Winston book us a short holiday in Italy. A gallery owner friend had told me about the beautiful sandy beaches of Rimini, a city on the east coast of northern Italy. It had a reputation for being one of the best seaside resorts in Europe, so that's where we went.

On the last Friday of April, Winston and I boarded a flight from London's Heathrow airport and enjoyed a relaxing two-hour journey, with gin and tonics and a paperback book each.

During the flight, I asked him what he was reading.

"Non-fiction, World War II stuff. How about you?"

"A pretentious fiction novel about a Scottish idiot who scours the globe searching for high value objects to trade for profit, with an oversized ape as his sidekick", I responded sarcastically.

"Sounds rubbish", he said, "I'm surprised anybody published a book like that."

Our plane landed at Rimini's airport in the late afternoon sunshine. After going through the passport checks and collecting our bags, a short cab ride took us to the Grand Hotel Rimini, which was to be our home for the next few days.

Built at the beginning of the 20th century, the hotel was a magnificent white stucco building, considered by many to be the most prestigious hotel on the Italian Riviera. It stood resplendent among a grove of trees, just a short walk from the beach.

At check-in, Winston and I were assigned adjoining rooms on the top floor facing the water. We each had our own private balcony that looked out onto spectacular views of the Riviera coastline.

We arranged to meet in the hotel bar at seven, so I took a nap in my room for an hour, then showered and got dressed for going out. I'd packed various outfits, suitable for both formal and casual occasions just in case, but for the first evening I selected a pair of blue jeans and a white shirt. I put on a pair of brown boat shoes and didn't bother with socks. I brushed my teeth and my hair, then sprayed on some of my bespoke cologne and I was good to go.

Winston was already sitting on a stool at the bar when I arrived downstairs. He was dressed in jeans as well, but wore a black, tight fitting, round neck t-shirt, which showed off his bulging biceps. He was halfway through his first beer and when I joined him at the bar he handed me a bottle of Moretti, a popular Italian lager.

"When in Rome, right?", he said, rhetorically.

"Thanks. You hungry?", I asked.

"I'm already on it, boss. The barman recommends Pizzeria del Secolo, in the town centre. One of the oldest pizzerias around. He says it's about a twenty-minute walk from here, but worth the effort. We could take a taxi if you want?"

"No, it's a nice evening, let's walk", I replied.

We finished our beers, then walked out the front of the hotel into the bright, but diminishing sunshine. Winston put on a pair of dark sunglasses and looked like he was in the American Secret Service.

The walk allowed us to take in the sights at an easy pace. We took a slightly indirect route, heading West along the side of a stretch of water, the Porto Canale. Tree lined walkways flanked the canal, which was flat calm and had dozens of small fishing boats tied up along the South pier.

At the end of the canal, we turned left onto Via Dei Cavalieri and arrived in the heart of Rimini's old town. Centuries old stone buildings towered above us on either side as we walked along the narrow, cobbled street.

We made a right turn onto Corso Giovanni XXIII, then took a left onto Piazza Luigi Ferrari Tempio Malatestiano, before making a final right turn that took us to the pizzeria. The smell of pizza filled the air. The fresh dough, tomato sauce and herbs, together with a smokiness, presumably from the oven, made an appetising assault on my senses and suddenly I felt famished.

Pizzeria del Secolo was a tiny, modest looking takeaway. Winston and I bought a large slice of Margherita each, then went outside to eat al fresco, along with a couple of cold beers.

A few local teenagers sat nearby on the street, eating pizza and smoking cigarettes. A couple of old Lambretta motor scooters were parked nearby, one in white and the other in a baby blue colour. The whole scene was typical of photos in a holiday brochure.

Winston struck up a conversation with the teenagers, who spoke a little English. He asked if there were any nice cafes or bars close by and they told us about a place that was just a couple of hundred yards down the street.

We washed down the remains of our pizza with the beer and walked off in the direction of the cafe. We rounded a corner and entered a small piazza, the centrepiece of which was Caffe Cavour, a palatial two-level building with stone columns and arched windows. A large cream coloured canopy covered thirty or so tables in the square outside it.

Winston and I sat down at an empty table and took in the scene around us. The area was filled with a Friday evening crowd that was probably similar the world over. Young couples enjoying a pre-dinner drink. Well-dressed business people relaxing at the end of the working week with a cocktail or two. Groups of friends chatting noisily at long tables with beer, wine and coffee flowing generously.

A waiter arrived and we ordered a large glass of local red wine each, along with a plate of antipasti to share. We enjoyed the casual atmosphere around us and spent a couple of hours people watching in the square. The sun had long since set and we talked about what we should do next.

The waiter arrived to clear our table and I asked him if he could recommend somewhere we could go for a change of scene. He told us about a hotel a few streets away that he said would have a lively bar on a Friday night and that it also housed a casino. I asked him if we were dressed appropriately.

"Sì, signore", he replied, "this is Italy, not England. In Rimini, you don't have to dress like a penguin to enjoy a night out."

"Fair enough", I said.

Winston nodded in agreement so I left some money on the table to settle our bill and off we went.

The Hotel Cesare was around a quarter of a mile away, back in the direction of the beach, which suited us perfectly. It seemed like every building we'd seen in Rimini so far was a spectacular ancient monument and the Cesare was no exception. An enormous pre-war stone building, the exterior walls were lit up by beams of coloured light dancing on the stonework, emanating from spot lights placed on the ground.

We could hear dance music coming from inside the hotel, a thumping rhythmic beat, accompanied by the unmistakable buzz of weekend revellers partying.

We went inside to the hotel's main reception area then turned left into the bar, which was crowded with young adults, all dressed up and shouting to be heard over the loud music.

Winston led us to the bar and bought a whisky for me and a glass of red wine for himself, which we carried outside through a door that led to a patio area. It had four large couches arranged in a square, each facing inward, with a small fire pit in the middle. The fire pit, although completely unnecessary in the warm Mediterranean air, gave off a glow of light that was a welcome addition to the overall ambiance of the setting and it was burning wood, which gave off a wonderful smoky aroma.

We joined some others that were already outside and took an end seat each on a couple of the couches so we were beside one another in a corner.

Winston introduced himself to a young Italian woman sitting along from him. They made small talk for a while, then they stood and moved off to the side together and continued chatting. She looked about twenty years old and had long black hair, tanned skin and wore a skirt so short it barely covered her backside.

I was happy to sit and watch the goings on around me whilst sipping my dram contentedly. Winston's new friend seemed quite taken with him and I watched in amusement as she made a fuss over how big and muscular he was.

Winston then called me over and I stood up to join them. He told me her name was Carla, I introduced myself and shook her hand. I asked her about the hotel's casino and she said it would be open soon if we wanted to go. We were then joined by one of Carla's friends, who had stepped outside from the bar for some air.

She introduced herself to us as Vittoria. She was a slim, beautiful girl about the same age as Carla, with big blue eyes and long dark hair. She wore a short black body hugging dress and was an absolute knock out. I asked if she was a fashion model and she blushed slightly. I then took an order for a round of drinks and disappeared back inside to the bar while Winston continued chatting with the girls.

Carla and Vittoria were both students, studying law together at the local University and both spoke English impeccably. They were sharp witted and they seemed to find my ironic humour entertaining. Over an hour or so, we enjoyed each other's company immensely, then Winston asked if they wanted to accompany us to the casino. They accepted his invitation and went off to tell their friends they were leaving with us, then Carla led us through to the hotel foyer and up an escalator to the casino on the first floor.

Winston and I had to register as new patrons. The two girls were already members and shared some banter with the doorman for a moment while we signed a couple of forms.

We entered the casino through a large revolving glass door and were immediately struck by the noisy excitement inside. There were several roulette tables, some black jack tables too and a couple of tables for three-card poker. Slot machines lined the walls on either side and there was a bar at the rear.

We followed Winston as he made for the bar and bought champagne for the four of us. He wanted to try roulette so we walked over to a table that had some space available round it. Winston, Carla and Vittoria each took a seat while I stood behind them, watching for now. All three exchanged some currency for chips and started laying down bets on the numbered green baize.

There followed a mixed bag of wins and losses over the next half hour, but everyone was having a good time. I excused myself and went to find the men's room. It was at the rear of the casino near the bar and as I approached, I noticed a glass door off to one side that revealed another area of the casino beyond it. I used the rest room, then strolled over to the door for a peak.

As I approached the glass I saw into a room that had a large oval table and a green baize top, with eight players and a dealer sat round it. A private poker game, I figured. A few others milled around the room away from the table, mostly women enjoying cocktails.

My attention was then drawn to someone at the back of the room. A tall figure, somewhat familiar, standing alone. He was pensive and alert. Watching the game, but also watching everyone in the room.

It was Archie, the Glaswegian guy we'd met in the Ritz hotel in Paris. His scanning eyes spotted me peering through the door and we both smiled in recognition. He beckoned me into the room with a hand gesture.

I entered the room quietly and walked over to shake his hand. He seemed pleased to see me.

"Where's Max?", I asked.

Archie pointed toward the table and I saw the overweight frame of Max Van Aanholt seated at the card game. He noticed me and waved, then held up a couple of fingers, and mouthed "two minutes", which I took to mean he would join us when there was a break in the game.

"Where's your English ape?", Archie whispered to me quietly.

"He's entertaining a couple of Italian beauties at a roulette table next door", I replied.

"Rascal", said Archie, winking at me.

"How are you and Max doing?", I asked.

"Generally, pretty well, but not tonight. Max is down a few thousand and he's in a foul mood", he replied.

I thought for a moment.

"I have an idea. Meet me through at the bar when Max takes a break", I said and left the room.

I went to the bar.

"Do you happen to have a bottle of Petrus, Pomerol, 1988 vintage?", I asked the barman.

He pulled a large notebook from under the bar, flicked over a few sheets of paper, then ran his finger down a page, stopped and looked up at me.

"Sì, signore. You want?", he asked.

"Si, una bottiglia e sei bicchieri per favore", I said.

I paid him in cash, then went over to the roulette table while he went off to a backroom in search of the Petrus.

I sidled up to Winston.

"How's it going?", I asked, but could see that he and the girls each had an enviable pile of chips stacked up on the table. Things had clearly gone extremely well while I was away from the table.

"Great. We're on a roll. Where've you been?", he asked me.

"I went to the bathroom, then discovered a private card game going on in a room round the back. You'll never, in a million years, guess who's here. Someone we both know from a few years back. Remember our search for the Chanel brooch?", I said.

He gazed upwards, thinking for a moment. The girls had turned their attention towards me and looked intrigued. Then Winston looked back at me. He'd figured it out.

"No way?", he said.

"Yes", I replied nodding, as we eyeballed each other and I assumed we were on the same page.

"The Prince of Wales is here?", he asked.

"The Prince of Wales?", said Carla.

"No, Winston, you idiot. Not the Prince of Wales. The posh fat guy, Max Van Aanholt. I just saw him and your thin body double, Archie", I replied.

"Oh", he said, upbeat.

"Oh", said Carla, downbeat.

"They're at the card game. Come on, let's join them for a drink at the bar. It looks like all three of you have had a good run, but it won't last forever. It's best to leave the table while you're up", I said.

They looked at one another, slightly forlornly, then reluctantly started counting out their chips. In addition to the sizable amounts they had stacked up on the table, both Winston and the girls comically produced chips from various parts of their clothing. They must have been setting some aside each time they won. Winston pulled numerous chips from his pockets, while Carla withdrew a couple of handfuls from her tiny clutch handbag. Then Vittoria, bizarrely, reached into her cleavage and pulled out some chips that she'd stashed inside her bra. It was ridiculous.

"Quite finished?", I asked.

They ignored my quip and went to exchange their chips for cash, then joined me at the bar.

Max and Archie emerged from the other room and approached our group with big smiles. Max and I embraced like old friends.

"Bronson, you smell great, what is that?", he asked.

"It's cologne. A perfumer in London made it for me", I replied.

I introduced Carla and Vittoria to "fat boy and slim", but used their real names, then Winston and Archie renewed their acquaintance with a simple hand shake.

Winston pulled a couple of nearby tables together then arranged six chairs around them and we sat down.

The waiter brought over the wine and six glasses on a silver tray. Max spotted the Petrus label immediately and bellowed out loudly, in his absurdly posh accent.

"Bronson, you bastard. You remembered my favourite tipple", his exclamation had us in stitches.

We then played catch up for an hour, as Max held court and entertained us with hilarious stories of what he and Archie had been up to since Paris, which included a tale involving Archie falling into a river in Antwerp, Belgium, whilst chasing after a pickpocket who'd relieved him of his wallet.

The best one of all, though, was a story about Max getting drunk at a whisky auction in Tokyo and paying a fortune for some new Japanese scotch that he was convinced would be the next big thing, but which he couldn't sell for peanuts and having tasted it, said it was bloody awful. This nearly brought us all to tears.

We enjoyed a few more drinks together. Whisky for the boys. Carla and Vittoria went back to champagne.

"Hey, what are you doing on Sunday?", Max asked me.

"No plans, why?", I replied.

"Archie and I are going to the San Marino Grand Prix. We've been invited by the head of the main Williams team sponsor, Rothmans, the cigarette company. I'm doing a trade with the head honcho, who's mad for Beatles memorabilia.

I'm giving him a limited edition "White" album, signed by the Fab Four, in exchange for a box of vintage Fuente Don Arturo AnniverXario Cuban cigars that he picked up from a chap at the Brazilian Grand Prix in March. You and Winston must join us, please say you'll come?" he asked.

I couldn't think of a single reason why we shouldn't.

"Alright", I said, "count us in."

"Excellent. I'll arrange for a car to pick you up around eleven o'clock. Which hotel are you staying at?", he asked.

"The Grand", I replied.

"Very nice", he complemented.

"Thank you", I said.

The six of us then called it a night and we went our separate ways. Max and Archie left the casino first, while Winston and I shared an awkward moment with Carla and Vittoria, as Winston enquired as to whether they would like to remain in our company for the rest of the night. They smiled and nodded happily so Winston invited them back to our hotel for a nightcap, then we went downstairs and out the front of the Cesare in search of a taxi.

After a very short taxi journey, we arrived back at the Grand just after midnight. We rode the elevator up to the top floor and I led us along the corridor towards our rooms. As I opened the door to my room, I turned to the others, about to ask if Vittoria wanted to join me, but watched in amazement as Winston disappeared into his room, accompanied by both Carla and Vittoria together.

Oh well, I thought. Archie must have been right. Winston is, in fact, a rascal.

127

ELEVEN

I awoke mid-morning on the Saturday after a sound night's sleep and telephoned for a room service brunch of poached eggs with toast and black coffee. I also asked for the European edition of The Times newspaper, then went back to sleep until the room door buzzed.

I took breakfast out on the balcony and enjoyed the welcome sea breeze on my face as I browsed through the paper. I felt like I was in paradise with the gentle sound of waves hitting rocks nearby and the cloudless blue sky above.

The sports pages headlined with a report of a crash that had happened during Friday's qualifying for the San Marino Grand Prix. Rubens Barrichello, one of the two Jordan team drivers, had been injured and taken to a hospital in Bologna. Poor bloke, I thought. Formula one must still be a dangerous sport.

Winston knocked on my hotel room door around midday. I opened the door to a bleary-eyed gorilla and invited him in.

"Well, how was your night?", I asked him with a smirk on my face.

He said he'd had the night of his life with Carla and Vittoria. The girls had now gone home and he asked if I fancied a dip in the hotel pool, which sounded like a great idea so I put on my swim shorts, a pair of beach sandals and grabbed a towel before heading downstairs.

Winston filled me in on some of the details about his night of lust, which sounded amazing. He joked that he'd never had the opportunity to disappoint two women at the same time before. I laughed and felt genuinely happy he'd had such a good night.

We lazed in the sun by the pool for the rest of the day, cooling off in the water from time to time and enjoying espressos from the pool bar.

I went back upstairs around five o'clock and left Winston asleep at the pool. I napped for an hour, then took a shower and dressed casually for dinner.

I met up with Winston down in the bar at seven and we ate a couple of steak dinners in the hotel restaurant. We shared a bottle of house red wine and talked about work. I'd been having thoughts about rare watches and sounded out Winston about maybe heading to America for a while to get into the market there. He agreed that watches could be lucrative, if we picked the high-end brands then worked out a strategy for buying low and selling high.

I slept well again that night and awoke in the morning feeling fresh and energised. I phoned room service for the same breakfast as the day before and a copy of the Sunday Times. I felt sad reading about another accident at Saturday's Grand Prix qualifying. The Austrian driver, Roland Ratzenberger, died tragically after his car collided with a concrete barrier. It was the first Formula One fatality in more than a decade.

Although some teams decided to take no further part in qualifying, Sunday's race was still set to go ahead.

I dressed in jeans, a t-shirt and a pair of running shoes, then grabbed my sunglasses and popped through to the room next door to collect Winston. Just before eleven o'clock, we made our way downstairs and waited outside in the sunshine at the front of the hotel.

The car that Max had sent to pick us up was a black, late model Audi saloon that gleamed in the bright sunshine. Winston identified us to the driver, then we both jumped into the back for our journey to the Autodromo Enzo e Dino Ferrari race circuit in San Marino.

An hour and a half later, we arrived at the Imola race track and were met by Archie who handed over some VIP passes and escorted us through a security checkpoint as we made our way into the paddock area.

I covered my ears with my hands as a cacophony of noise enveloped us while we climbed a flight of steps up to the hospitality suites. The sound of revving engines and pneumatic tools was deafening and I was glad when we made it inside the building.

We entered a big open floor filled with hundreds of guests and a waitress handed me and Winston a glass each of chilled champagne, before Archie led us over to a private hospitality box that had large full height windows overlooking the race track below. Max heralded our arrival with a hearty welcome and introduced us to, firstly his host, the guy from Rothmans, then the other half dozen guests also in attendance.

Much of the talk in the room was about the crashes during qualifying and what could be done to improve driver safety in the sport. The Williams team boss arrived in our box and introduced everyone to his star racing driver, the Brazilian, three-time Formula One World Champion, Ayrton Senna who, despite a disappointing start to the season, had qualified in pole position for the San Marino Grand Prix and would start the race at the front of the grid.

Even though he was only in our box for a few minutes, we all got a huge kick out of meeting Senna, who was already a legend and widely regarded as one of the best racing drivers ever. He and the Williams team boss left to make their final preparations for the race and our group sat down to a lunch of smoked salmon, langoustines and scallops, which we washed down with the champagne.

During lunch, Max left us for a time and when he returned he was accompanied by a very attractive blonde woman wearing a royal blue summer dress and cream coloured stilettos.

"May I have your attention please, everyone", he announced, "I'd like to introduce my lovely wife, Rebecca. Please be nice to her, she's very shy and retiring", he kidded.

"Like hell I am. You big oaf", she responded and gave him a slap on his backside, which got a roar of approval from everyone at the table.

Rebecca sat down with a glass of champagne in her hand and began to work the room like a pro. Max sat down next to me and we got the chance to chat for a while.

"Tell me Max, how's your search for the Jefferson wines going?", I asked him.

"It's a bloody disaster, my boy. Remember the French chap I mentioned to you that was overheard in Prague talking about the collection?", he asked.

"Yes, the recluse, right?"

"Yes, him", he confirmed.

"Did you find him?"

"Yes, we tracked him down to a town in the South of France."

"And?", I asked.

"He's fucking dead, my boy. Would you believe it?"

"Oh no", I said with sympathy, "did he have the wines though?"

"No. However, my lawyer made some enquiries with the executors of his estate, and it turns out they found some paperwork in his house that seemed to indicate this guy, Francois Albert was his name, may have sold the Jefferson wines to his cousin.

"Now, Albert's cousin is a man called Louis Morel, who's also a well-known collector that deals mainly in the very high-end stuff", said Max.

"And, did you manage to track him down?", I asked.

"Yes, but he lives in America and likes his privacy. Apparently, he lives up a bloody mountain or something. The only way I'll get near those wines is if the current owner decides to put them up for sale at auction".

"Does anyone know what they look like?", I asked.

"There are no photographs, but an American friend of mine discovered a written description of them in the archives of the National Museum of American History in Washington, D.C. He was there doing research for a magazine article he wrote on the history of French wines", he replied.

I listened, fascinated as he continued.

"Apparently, there are no labels on the bottles. There are three reds: a Laffite, a Mouton and a Margaux, two whites: both Yquems and a sherry. They're all 18th century and each one has Jefferson's initials etched on the bottle".

"Do you think he has them?", I asked.

"Morel? Who knows?", he said and became distant for a moment as I sipped my champagne.

The atmosphere was building out on the track as hordes of people amassed around the cars down on the starting grid. A large screen was mounted at one end of our box, which showed live pictures of interviewers getting some pre-race thoughts from a couple of drivers. A few minutes later, everyone stood as a brass band played the Italian national anthem, then the crowds dispersed from the track to leave only the cars and drivers.

Spectators in the grand stand opposite cheered loudly as the starting lights went on and off in a sequence that signalled the start of the formation lap and the cars set off in the direction to our left for a single circuit of the track. A minute or two later, the cars re-appeared around a corner to our right and slowed to a stop in their respective starting positions on the grid.

The revving of engines reached a crescendo as the four red starting lights came on in order, then all went out at the same time to start the race.

The crowd roared the racers away, but there was mayhem instantly when one of the cars in the middle of the grid, a Benetton, didn't move. Then one of the cars further back, unsighted by those in front, accelerated straight into the stationary Benetton, sending debris everywhere, including into the crowd.

I felt a rush of excitement seeing and hearing all this live and in that moment, I completely understood the allure of this supremely glamorous sport. Winston handed me a bottle of cold beer and we turned to the big screen to watch replays of the crash while marshals cleared up the mess down below us and the Race Director organised the remaining cars for a re-start.

A short while later, the race began again under a rolling start on lap five after the cars had been led round the track in race order by a safety car for a few laps while the debris was cleared.

At the end of lap four, the safety car left the track, signalling the official re-start of the race and our group watched the screen closely as the Grand Prix finally got underway.

Having drunk several glasses of champagne and cold beer I needed to make a pitstop of my own, so I excused myself and left the noisy excitement of the private box to go to the men's room.

When I returned though, there was complete silence.

Everyone in the box sat motionless, staring at the screen as if they were all in a trance. I turned to Winston.

"What is it? What's wrong?", I asked him worriedly.

"It's Ayrton Senna. His car just slammed into a wall at the Tamburello corner. It looks bad, Bronson. He's not moving."

I immediately felt a tingling numbness all over. I struggled to comprehend what Winston had told me. I glanced round the faces of everyone in the box as they continued to stare at the big screen, frozen in shock.

I was dumbstruck with horror at the pictures on the screen. The car was unrecognisable and there was debris from the crash all over the track. Nobody touched the driver while they waited for the onsite medical team to arrive at the scene of the accident.

No one spoke as we looked on helplessly at the tragedy unfolding before our eyes. I'd never been an avid motor racing fan, but being there in person had somehow made me feel like I was, momentarily, part of the sport. An hour earlier, Ayrton Senna had been standing right next to me. It didn't seem real.

Winston disappeared from the box for several minutes, then returned with a bottle of scotch and some glasses from the bar, offering anyone who needed a stiff drink to help themselves.

After much incredulity and shaking of heads, those around me gradually began to wake up from their trance like state when Senna's car was removed from the track and he was flown to hospital by helicopter.

The race organisers, unclear about the extent of Senna's injuries, but knowing that he was on his way to Bologna for the best medical attention available, decided to restart the Grand Prix for a second time.

Winston's bottle of whisky didn't last long as we all gulped down a few shots to try and ease off the shock of the crash, and there was a subdued mood inside the box as we observed the remainder of the race through the windows and on the screen with little real interest.

In the end, the German driver, Michael Schumacher, won the race in his Benetton car and collected his third straight win in a row. The prize giving ceremony on the podium was a very sombre affair, with no signs of celebration and certainly no spraying of champagne.

With the uncertainty of Senna's fate hanging in the air, nobody felt like staying on to party at the track after the race. Max and his wife invited Winston and I to join them for dinner back in Rimini along with Archie and we accepted.

We left the Imola circuit in two chauffer driven cars, with me and Winston in one and our hosts in the other as we made the return journey in relative silence.

We were dropped off at the North side of Porto Canale outside a fine dining establishment called Ristorante Emelia. Max emerged from the front passenger side of his car with a box of Cuban cigars tucked under his arm. His wife, Rebecca, and Archie got out of the rear and we all entered the restaurant together. We were shown to a table at the back and Max ordered some limoncello in a bid to revive our dented spirits.

The drinks arrived and were quickly despatched as we looked over the menu. I chose a risotto with asparagus and Parma ham, topped with Parmigiano Reggiano cheese. The others all picked fillet steaks, except for Archie who opted for a pasta dish.

Max allowed me to choose the wine, so after studying the list I ordered two bottles of Brunello di Montalcino 1983, which seemed to impress my host, as well as some San Pellegrino sparkling water.

"What a day", Max exclaimed, voicing the thoughts of everyone at the table.

"Not quite what we expected", I said.

"It's terrible, of course, but it's a very dangerous sport. I'm sure the drivers know that", said Rebecca.

"I'm sure they do darling, but I don't think a sport should be as brutal as we saw today", Max responded.

"I really hope that Senna chap's alright", said Rebecca, "and what about that business at the start, with that car that didn't move getting obliterated from behind by one of the others?"

"His race ended before it even began", I said.

"Would he still get paid for that?", asked Rebecca.

"Which one, the driver who sat still or the one who ran into him?", I responded jokingly, which drew some smiles and we started to relax.

Our meals came and we thoroughly enjoyed the food, along with the wine, which everyone loved. Rebecca and Archie ordered dessert and the rest of us had coffee. Max and I then excused ourselves and went for a stroll along the canal.

Max offered me one of his new cigars and we enjoyed a relaxing smoke as we ambled along the water's edge, chatting easily about all kinds of things. We spoke about wine and art, cars and property, as well as other topics that we shared a keen interest in.

"What's your favourite scotch, Bronson?", he asked.

"Probably the Macallan, eighteen or twenty-year-old. I've never tried a fifty-year-old, I bet that would be something."

"I saw a fifty-year-old Macallan come up at auction once", said Max, "it went for over $15,000, if I remember rightly. I bet it was lovely though, assuming the buyer drunk it, of course."

"How about you, Max, what would be your choice?"

"Oh, that's a tough one. A forty-year-old Balvenie perhaps. Or, maybe a fifty-year-old Highland Park".

"Have you ever tasted a fifty-year-old Macallan?", I asked him.

"No, but I hear it's quite wonderful."

"I've heard some rumours recently. Apparently, Macallan's going to release a very special fifty-year-old single malt in 2006", I told him.

"Is that right?", he asked.

"That's what I hear. It's always been my dream to have one of those, Max. When I heard about it, I made a promise to myself that, come 2006, if I'm wealthy enough, I'm going to buy one", I said.

"I'm sure it'll be worth waiting for, my boy."

"I hope so. Thanks for the cigar, by the way", I said.

"Don't mention it", he replied, "Come on, we better go back and re-join the others at the restaurant."

We returned to the Ristorante Emelia and I paid the bill, as a thank you to Max for taking us to the Grand Prix. As we were leaving, a waiter told Archie that news reports had confirmed that Ayrton Senna had died and he relayed the news to the rest of us.

It was so sad and none of us knew what to say.

We parted company outside the restaurant. Max gave me his card and Winston gave Max one of mine from his wallet. We didn't make any plans to meet up again, but I think we all knew this wouldn't be the last time we bumped into one another. The business Max and I were in was bound to pull us towards the same objectives at some point.

Hopefully, as and when that happened, it wouldn't end in conflict between us.

Winston and I walked back to the Grand and enjoyed the cool breeze coming in off the sea. We talked about having a nightcap back at the hotel bar, but when we arrived, the emotion of the day, along with the fresh air in our lungs, brought on a sudden tiredness and we chose to get some sleep instead.

In the morning, we packed our bags and took a taxi to the airport for our flight back to London. In the end, I had mixed feelings about our trip to Rimini and was looking forward to going home.

TWELVE

Winston and I spent the remainder of the 1990s continuing our pursuit of profitable deals, making more money than we ever dreamed of and building enough wealth to ensure that the option of an early retirement was all but guaranteed, provided we didn't blow it all on a series of bad investments.

The more things we traded in, the more experience we gained. We mostly got the timing of our purchases and sales just about right, though not always, and I made a point of trying to learn from our mistakcs, so as not to repeat them.

Winston was now indispensable on the business front. Doing most of the legwork researching markets for me and digging around to find out who owned certain pieces we were interested in. As a result, I increased his share of our profits to one third, which he more than deserved.

Together, we had done extremely well trading in works of art, rare wines and jewellery, and as the end of the decade drew closer, with me in my mid-thirties, I put the final part of my plan to enter the watch market into action.

Through contacts at Sotheby's, I'd spent the winter months of 1999 laying the groundwork with a New York investment banker based in Manhattan, to buy a rare watch from him that I reckoned could double in value over the next ten years. Sometimes, you've got to play the long game to maximise returns.

The banker's name was Michael Barker and he'd used part of an annual bonus to buy the watch back in 1988. It was a very scarce, stainless steel Patek Philippe 1518 model. Made in 1943, it had features such as a moon-phase indicator, Arabic hour markers and a tachymeter scale.

Barker had paid just under $200,000 for it back in '88, at a time when there were thought to be around ten such timepieces left in existence. Twelve years on, he was looking to sell it on for big money to bolster his pension fund, as he coasted towards retirement at the end of his career.

As the new millennium approached and the world braced itself for a much-hyped digital Armageddon, which never came, Winston's extensive research had concluded that there were only six 1518s remaining in circulation and no examples had been seen at auction for nearly twenty years.

Therefore, my biggest problem was putting an accurate valuation on Barker's watch in the current market. Like most things though, I figured it would ultimately depend on its condition.

Through long distance telephone conversations with him, I managed to convince Barker I was a serious buyer, with the means necessary to make a genuine offer for his Patek Philippe. During a phone call in late April 2000, he told me that he and some golf buddies had booked a trip to Europe in the summer and would be spending a fortnight in

Scotland at the end of July. They planned to play golf on some of the country's best courses, followed by four days spectating at the Open Golf Championship during their visit, which would be contested by the world's best players at the home of golf, the Old Course in St. Andrews.

A week before the tournament, Barker and I made plans to meet in person on the final day of the Championship, Sunday 23 July, and thrash out a deal for the watch. I chose the cocktail bar on the top floor of the Old Course Hotel, which overlooked the golf course, as our meeting place. We agreed to meet there at seven o'clock in the early evening, by which time the tournament should be finished.

Winston booked us a room each at the Old Course Hotel for four nights and bought tickets for each day's play with hospitality included, so we could enjoy watching golf's elite in action.

We flew up from London to Edinburgh first thing on the Thursday morning and took the train north to St. Andrews, an hour and a half away. After a short taxi ride, we arrived at the hotel at eleven o'clock, just in time to drop off our bags and head out to the course to watch the action.

I'd been to the Old Course once before, with my father when I was a teenager and saw the likes of Jack Nicklaus, Gary Player and Tom Watson play. Winston and I were both looking forward to seeing the present day's golfing heroes in person, especially Tiger Woods, the twenty-four-year-old sensation who had taken the modern game by storm. Tiger already had three major tournament victories to his name prior to his arrival in Scotland for the 129th Open.

I led Winston out to the northern most end of the course, where we sat in a grandstand that gave us a great view of four entire holes from the same vantage point. We spent a couple of hours there watching numerous groups of the top golfers go by and witnessed some fantastic shots.

Noises from Winston's stomach told us it was time for some food, so we left the grandstand and walked south to the hospitality area. It was nicknamed the 'tented village' on account of the huge array of white marquee tents that were set up in an area next to the course offering food, drinks and souvenirs throughout the championship.

Our passes afforded us entry to a large indoor corporate dining area and we sat down to a splendid late lunch of Scottish smoked salmon pate, followed by crab filled ravioli in a white wine sauce. We also drank a couple of glasses of wine and almost decided to stay put for the rest of the day, but I was too keen to watch the golf and I managed to persuade Winston to join me back out in the sunshine. There's no way he would have joined me if the conditions outside had been more like Scotland's typical summer weather of gale force winds and hail stones.

By six o'clock, the day's early start and the travelling, along with the fresh air, finally caught up with us and we went back to the hotel. I ate a room service dinner then crashed out before ten o'clock.

Day two of the Championship was fantastic for all the spectators, who were treated to a Tiger Woods masterclass as he ended the day at the top of the leader board. Winston and I had as good a day as anyone, enjoying the golf and the weather, which was uncommonly dry and bright again, as well as the refreshments in the 'tented village'. We ended the day with a steak dinner in the hotel's informal restaurant on the ground floor and sampled a couple of whiskies before heading off to bed.

On the Saturday morning, Winston and I ventured into the town of St. Andrews and window shopped for a couple of hours around the quaint little town centre. It was full of boutique book shops, cafes and old stone buildings that were steeped in history.

At lunchtime, we walked back to the golf course and had some food at the Jigger Inn, a traditional Scottish pub situated on part of the hotel's grounds right next to the seventeenth fairway. We then hiked off to the southern end of the course to watch the remainder of round three.

Tiger was still leading the tournament at the end of the day and Winston and I had a few beers in the evening as we looked forward to watching the final round on Sunday.

The next morning, we went to the 'tented village' for a walk around the merchandise tent. Every golf product imaginable was for sale inside the enormous covered emporium.

We popped into the hospitality area for lunch, then Winston bumped into an old army buddy. They had a lot of catching up to do, so I left them to it and went out onto the course to watch the golf. I told Winston I'd meet him back in the hotel bar at six o'clock.

I'd brought a small portable radio with me and walked around the course listening to the local station's coverage of the final round as I watched the drama of a tense final day's play unfold before me.

Around four o'clock I heard an amusing radio report of a brawl involving drunken fans in the Bollinger Champagne tent. An hour later, I was positioned near the eighteenth green to watch an unstoppable Tiger Woods claim his fourth major title with an emphatic win.

On my trek past the hospitality tents on my way back to the hotel, I caught a glimpse of some golf highlights being replayed on a gigantic outdoor screen. I watched for a couple of minutes, then got the shock of my life when a video clip showed footage of the fight in the champagne tent from earlier in the afternoon.

The huge screen showed a magnified version of Winston's hulking frame, as he threw two men out of the tent, one in each hand, with his army buddy behind him, smashing another bloke to the floor with an expertly timed roundhouse kick. Two more idiots stumbled out of the tent and fell onto the grass outside, their faces puffy and bloodied.

The clip ended and the footage moved on to a shot of Tiger receiving the claret jug trophy. I resumed my journey back to the hotel, looking forward to hearing Winston's version of what had happened in the champagne tent.

My walk took me past several spectator buses, filling up with golf fans as they readied themselves to leave. I then spotted Gary Lineker, the former England footballer, walking in my direction alongside the buses.

After retiring from football, Lineker had started a second career as a television presenter on the BBC's Match of the Day programme. He had also become the face of Walker's crisps, a well-known British potato chip brand, starring in the company's TV commercials as a fiendish pilferer of other people's crisps.

As Lineker walked by, some golf fans in one of the buses recognised him and, in a wonderful moment of spontaneous mocking, knocked on the windows to get his attention, then thrust half a dozen packs of Walkers crisps against the windows, with broad grins on their faces. His reaction was priceless.

He raised his hands defensively and offered them a congratulatory nod, as if this type of thing happened to him every day, while the guys in the bus fell about laughing. Ah, the British, I thought. That's one they'll tell their grandchildren about.

I finally reached the hotel and went up to my room to shower and put on some fresh clothes. I then took the elevator up to the bar and picked up a bottle of lager on my way to join Winston who was sat in a leather armchair. He was gazing out of the impressive full height windows at a spectacular twilight view of the world's most famous golf course down below.

I sat down beside him and considered how to word my opening salvo.

"Been in the wars, have we?", I asked with my eyebrows raised.

"How'd you know?", he replied.

"You and your army buddy were caught on TV, throwing some peasants out of the champagne tent."

"They deserved it", he said.

"No doubt. Alright, let's hear it."

Winston told me how he and his friend had gone to the Bollinger tent after I left them and had a few glasses of champagne. At some point, they became aware of three young women in cocktail dresses taking a load of verbal abuse from five drunken morons, who had tried to chat the girls up, then turned aggressive when they were rebuffed.

The dynamic duo then kept half an eye on the situation and stepped in when one of the louts grabbed one of the women roughly by the arm. I didn't need to hear the rest of the story. There wasn't a mark on Winston and I'd seen the end of the bout on TV.

"Is your friend alright?", I asked.

"Yeah", he laughed, "Sully turned into Jackie Chan and the jerks started dropping like bowling pins. A squad of local police constables showed up when we were outside the tent.

"The girls told the bobbies what happened and they had a good laugh when they found out Sully and I were ex-military. The boys in blue escorted the poor thugs off to the first aid centre and the girls thanked us for our help, then we left. I feel bad for hurting the boys, though", he said, looking a bit subdued.

"Nonsense, they were asking for it. If it hadn't been for you two, they might have hurt those poor ladies", I said, trying to make him feel better.

I went up to the bar and returned with two cold bottles of beer and we both sat looking out of the window for a while. We ordered burgers and ate them where we sat, enjoying the view and the comfort of the armchairs.

When seven o'clock came around, I adjusted the angle of my chair so I had a good view of anyone entering the bar area as we waited for Barker to show up.

At a quarter past the hour, a seasoned looking group of four men approached the bar and I overheard one of them mention my name to the barman. It was show time.

Winston and I put our game faces on and rose from our chairs. I walked towards the lead guy, offering my hand and a friendly smile, while Winston remained a step or two behind me.

"Bronson Larkin", I announced and one of the men shook my hand.

"Michael Barker. Good to finally meet you, Bronson", he said, then introduced his friends, pointing at each one in turn.

"This is Rick, Bob and Steve", he said.

I introduced Winston and everyone shook hands. Rick looked at Winston.

"Have we met somewhere before?", he asked.

I frowned at my man-beast, remembering his appearance on TV earlier and he shrugged his shoulders.

"I don't think so. Maybe I just have a familiar face", Winston replied.

"I'm not sure people recognise you by your face. More likely by your size. You look like a house with legs", said Rick and we all laughed.

"So, how about your watch then, Michael? Do you have it with you?", I asked.

"Yeah. We're staying in this hotel. I have the watch in my room safe. Why don't we go downstairs and you can check it out?", he suggested.

"Sure, let's go", I replied and the six of us headed towards the elevator.

Barker's room was on the second floor and was even more luxurious than mine. It was a suite with a lounge and a separate bedroom and must have cost him a fortune during Open Championship week. His three friends and Winston sat on a couple of couches. I stood by, slightly nervously, as Barker got the watch from the safe. He brought it out, in its original box and laid it on a table, then opened the box, took the watch out and handed it to me.

It was beautiful. Easily the most elegant timepiece I'd ever seen. I looked closely at the glass, the steel case and the crown. There wasn't a scratch on it. I glanced over at Barker.

"Have you ever had this thing on your wrist?", I asked, bewildered by how pristine the watch was.

"Not once", he replied smugly.

I could tell that Barker knew his example was in mint condition and I figured I would have my work cut out to prize it from him.

"It's mint, Michael. Just as you promised. What's it going to take for me to wrest it from you?", I asked, dreading how much he would want for it.

"Do you have an offer in mind?" he asked, as the others in the room watched us from the sofa. You could've heard a pin drop and I think my knees may have been shaking.

Here goes, I thought.

"Well, Winston and I have been researching the 1518 market for the past few months, so we know there are very few left in existence. There have been no reported sales in the last two decades, so putting a price on your watch is very difficult. Granted, we'd be unlikely to find another one in better condition than yours, but the fact is, there are other examples out there", then I paused, to see how he reacted.

Nothing. He neither spoke, nor changed his facial expression. I had a fleeting thought that I wouldn't want to play poker against this guy, but then realised that in a way, I already was. I took a deep breath and continued.

"You said you paid just shy of $200,000 for it twelve years ago, right?"

Barker nodded and waited for my opening offer.

"For this watch, in this condition, I'm willing to make you a premium cash offer of $450,000", I declared, then watched him for a reaction.

Again, nothing.

"I see", he said with a slight grimace.

"Believe me, Michael, that's a top offer", I said, trying to convince both Barker and myself.

He was silent for a moment, then walked to the other side of the lounge, past the others who were on tenterhooks, and looked out of the window, thinking.

I looked at Winston, who shrugged his shoulders. Neither of us had a clue where we stood, as Barker mulled over my offer. Finally, he turned and faced me.

"I'm sorry Bronson, but I can't sell it to you for that. I honestly think if I put it up for auction, say, in London or New York, it would fetch a higher price", he said.

I was gobsmacked. Did Barker know something I didn't? How could he be so confident that my offer would be surpassed at auction?

"I really am very sorry", he said.

"So, what will you do?", I asked, unwilling to make him an improved offer, which I assumed is what he expected, but he didn't hesitate.

"I've already made preliminary arrangements with Sotheby's in London for the watch to be auctioned there next week, before I return to New York. My fall-back plan, in case you and I didn't reach an agreement", he said and I realised there and then that I'd been played.

He never intended to sell it to me. He just wanted to see how much I would offer to test the market and help him decide what to set the reserve at for next week's auction.

"What day next week?", I asked him, coolly.

"Friday afternoon, 28 July, at two o'clock. Will you go?", he asked.

"I'm not sure. To be honest, right now I'm a little disappointed, and surprised. I thought my offer was more than fair, Michael. But what the hell, you can't win them all, right?"

"No hard feelings?", he asked.

I hesitated before responding, then reluctantly accepted defeat.

"No hard feelings", I repeated.

"Let me buy you guys a drink?" Barker offered.

"Sure, why not?", I replied.

My acceptance of his drinks invitation seemed to ease the awkwardness that followed his rejection of my offer. The others stood and we all left the room for the bar upstairs.

Barker got the first round in, so I crucified him by ordering a twenty-year-old Glenlivet, which must have dented his wallet, but I felt no remorse. Not only had I invested many hours of my time on this deal with Barker, I'd also dropped over £4,000 on our visit to St. Andrews to meet him, with no end result.

Winston stuck to bottled beer, as did the others, and we ended up having a pretty good evening with them, all things considered.

Barker and his pals had plenty of funny Wall Street stories that were very entertaining. We took turns paying for drinks and shared some nibbles as we sat in comfy chairs around a knee-high table. I ordered pistachio nuts and salted cashews, which went down a treat.

Barker's pal, Rick, had this annoying habit though, of piling up his discarded pistachio shells into a neat little circle on the table, then he kept adjusting the edges. I saw Winston notice it too.

We left Barker and his buddies at the bar around midnight and went off to bed, with me promising to think hard about making another bid for his wristwatch at the auction next week.

I didn't sleep well that night and beat myself up a little for not having seen Barker's play coming. Yet another lesson I learned about the trading business. Don't go into any deal with a pre-conceived notion that the person on the other side holds themselves to the same standard of integrity as you do. Trust, must be earned.

Winston and I got up early on Monday morning and left St. Andrews on the first train to Edinburgh, then caught a late morning flight back to London. I thought about my failed bid for Barker's watch during the flight and arrived at Gatwick with a renewed appetite for giving it another go at Sotheby's in a few days' time.

THIRTEEN

When Friday came, Winston and I took a taxi from our apartment to Sotheby's auction house on New Bond Street and arrived just after one-thirty in the afternoon.

We were escorted through to a small sales room on the ground floor and accepted our hosts' offer of tea. The room was much smaller and more intimate than the one we'd been in at Christie's. There were only a dozen seats set out in three rows of four, but there were a couple of tables off to one side with telephones, two of which were already in use by auction staff, presumably touching base with a couple of remote bidders.

Winston and I perched ourselves on a couple of unoccupied chairs in the back row and before long all the seats in the room were taken. Barker's watch would be lot number four.

As the long hand on a wall clock behind the auctioneer's lectern struck the hour mark, a small man promptly made his way up onto the raised platform and announced that just five timepieces would be included in the day's auction.

I readied myself as the auctioneer kicked things off with lot number one, a 1968 Rolex Daytona Chronograph in yellow gold. After a slow start, followed by a flurry of bidding from three people in the room, the Rolex sold for £18,500.

The next watch, a rare 1981 white gold George Daniels automatic, leapt way beyond its £75,000 upper estimate as the auctioneer's hammer was brought down at £126,000 to a telephone bidder and brought a wave of excitement among those in the room.

Before the auction resumed, a late participant had arrived and a member of the auctioneer's staff asked if anyone seated was willing to give up their chair. Since Winston wasn't there to bid, he stood and offered up his seat to the new arrival, who accepted his gesture gratefully and sat down next to me.

Winston stood at the back of the room near the door as the auctioneer at the lectern announced the details of lot number three, a 1946 yellow gold Lemania chronograph, presented with a brown leather strap. It was a beautiful watch in excellent condition, but surprisingly nobody in the room, or on any of the telephones, made an opening bid above its reserve and it remained unsold.

I steeled myself for lot number four and thought about the strategy Winston and I had settled on. The $450,000 I'd offered Barker in St. Andrews equated to just under £320,000 and I'd decided that I was prepared to offer no more than £375,000 this time round.

The room fell silent as the auctioneer announced the details of Barker's timepiece and asked for an opening bid of £295,000. I waited to see who I'd be up against.

A telephone bidder, as it turned out.

A smartly dressed woman at one of the phone tables announced an opening bid of £295,000 on behalf of a remote bidder on the other end of her telephone.

I scanned the room to see if there would be others, noticing that Winston had disappeared from the room, which startled me. Nobody in the room made a counter bid, so I raised my bidder paddle, which was number six this time, and offered £300,000.

The auctioneer went through his routine to invite more offers and seconds later the woman with the phone called out an increased bid of £305,000.

I looked behind me to see that Winston was still missing in action. Where the hell had he gone?

I then nodded to the auctioneer signalling a move up to £310,000.

Over the next few minutes, the auctioneer went back and forth between me and the woman on the telephone, as the bidding reached £355,000 with no signs of slowing down.

Then, during a pause, with my opponent's most recent bid of £355,000 hanging in the air, I nearly jumped out of my seat when someone tapped me on the shoulder from behind.

It was Winston.

"Boss, we've got a problem", he said.

"Where the hell have you been? What problem?", I replied.

He whispered an explanation as all eyes in the room were trained on me, waiting.

"I was chatting with one of the auctioneer's staff at the back, who told me remote bidders on the telephones may not necessarily be hundreds of miles away. I asked what he meant and he said there's a room along the corridor they use to seat people who come to take part, but who wish to remain anonymous. They phone in bids from there through to the sales room", he said and I knew he had more to tell me.

"Sir?", the auctioneer called out to me, "the gentleman at the back, are you all done, sir?", he asked.

"No, not yet", I replied, "may I have just a moment please to confer with my associate?", I asked, not knowing if that was even allowed, as Winston continued whispering in my ear.

"I went down the corridor and tried a couple of doors that were locked, then came across one that wasn't. I opened the door slowly and when it was about halfway ajar, I heard a panicky American voice saying it was a private bidding room and nobody was allowed in there. I said I was looking for the men's room and closed the door, but I got a glimpse of someone's arm and a hand resting on a table, right next to a neat circular pile of pistachio shells.

"It's Barker's buddy, Rick!", he said with alarm.

I recoiled in horror and quickly tried to figure out what was going on, then it struck me. Barker was using his friend to drive up the price, with me as the only other bidder. That sly bastard, I thought.

"Sir?", the auctioneer called out again.

I had to think fast. Barker's strategy was for his man to keep outbidding me until he was happy with the price I offered, but he was taking a big chance. He couldn't possibly know how high I was willing to go. All I had to do was leave Rick's telephone bid on the table and not make another counter bid and Barker's ploy would fail. I wasn't going to be played by him a second time.

I shook my head towards the auctioneer, signalling that I was all done. I smiled at Winston and he realised what I'd done.

"Well done, boss", he said, "do you want me to go and break Rick's skull?", he asked menacingly.

"No. Not yet anyway", I said calmly, "let's go and see what he has to say for himself though", I said, then Winston and I left the sales room.

By the time we got to the other room, Rick was gone, but he had indeed left a neat little circle of shells behind. I stared at the table for a moment with mixed emotions. I was furious that Barker had tried to screw me over twice, but was glad I'd managed to thwart him, if only by a whisker.

"Let's get out of here", I said and we left.

FOURTEEN

My assault on the rare watch market hadn't gone to plan and I licked my wounds for the next twelve months, while Winston and I turned our attention to other things.

Then mid-way through 2001, I read in a Financial Times, weekend edition, Collectables supplement that a 1943 stainless steel Patek Philippe 1518 model had sold for $523,000 at a Bonham's auction in San Francisco. I read the article with interest and was somewhat surprised to learn that it wasn't Michael Barker's watch that had changed hands. The seller was reported to have been a Japanese watch enthusiast, but no details were included about the buyer, who must have requested anonymity.

I showed the piece to Winston, who read it and smiled, amused.

"How do you think Barker would react to this news?", he asked.

"I have no idea. Why?", I replied.

"A year ago, you were the only genuine bidder at the auction he chose to sell his watch at, right?"

"Yes", I answered, wondering where he was going with this.

"Well, suppose you were Barker, would you take the news of this sale as a sign that the market for reference 1518s was about to be rekindled, or, would you be fearful that the list of potential buyers for your own watch had just diminished by one?"

Winston had made a very interesting point. He continued.

"Didn't you say he wanted to sell his watch to boost his retirement funds? What if he's running out of time? The previous reported sale of a 1518 before this one was twenty years ago. Surely Barker can't wait another twenty years to sell his one?", he said.

"You know Winston, you're not just a pretty face, are you?"

"I have my moments, boss", he responded, looking pleased with himself.

"How about I give him a call? It would give him a chance to apologise and I could take his temperature about resurrecting a deal for his watch", I suggested.

"What have you got to lose? Who dares, wins, right?", said Winston.

"Isn't that the motto of the British S.A.S.? Back when you were in the military, Winston. You weren't, by any chance, in the Special Air Service, were you?", I asked.

"Well, if I was, I wouldn't be allowed to admit to it, would I?", he replied and I left that conversation there.

I went to the office and found Barker's telephone number, then checked my watch to work out what the time would be in New York. It was almost mid-day in London, which meant it would be nearly seven o'clock in Manhattan. I picked up the phone and dialled. If I got Barker out of his bed on a Sunday morning and it annoyed him, that would be a nice bonus.

It went straight to his answering machine, though, so I left a message.

"Good day to you Michael. This is Bronson Larkin calling from London. I can't believe it's been a whole year since you tried to screw me over. Twice. Anyway, I was just wondering if you'd seen the reports from San Francisco that a 1943 stainless steel Patek Philippe 1518 just changed hands there. That can only mean the number of potential buyers for your own watch just reduced by one. If this news, in any way, prompts you to consider selling your watch to me again, then I would be interested, provided you're prepared to play fair. Dishonesty may be an admirable quality in the Investment Banking business, but it certainly is not in mine. If you're interested in discussing it, you can reach me at the same number you used last year. If not, then no hard feelings and all the best", then I hung up and turned to Winston.

"What do you think?"

"Well, you left the door open for him, so let's wait and see. My gut says he'll call. He's not getting any younger", Winston replied.

I wasn't sure, but I supposed we would find out in a day or two.

As it turned out, it didn't even take a day. At seven-thirty in the evening, London time, the phone rang and it was Barker.

"I just listened to your message, Bronson. It's great to hear from you", were his opening words, "I must apologise for my behaviour last year. I guess I was being too greedy and, in the end, I got what I deserved", he said.

"I'm glad to hear you say that, Michael. Maybe your soul can still be saved after all", I responded.

We got straight down to it and he said he planned to retire at the end of the year and asked if I was serious about making another offer for his watch, considering how things had turned out the last time. I told him that, although his duplicity had infuriated me at the time, I was a business man and if we could still come to an arrangement that suited us both, then the past could be forgotten. This sounded promising to Barker so we agreed to sleep on it and arranged to talk again in a few days, to make sure neither of us was being rash.

Over the next month, Michael and I had several telephone conversations, bartering over price, until we eventually struck a deal. He agreed to sell me the watch for $490,000, which, based on the dollar to pound exchange rate at the time, equated to £350,000, the exact amount of my final bid for his watch at Sotheby's in July 2000, before Winston rumbled his scam and I withdrew from the auction. I thought I was being more than fair, giving him a second chance at that price, considering he'd been a total prick the year before.

For my part, I agreed to travel to New York so that the deal took place in Barker's own back yard, and for his part, he promised there would be no bullshit this time. I warned him that Winston would accompany me to make sure there wasn't.

Winston booked us business class flights from Heathrow to New York's JFK airport and made reservations for two adjoining rooms at the world-famous Plaza Hotel.

We left London on the morning of Monday 10 September 2001 and travelled the 3,500 miles to New York in style, enjoying fine food and great wine. We even managed to get some sleep on board during the six and three-quarter hour journey. We landed at JFK in the early afternoon, local time, and despite not hearing a peep from a soundly sleeping Winston at any time during the flight, I couldn't resist the temptation to get up to my old tricks as we prepared to disembark.

"Winston", I said, loud enough for the other business class passengers and flight attendants to hear, "you owe everyone an apology for snoring throughout the flight and keeping us all awake", I scolded.

"Not again, boss. I'm really sorry everyone, I can't help it", he said sheepishly, which drew a few smiles from the others, who realised I was pulling his leg.

"Well, we really must get that sorted out, Winston", I said, as I winked at one of the stewardesses behind Winston's back to let on I was just kidding, but she looked back at me as if I was a horrible person for doing that to my friend. Ah, the British sense of humour strikes again, I thought.

Inside the terminal building we spent an hour waiting in line at immigration, which we cleared successfully, then collected our bags and rode a yellow cab into Manhattan. We arrived at the Plaza just after two in the afternoon, on a bright sunny day in New York.

Everything about the Plaza was the ultimate in luxury, from the huge mirrored archways and highly polished floors, to the spectacularly opulent Palm Court restaurant, with its marble pillars and potted palm trees, interspersed among the dining tables. Above the restaurant was a wonderful, ornate stained-glass ceiling, a very impressive recreation of the original Edwardian version from 1907 that was destroyed in 1944.

We checked in, then took one of the art deco elevators up to our tenth-floor rooms, which were classy and palatial.

Since the weather was so nice, we decided to go for a walk to clear away the cobwebs from our hours of travelling. We set off north from the hotel towards Central Park and my first impression of New York was that it was just like the movies.

There was steam emanating from orange and white striped vent pipes that protruded up through the street and I could hear the rumble of subway trains from down below. The scale of the skyscrapers was like nothing I'd ever seen and I spent much of our walk looking upwards at the concrete giants surrounding us.

We entered the park, which was a lot busier than I expected for a weekday afternoon. There were tourists riding along in horse drawn carriages, we passed a dog walker exercising five dogs at the same time, as well as a few runners braving the formidable mid-afternoon heat.

We were passed by a peloton of around fifty cyclists competing in an official race and we even saw a photo shoot taking place at Bethesda Fountain with models dressed in bridalwear as a couple of dozen curious bystanders looked on.

Bearing in mind the business we were in, we couldn't be in New York's Upper East Side and not visit both the Metropolitan Museum of Art and the Guggenheim. We only had time to spend about an hour in each though, which was a real shame, but it was still worth it to see a few of the world's finest artworks up close.

We took a rickshaw back to the hotel, which I found very amusing. Our shorts wearing pedicab rider had enormous calf muscles on show, pedalling manically as we zipped through the Midtown traffic at a surprisingly fast pace.

For dinner, the concierge at the Plaza recommended a terrific Italian restaurant called Trattoria Dell'Arte, which was just two blocks west of the hotel, over on Seventh Avenue. He made a reservation for us and we headed over there at eight o'clock. I enjoyed a beautiful crab linguine in a white wine & cream sauce, while Winston ate a fillet steak and we shared a bottle of red Italian house wine. On the way out of the restaurant, we were encouraged by the manager to touch the back side of a female bronze sculpture for luck, which we did. Strange custom, I thought, but you never know.

After dinner, we went back to the hotel and enjoyed a couple of whiskies in the Plaza's Oak Room bar, a stunning wood panelled masterpiece that I didn't want to ever leave, but we were there for business so we both went up to bed around eleven-thirty and agreed to meet downstairs in the Palm Court at eight the next morning.

I slept soundly that first night in New York and in the morning, once I'd showered and dressed, I felt more prepared than ever for our ten o'clock showdown with Barker.

Winston and I left the hotel just after eight and walked south for a couple of blocks until we found a diner for breakfast. I ordered fried eggs with bacon and Winston had the works, a mountain of sausages, bacon, scrambled eggs, hash browns and toast. We both enjoyed several cups of strong black coffee as our diligent waitress re-filled our mugs every few minutes.

The diner was noisy and packed full of customers, more than a third of whom were uniformed cops, presumably about to start a shift, or maybe having just finished one. The other customers were a mix of business people and tourists. I was impressed by all the waiting staff bustling around the place, seemingly taking orders, delivering breakfasts, refilling cups and clearing tables all at the same time. All the checks were paid to a supervisor at a cash register near the door.

We sat back enjoying a final cup of coffee, taking in the scene around us as we allowed our food to settle, not realising that the whole world was about to change forever.

At around ten minutes to nine, the din inside the restaurant was pierced by a series of high pitched beeps that I initially thought was a smoke alarm sounding in the kitchen. All the cops around us reacted at once, grabbing hats and exiting the diner hurriedly when their beepers went off, handing money to the cashier as they bolted out the door.

Winston and I were baffled by the scene, as were the others who remained inside the restaurant. It was time for us to leave, so I paid our check at the cash register and we stepped out onto the street, where all hell was breaking loose.

Sirens filled the air as fire trucks and police vehicles sped south. Pedestrians stood motionless all around us, staring down towards Lower Manhattan, with mouths gaping open, looking shocked and confused. We followed their gaze and turned to see what they were looking at, then saw, to our horror, a huge cloud of smoke billowing out from the upper floors of one of the World Trade Centre's Twin Tower buildings.

We were too far away to make out any sign of flames coming from the damaged skyscraper, but I remember feeling a jolt of heartbreak as I instantly thought of the poor folks inside the building.

"Holy shit", I said.

Beside me, Winston stared at the carnage off in the distance, but said nothing as emergency vehicles continued to stream past us with horns and sirens blaring.

Some of the onlookers around us started crying, as they too, began to realise that scores of people inside the building were bound to be suffocating from smoke inhalation and that, but for a miracle, many would surely perish.

Winston grabbed my upper arm and turned me round to face the opposite direction.

"No good can come from us standing here watching this. We need to start making our way uptown", he said.

I reacted to his words by forcing my feet to take a step forward, then another, and before long we were striding along at pace leaving the scene from hell behind us.

When we reached the corner of Central Park South where it meets Fifth Avenue, we heard screams from others around us. I turned to look south and saw that the other tower now had smoke billowing from it too.

"What the hell's going on, Winston?", I said, completely bewildered by what I was seeing.

"Who knows what this is, but my nose is telling me that, with both towers damaged in the same way, around the same height, at the same time, this isn't an accident. More likely it's an attack of some kind. Let's keep moving north, boss."

We crossed over Fifth Avenue at East Sixty-First Street, then walked one block east and turned north on Madison Avenue as we continued our journey uptown towards Michael Barker's apartment building.

We found his address at twelve, East Eighty-Sixth Street, just before ten o'clock. The building was a traditional beige-brick mid-rise, built in the early 20th century that used to house The Croydon Hotel before it was converted to apartments in 1976.

Winston gave our names to the doorman and told him we were there to see Barker. He called up to Michael's penthouse apartment on the fifteenth floor and announced our arrival, then showed us to the elevator.

Barker's wife Trudy, opened the door to the apartment and we introduced ourselves. She was a slim brunette who looked ten years younger than the Michael Barker we'd met in Scotland a year ago. She led us through an impressive foyer, then along a central hallway, past half a dozen or so doors that I assumed led to other parts of their home, which I soon realised took up the entire fifteenth floor of the building.

We entered a large drawing room at the end of the hallway, which had full height windows giving an enviable view of Central Park. The walls were panelled in a very dark wood and the room was filled with French style antique furniture. Michael greeted us with half-smiles and limp handshakes. He had the television tuned to a news channel and seemed pre-occupied with what was going on down at the Twin Towers.

Trudy asked Winston and I if we wanted something to drink and we both declined, so she remained in the drawing room and sat down on a couch. Her eyes were glued to the TV screen, which showed live pictures of flames and smoke continuing to stream from both buildings.

"I have hundreds of friends and colleagues in the North Tower", said Barker, absently. He was clearly rattled.

"I'm very sorry to hear that, Michael. I'm sure the emergency services are doing all they can to rescue as many people as possible", I said.

"The news is reporting it as a co-ordinated attack and that both towers were hit by aeroplanes turned into missiles by anti-American terrorists", he revealed.

"That's horrific. Those poor people", I responded, then feeling sympathy for him, "Look Michael, we don't need to do this now. Winston and I can come back, when you're…"

"It's alright Bronson", he stopped me mid-sentence, "you've waited long enough for today. Thanks for agreeing to do the deal here in New York, by the way", he said.

"No problem", I replied, as he left the room and returned a moment later carrying the same box we'd seen in St. Andrews.

He muted the TV volume with the remote and handed me the box, which I opened and carefully took out the Patek Philippe. It was still in first class condition; the steel was polished to a high shine and there wasn't a single scratch on it.

"This is terrific", I said to him, with genuine admiration for the state of his watch, "Let me have your bank details and I'll make a phone call to have the $490,000 transferred into your account right away."

He handed me the details on a slip of paper. I took out my cell phone and dialled, then a few seconds later I was put through to the right person. After correctly answering a series of security questions to confirm my identity, I requested the transfer and was advised that the money would be in Barker's account within a few minutes. The guy on the other end of the line confirmed the exchange rate for the transaction as $1.496 to the pound Sterling, then I thanked him and hung up.

Barker turned the TV volume up and the four of us watched in continued disbelief as a news reader was saying that another hijacked plane had crashed into the Pentagon in Washington and authorities had lost contact with a fourth aircraft, which was now presumed to be under terrorist control.

The President was being protected by tight security at a school somewhere, while the Vice President had been squirrelled away into an underground bunker along with some other senior White House officials. Meanwhile, the FAA were grounding flights and the main road and rail transport routes into Manhattan were being closed.

The United States was under attack, with the entire country facing a complete lockdown as confusion reigned over whether there were any more threats out there.

Barker called his bank from the landline in his apartment and having been satisfied by the person at the other end that the money was safely in his account, he clicked off and looked over towards me.

"It's done, Bronson. You have the watch and the money is in my account", he said, then rose from his chair and approached me, offering a final hand shake.

"Thank you, Michael. I'm glad we were able reach an agreement in the end. And, I really do hope you hear some good news about your friends at the World Trade Centre", I said.

"Thank you, Bronson. Good luck to you both", he replied, then Trudy escorted us to the front door, leaving her withdrawn and sombre looking husband behind in the drawing room, staring at the TV screen.

Outside on the street, I handed the watch, in its box, to Winston for safe keeping and hailed us a cab on Madison Avenue. We went straight back to the Plaza, where I had the concierge put the watch into the hotel's master safe, then we both went upstairs to my room and spent the rest of the day watching the news, as more details of America's worst nightmare began to emerge.

We were stunned by footage from earlier in the day showing each of the Twin Towers collapsing, one after the other, engulfing lower Manhattan in a gigantic cloud of dust and debris.

Dinner that night was room service sandwiches and bottled beers as Winston and I remained glued to the TV until he went back through to his own room around ten o'clock and I went to bed, wondering what kind of world would be waiting for me in the morning.

Wednesday's breakfast was bagels with cream cheese and smoked salmon, or more likely lox, since it was more common for the fish to be cured in a slightly different way in America. We bought our food 'to go' from a nearby delicatessen, along with black coffee and went to Central Park to find a seat.

There was an unmistakable sense of quiet around the city, as the sheer magnitude of the previous day's brutality began to sink in. We claimed a park bench on The Mall, Central Park's famed tree lined avenue, and finished off our bagels.

"What rate did you get, boss?", Winston asked.

"Pardon?"

"For yesterday's money transfer. What dollar to pound exchange rate did the bank give you?"

I cast my mind back to the previous day's phone call.

"$1.496 to the pound, why?", I asked.

"Well, I remember you working out the value of the deal when you agreed the price with Barker back in July. The conversion rate for the £350,000 you were prepared to pay was based on the rate at the time, which was $1.400 to the pound. That's how you arrived at $490,000, right?"

"Yes", I answered, then did the calculation in my head.

$490,000 divided by $1.496 to the pound, worked out at around £327,500.

"Oh my God", I said, "the dollar rate must have spiked in reaction to the attack on the Towers. Even allowing for some commission charges, I've ended up paying £20,000 less for the watch than if the rate had been the same as it was two months ago", I said, incredulous at how a rate change of less than ten cents per pound Sterling could result in such a difference due to the size of the overall transaction amount.

Winston had already figured this out himself and wore a knowing expression on his face throughout my response.

"Yup", he said.

Poor Michael Barker I thought, but felt no satisfaction in having eventually gotten the better of him, as my thoughts turned to the fate of his friends who had been in the North Tower, as well as that of thousands of others who were thought to have perished on Tuesday morning. It was gut wrenching.

Winston and I spent another couple of days in New York as the city took some time to reverse the imposed travel restrictions. This gave us the opportunity to do justice to Manhattan's museums and we wrapped ourselves in a cocoon of culture to try and keep away from the depressing twenty-four-hour news bubble.

In the days following the mayhem in New York and Washington, America seemed to have already made up its mind who was responsible. A man named Osama bin Laden, the founder and head of an Islamist group, called Al-Qaeda, was named constantly in the news as being the undoubted mastermind behind the 9/11 attacks.

Neither Winston, nor I, had ever heard of the guy or his group before, but based on the latest reports, Bin Laden had become the one and only subject of a worldwide manhunt.

When transatlantic air travel out of JFK finally resumed, we were relieved to board our flight back to London. However, as the plane began its south west ascent, then banked round to the east, I saw the destruction at the World Trade Centre site far below. I was stunned by the scale of the mess, and by the huge clouds of smoke still emanating southwards in the wind from days old fires that were somehow still burning.

I got my head down on the plane and must have fallen asleep, since Winston shook me awake halfway through the flight and said I'd been snoring loudly. I laughed, defensively, while ironically refusing to believe that I'd been snoring, since I had not heard myself doing so. A couple of hours later, the plane began to descend as it started its approach towards Heathrow and I felt glad that in a short while we would be back home, safe and sound, with a bargain priced vintage Patek Philippe stowed away in Winston's cabin bag.

FIFTEEN

London, England
June 2005

In the four years since 9/11, Winston and I continued our pursuit of wealth, whilst having loads of fun along the way. My investment in the purchase of Michael Barker's Patek Philippe wristwatch looked like it was going to pay off, as industry insiders let on to Winston that the rare vintage watch market was booming, especially in London, where numerous Russian billionaires had started acquiring residential status in England's capital.

The country's new arrivals began buying up mansions in Surrey and competing against one another in a constant game of rich man's one-upmanship. Tit-for-tat purchases of flashy boys' toys was the latest fad, with supercars, Savile Row suits and rare timepieces being the most popular, especially with the under thirties.

Nevertheless, I decided to keep the 1518 safely locked away in my safe for the time being, happy to wait patiently for the right moment before, hopefully, cashing in big.

Our trading enterprise had now made both Winston and I millionaires. On paper at least. We had both built up an admirable collection of high value assets, such as property, which we rented out, some equities and bonds, the boring ones as I saw them. But we had also made a few sexier acquisitions, like my purchase of an original Picasso and Winston's procurement of one of the late Steve McQueen's Tag Heuer watches, although not the iconic one he wore in the motor racing movie Le Mans, but still a very cool and much sought-after timepiece.

We also had a worryingly large amount of cash in various currencies, piled up in the safe in our apartment. Sure, we had bank accounts with enviable balances earning decent interest, but we found that having plenty of foreign currency around allowed us to take advantage of exchange rate swings from time to time, swapping one currency for another when the rate was favourable, then back again several months later when the situation was reversed. We thought this was a little perverse, making money on our money, for free, but we also found it good fun, as if we were somehow beating the system.

In early June 2005, I was invited by a friend to attend the launch party of his new restaurant, Via Milano, an Italian place a few streets away from my apartment. It was a Saturday night and the place was already buzzing noisily when I arrived on my own, just after eight o'clock. Winston didn't fancy it and said he wanted to stay in and watch TV instead.

My friend, Gino, who I'd gotten to know through his sister, Monica, the owner of a gallery that Winston and I frequented often, welcomed me with a huge embrace and a glass of champagne. This was his big night and I was thrilled to be there for his launch. The restaurant was full, the food and wine were amazing and I had a terrific evening, which seemed to be a great success for Gino and his wife, Antonia.

As the curtain came down on the owners' glorious opening night party, they and a few others didn't want the evening to end, so I happily went along with the crowd as we went off to a local bar that had a one o'clock license. Gino got his front of house man, Carlo, to close the restaurant and off we went.

The pub was a cosy little place called the Wiltshire Arms and was just a few hundred yards away from Gino's restaurant. When we entered, I made sure I got to the bar first so I could buy a round of drinks, since I'd been eating and drinking at Gino's expense all evening back at the restaurant. There were eight of us and within an hour we were all the best of friends and very merry, as toast after toast was made in honour of Via Milano.

Around midnight, the door to the pub opened and in walked two women who looked slightly worse for wear. I recognised Rebecca van Aanholt immediately and went straight over to say hello.

"Oh, Bronson", she exclaimed loudly when she spotted me heading towards her. She gave me a big kiss on the cheek and wrapped her arms around me in a bear hug.

"Girls night out?", I asked, looking at Rebecca who hadn't aged a bit in the ten years since I'd last seen her.

Although clearly only a couple of drinks shy of being drunk, she looked as classy as ever in an elegant black dress and killer heels, but then she opened her mouth.

"What the fuck are you doing here, Bronson?", she slurred, "Oh God, I've missed that cologne of yours. Come here", she said nuzzling her face into my neck and taking a good sniff.

"I live here. In Kensington", I replied and this seemed to puzzle her. "I've been at a launch event at my friend's new restaurant up the road and a few of us came here afterwards to keep the party going", I explained.

"Holly, come and smell his neck, it's amazing", she said to her companion, but a rather pale looking Holly excused herself and went off to find the ladies room instead.

I did my best to hold Rebecca upright as she started to flag and made her drink some water I got from the barman. Then moments later Holly returned, her face looking as white as a ghost.

"I think I better go home now, Becks", she said, "I'm afraid I've just been a bit unwell in the ladies' bathroom. I've called Richard and he's on his way to pick me up", poor Holly looked done, make-up smeared around her eyes and beads of perspiration on her forehead.

"Bloody lightweight", Rebecca told her, but not with any sincerity.

"And where is Mr. Van Aanholt this evening?", I asked Rebecca.

"He's out with the boys at a private gentleman's dinner, at some club in Pall Mall", she answered, "He's probably more drunk than I am right now. Then he'll go on to the casino and throw some money away, the daft old sod", she giggled.

Holly then said a very quick goodbye and bolted for the door, as if she were about to be 'unwell' again out in the street.

"Call me in the morning", Rebecca screeched after her, then I got a water refill from the barman and made her drink it. I propped her up on a bar stool and went to tell Gino's crowd that I'd met a damsel in distress, the wife of an old friend, who I needed to escort home safely. We said our goodbyes, I congratulated Gino and Antonia once more on the success of the restaurant opening and returned to a nearly asleep Rebecca, whose head was now resting on the bar.

When we made it out onto the street, there was no sign of Holly so I presumed she'd been collected and I scanned the road for a passing taxi, as we walked north in the general direction of Kensington High Street.

Rebecca felt cold, so I took off my jacket and draped it over her bare shoulders. She seemed to rally a little in the fresh air and apologised for being so drunk. I hailed a passing black cab and when we got inside I asked Rebecca where she and Max lived.

"Eaton Terrace, Belgravia", she said, and I relayed this to the driver, who made a U-turn and we sped off in the opposite direction.

Rebecca rested her head on my shoulder as we rode along the quiet streets and ten minutes later we arrived outside her house. I asked the driver to wait while I helped Rebecca out of the taxi and into her house. She struggled to locate her key for a moment, then pulled it out of her bag and opened the front door.

She thanked me for getting her home safely, apologised again for being so drunk and promised to give my best to Max. We then embraced in a hug and she went inside, closing the door without realising she was still wearing my jacket. I knocked gently and the door opened again.

"Oops", she said, giggled once more, then took a long sniff at the collar of my coat and handed it back to me.

"That cologne really is wonderful, Bronson. Thank you again, my Knight in shining armour", then she winked, kissed me on the cheek and closed the door.

I hopped back into the cab and told the driver my address, then we set off again along the quiet London streets back to my apartment. I paid the fare, adding a generous tip, then climbed the stairs up to my home and went off to bed.

In the morning, I told Winston all about the party at the restaurant and who I'd bumped into in the pub afterwards. He said he was sorry to have missed seeing a drunk Rebecca van Aanholt and admitted that he'd been quite taken with her back in Rimini, albeit that she was a married woman.

On hearing that I told him it was probably a good thing he hadn't been out with me then. I didn't want any conflict with Max over his wife.

SIXTEEN

Several months later, in early 2006, I heard the news I'd been eagerly anticipating for over a decade, ever since I was told about the Macallan distillery's plans for releasing a fifty-year-old special edition single malt. The distillery had finally announced that it's fifty-year-old would soon be released, but that only 470 bottles would be produced.

I couldn't contain my excitement as I made enquiries directly with the distillery's sales team, but was somewhat dismayed when I was told that there appeared to be far more buyers interested than there would be bottles available. Demand outstripped supply by more than ten to one, so they had decided to conduct a ballot as the only fair way to choose who would be invited to make a purchase and sales would be limited to one bottle per buyer.

They told me that names would be drawn out at random on the morning of 6 March, at Macallan's Craigellachie headquarters in the Scottish Highlands and that, successful or not, everyone in the ballot would be notified of the result by telephone the following day.

I entered both Winston's name, and my own name to the ballot immediately, to try and improve my chances of being selected, albeit marginally.

I desperately wanted to get my hands on one or more of the 470 bottles, since I figured that, in time, as numerous bottles were consumed by avid whisky drinkers and the number left in circulation diminished, the value of each remaining bottle would rise, maybe exponentially.

When 7 March came around, I felt wired with anxiety, which was not helped by the several strong cups of coffee I'd had at breakfast. The telephone in our apartment didn't ring all morning, which I felt was not a good sign, since I presumed the successful buyers would be notified first.

Then, shortly after noon, the phone rang.

"Bronson Larkin", I answered, with urgency.

"Good afternoon Mr. Larkin", said a female voice, "it's Claire from the Macallan distillery here", she said, then paused.

"Yes", I replied, fingers crossed.

"I'm afraid your name wasn't selected in yesterday's ballot for our fifty-year-old special edition. I really am very sorry", she told me, sounding genuinely apologetic as if she appreciated the level of disappointment her round of phone calls would bring to people that afternoon.

"What about my colleague, Winston Murchison?", I asked, "His name was entered too."

"Oh", she exclaimed in recognition, "I think his name was one of those selected. Hold on a moment and I'll check."

This brought on a wave of optimism inside me, as I pleaded silently with the universe for Winston's name to have been picked out.

She came back on the phone.

"Oh, no sorry, Mr. Larkin. I was wrong. I was thinking of a chap I called this morning, his name was Wilson Murison. The name sounded so similar. No, Mr. Murchison's name was not selected either. I'm so sorry."

Then, attempting to console me, she said that if I was still interested, one or two buyers may choose to auction off their bottle over the coming years, if I was prepared to wait. I thanked her anyway and ended our call, feeling absolutely devastated.

"Pub?", asked Winston, reading my mind.

"Absolutely", I replied and off we went, but alcohol would bring me little consolation.

A few days later, articles started appearing in the press about the lucky few who had been able to purchase a bottle of the once in a generation special edition. Enthusiasts who had been lucky enough to taste it, were already declaring the fifty-year-old as the best single malt whisky ever produced.

My misery was further compounded when details were revealed of how the whisky had been presented. The distillery had partnered up with the renowned French glass making company, Lalique, which had designed and crafted an exquisitely beautiful crystal decanter.

As a combination, the decanter and whisky together, were being described in the media as one of the first genuine masterpieces of the new millennium.

I had to wait a whole year before getting another chance to own a fifty-year-old Macallan Lalique. In late March 2007, an acquaintance of mine from Bonhams sent me a sale catalogue for an upcoming fine wines and rare scotch whisky auction that was scheduled to take place on 25 April at Bonhams' New Bond Street premises in London. The auction was to include a Lalique fifty.

It would be the first such bottle to appear in an auction since the whisky's release the year before. It was aptly listed in the catalogue as lot number fifty, with a pre-sale estimate of between £8,000 and £12,000, and its reserve would be set at £6,500.

I registered my interest and set up an account with the auctioneer, into which I transferred £35,000. An amount that was way more than I should need to secure the bottle, including the buyer's premium, and for that matter much more than I would be prepared to pay for a single bottle of malt whisky. Sure, I wanted it badly, but I wasn't crazy. Each bottle had been bought from the distillery for less than £2,000 when it was released only a year ago.

I hoped this would be my time.

On the morning of the auction, which was scheduled for eleven o'clock, Winston and I made it to New Bond Street at ten-thirty by taxi. We were welcomed into Bonhams by the guy I knew, who ushered the two of us upstairs to a huge sale room with what looked like a couple of hundred chairs laid out in neat rows, the front ten rows of which were already fully occupied.

I had requested a special bidder number for the auction. I'm not normally a superstitious person, but on this occasion, I figured a lucky charm couldn't hurt. The guy who'd escorted us upstairs smiled, as he handed me a circular bidder paddle with the number fifty stencilled on both sides. He wished me luck, then left the room.

Winston picked up a full glass of Prosecco from a table at the back of the room and handed it to me. I immediately gulped the whole glassful straight down, but declined the refill he offered. We then picked two seats at end of the back row, which afforded us a view of all the potential bidders in the room, as well as a sightline to the phone attendants at the opposite side of the room who would take part on behalf of any remote bidders.

At just a minute or so before eleven o'clock, I was browsing through the catalogue in my lap when Winston nudged me and I looked up. He motioned towards a figure who had just strolled in and who was heading for the one remaining vacant seat in the front row.

I recognised the unmistakable gait of Max van Aanholt and was disappointed he hadn't spotted us. The auction was about to start so I didn't get a chance to say hello before things got underway. Winston and I both turned to look behind us though, out of instinct I suppose, and spotted Archie, the thin giant, standing at the back of the room next to the refreshments table.

I gave him a wave, along with a goofy smile and Winston nodded at him with much more decorum. Archie acknowledged us with a simple military style salute.

The lights in the room then dimmed, ever so slightly and a tall suited man strode confidently up onto a stage at the front, before gently tapping a wooden hammer to quell the excited pre-auction hubbub. He introduced himself as the head auctioneer and went through the ground rules, in case anyone present was an auction rookie. I didn't think that was likely, but one never knew.

He got things underway with a series of multi-lots, mostly cases and half-cases of rare fine wines, all of which sold within the upper range of their catalogued estimates.

Before long, lots thirty to forty went within a quarter of an hour's bidding at a lightening quick pace and the auctioneer in charge did well to maintain control of proceedings, as bidder numbers popped up from all corners of the room.

I was slightly surprised that Max hadn't ventured into the fold yet. He seemed content to allow several prominent vintage wines to pass him by, which made me presume that he was waiting for a specific lot to come up, just like me.

The final wine lots came and went without Max making a single bid, then the auctioneer started with the rare scotch whiskies at lot number forty-eight.

Five minutes later, my long-awaited moment finally arrived, as the auctioneer called lot number fifty, then went through a brief description of the fifty-year-old Macallan, as it was paraded in front of the stage from one side of the room to the other in its sublime Lalique crystal decanter.

The bidding started at £6,000, then rose to £8,500 within a minute, as two participants went back and forth in the early exchanges. I waited patiently for things to slow down before I joined in at £9,750, but was immediately outbid by another new bidder on one of the telephones.

The two early bidders faded away as I battled it out against a mystery bidder, who's latest telephone bid took us up to £11,000. I pressed on, with a counter bid of £11,250 and thought it wouldn't be long before my adversary withdrew, as my latest bid brought us ever closer to lot fifty's pre-auction upper estimate of £12,000.

We continued for a few more rounds, outbidding one another in increments of £250, until the telephone attendant announced that her remote bidder was finally out, leaving me with the winning bid of £13,500.

To my delight, the auctioneer raised his gavel and went through the motions of declaring fair warning to the room. Winston placed a congratulatory hand on my shoulder as the hammer started its descent.

"£14,000", a voice suddenly called out loudly.

I scanned the crowd to see where this late bid had come from and my eyes narrowed with confusion, as they settled on the raised hand of Max van Aanholt, holding his bidder number aloft in the front row, staring ahead blankly.

"What the fuck?", I looked at Winston, who seemed as shocked as I was.

I turned around to Archie behind us and raised my eyebrows, mouthing "what's he doing?"

All I got back was a shrug, as if he was as bewildered by Max's interjection as we were. Meanwhile, the auctioneer was prompting me for a counterbid, seemingly excited by the sudden drama of a last-minute entrant.

I had told Max in Rimini, more than a decade ago, that my dream was to one day purchase a fifty-year-old Macallan and yet, here he was putting up a late challenge against me, just as I was reaching the finish line.

What the hell was going on? I thought this guy was my friend. There was no way in hell that he didn't know I was in the room bidding for this Macallan.

I needed to get a hold of myself quickly, or I would end up losing out, which I now presumed was what Max's aim must be, even though I had no idea why. I raised my bidder paddle.

"£15,000", I said and the auctioneer acknowledged me with an eager nod, as he realised that Bonhams' commission for lot fifty was about to exceed all expectations.

Max came back with a counterbid of £16,000, all the while maintaining his straight-ahead posture, giving no hint of looking back at me.

"£17,000", I said, but Max immediately nodded an increased bid in response, which the auctioneer announced to the room with glee.

"£18,000, I am bid. The gentleman in the front row, to my right. Do I here £19,000? The gentleman at the back. Do you wish to respond, sir?", he asked.

I did, and nodded my affirmation to go up to £20,000. This was becoming ridiculous.

Winston left my side to have a word with Archie, but returned almost immediately, saying that Archie hadn't a clue what Max was up to, saying only that his boss must have a good reason for wanting to beat me to this particular lot.

We carried on bidding.

Around five minutes later, we had reached £29,000, which was my own bid, and I was frantically doing calculations in my head, factoring in the buyer's premium of twenty percent. In doing so, I realised that I was at my limit of the £35,000 I'd deposited with the auction house and that one more bid from Max would see me missing out on my dream. This felt so cruel.

I watched in horror as Max yet again raised his bidder number and the auctioneer called out £30,000, before retraining his eyes back on me to solicit another £1,000 increase.

I was in shock. I slowly shook my head from side to side, and mouthed 'no more' to the auctioneer, then sat with my head bowed, as he went through the motions of fair warnings to the rest of the room, then finally brought his hammer down with a loud crack that signalled my defeat was now official.

Max stood up and made for the door as the auctioneer began announcing lot fifty-one. Winston and I left our seats too, but before I could get to Max, Archie stepped in between us, blocking my path as Max slipped out of the sale room, without making eye contact.

I was completely baffled by what had just taken place. Archie followed his boss out of the room, then Winston and I stepped into the hallway and pursued them along the narrow corridor.

"Max", I called out, but he ignored me and kept walking.

"What the hell was that?", I shouted after him, as he and Archie changed direction to descend the stairs.

When Winston and I made it down to the ground floor, there was no sign of them.

I approached a nearby member of Bonhams' staff.

"Where do the lots get collected from?", I asked.

"Along there", a young male answered, pointing, "last door on the left at the end of the hall."

I went straight towards it, Winston by my side. The door was ajar and Winston pushed it fully open as we entered a large office. Max and Archie were seated at a table, with their backs to the door, paperwork on a desk before them. A Bonhams' representative was explaining something to Max about the documents in front of him and looked up, startled by our intrusion.

"Why the fuck did you just do that Max?", I demanded. The Bonhams' guy raised his eyebrows, but said nothing.

Archie stood up, ready to protect his boss. I felt Winston tense up right beside me, as Max calmly turned to finally face me.

"You know why, Bronson", he said quietly, which had a disarming effect on the sudden heightened tension in the room.

"What?", I asked, confused beyond words.

"There are some rules that you do not break, Bronson. You think I don't know, but I'm not an idiot. You know what you did was wrong, my boy. Today is your punishment."

What the hell was he talking about? Had the old codger gone mental?

Archie took a step closer to where Winston and I were standing, but not in a threatening way, more like placing himself between Max and I as a physical barrier, just in case.

"I think it would be best if you took off and let whatever this is blow over, without any more animosity, for now at least", said Archie, in a calm and reasoning voice.

I fought the urge to lunge at Max's throat, as Winston put his arm around my back and led me out of the room. What the hell had just happened? Why had Max outbid me for my dream scotch? Had I done something wrong?

Out on the street, Winston hailed a black cab and guided me into the back seat, then we left New Bond Street and headed for home. I was completely and utterly bewildered.

SEVENTEEN

Milan, Italy
October 2010

That was the last time we saw Max and Archie for several years and I felt bitter about not knowing why Max had wanted to punish me. Nevertheless, our intermittent friendship, a relationship that I thought had been one of kindred spirits, based on a mutual passion for trading beautiful things, was clearly at an end.

Winston and I had not slowed down in the three years that followed the Bonhams' auction debacle. We'd done very well buying and selling scarce artworks, Renaissance paintings and centuries old stone sculptures, as the appetite of London's elite for such treasures continued to grow.

In early October 2010, I received a phone call out of the blue from the personal assistant of an American politician based in Boston. The caller introduced herself to me as Melinda Baker and told me she that worked for a man called Benson Ashley, who was the incumbent Senior Senator for the US State of Massachusetts, an important American Democrat politician.

She asked if I would accept a call, momentarily, from the Senator and I responded cagily, asking how she had obtained my home phone number. Apparently, Senator Ashley had tracked me down himself, by making some guarded enquiries with a political contact in the United States, to whom he revealed that he had a need for the services of a trustworthy and capable individual with a proven track record of finding illusive items of exceptionally high value, whilst maintaining the utmost confidentiality. His contact led him to an unnamed British aristocrat across the Atlantic, a member of the United Kingdom's House of Lords. The hereditary peer had, in turn, put Ashley in touch with Sir Philip Rathbone at Kensington Palace, who had subsequently provided the Senator with my details.

After thinking through this explanation, I figured Baker was being genuine, so I agreed to accept the phone call. She told me he would call in a minute or two, then hung up and I beckoned Winston through to our lounge so he could hear the imminent phone conversation first hand.

A moment later, the phone rang and I pressed the speakerphone button.

"Hello, Bronson Larkin", I announced, then the sound of Benson's voiced filled the room.

"Hello Mr. Larkin. Benson Ashley here. Thanks for taking my call. I understand from a mutual acquaintance, Sir Philip Rathbone, that you helped his boss, the Prince of Wales, with a personal errand a few years back. Is that right?", he asked.

"Yes, that's right. Your assistant told me you might want my help to find something."

"That's correct. A musical instrument. My daughter's cello. Someone stole it", he said.

Senator Ashley then told us an incredible, heart wrenching story as Winston and I listened in silence.

He had married his high school sweetheart, a beautiful young woman called Cindy Jackson, who was the daughter of a local Boston furniture maker and his school teacher wife.

After high school, the couple survived a difficult, long-distance relationship, as they continued their education at universities in separate parts of the country. Then, the pair married and moved into their first home together, a small apartment in central Boston as they both embarked on their respective careers. Benson joined a prominent law firm, while Cindy began her own interior design business.

They worked hard and prospered. Being high earners living a relatively modest existence, Benson invested a sizeable percentage of their surplus income every month, which, after only a few years, saw them well on their way to financial independence.

In 1986, Cindy became pregnant and they moved to a large detached house on a tree-lined street. They were blessed with a daughter, Christina, who would be their only child. Christina showed a talent for music from a very young age, starting both violin and piano lessons at the age of three. She developed a life-long love for playing classical music and, with hard work, would ultimately go on to play professionally.

By the time Christina had reached high school age, Benson's passion for the law began to wane and he became more interested and active in politics. Firstly, as an ordinary member of the Democratic Party, then as his leadership qualities, political astuteness and natural charisma as a public speaker revealed themselves, the party leadership offered to support him as a candidate.

With their help, Benson established a campaign committee, consisting of a well-respected and seasoned campaign manager, a public relations expert and an experienced fund-raising manager. He quit his job as a lawyer and, with his team around him, devoted several months to campaigning, after which he obtained the requisite number of registered voter signatures to get his name on the ballot for election to the United States Senate.

He won in a landslide against an aging and jaded Republican opponent and was duly elected as the Junior Senator for the State of Massachusetts in 2003. At that time, Cindy decided to give up her own career to support her Senator husband, which Benson said he had not encouraged, but was nevertheless, very grateful for. He told Winston and I that he had been completely humbled by his wife's selflessness.

He and Cindy were a formidable couple, with Cindy championing women's issues and working tirelessly in the community on charitable projects, and Benson working long hours as a dedicated public servant.

In 2006, Christina landed her dream job as a cellist with the Boston Symphony Orchestra and her parents couldn't have been prouder. However, it was then that the Ashley family's fairy tale life together came to a shattering end with the devastating news that Cindy had been diagnosed with a highly aggressive form of breast cancer.

Benson desperately reached out to the country's best doctors in search of a lifesaving treatment for his wife, but his efforts were fruitless. The cancer had grown too large, too quickly, for any treatment to have a chance. Cindy would have only a few months to live, at best.

In the Autumn of that year, with her condition worsening at a frightening pace, Cindy asked Benson to buy an heirloom quality gift for her, so she could give it to their daughter before she died.

The Senator contacted musical antique dealers and auction houses throughout America, with the intention of finding a cello worthy of being his wife's parting gift to their daughter.

After a few days, one of the dealers he'd contacted in New York telephoned Benson with news that he had a solid lead on an original, one of a kind, Stradivarius cello built by Antonio Stradivari in 1709, which had been nicknamed "Boccherini, Romberg" after Luigi Boccherini, the cello's first owner.

The dealer told him it was owned by a female member of the Rockefeller family, who, after hearing the tragic circumstances behind his enquiry, said that she would be willing to sell it to Mrs. Ashley for the same $475,000 she had paid for it herself.

Benson travelled to New York and bought the cello, then brought it back to Boston so that Cindy could present it to Christina from her hospital bed. The family shared a tearful evening together, as Christina was bowled over by her mother's bittersweet gift.

A few days before her mother died, Christina broke the news to her parents that she had been offered an overseas opportunity to play her cello in the United Kingdom with the London Symphony Opera. It would be a two-year secondment offering her the chance to broaden her experience and further develop her musical abilities, by working with different musicians and conductors in a new environment. Benson and Cindy were overjoyed for her and Cindy urged their daughter to accept the offer.

Cindy's funeral was attended by hundreds, including several members of congress and even the Vice President. A few weeks later, Christina left for London, leaving Benson on his own in Boston. He put all his energy into work, but was unable to mask the sorrow of losing his soul mate.

Three years later, with Christina back in Boston staying with her father, their home was burgled during the night while they slept. Benson awoke to a ransacked mess downstairs and discovered to his horror that Christina's Stradivarius was missing.

Months went by with the Boston Police Department making no progress solving the crime, and Christina heartbroken by the loss of her treasured cello.

Although Benson collected $500,000 from an insurance claim, he continued trying to recover the missing instrument through a private investigator, but was unsuccessful.

Then, in the late summer of 2010, with Christina playing in Europe, Benson's search led him to me, feeling that this may be his last chance to find the stolen cello.

Winston and I had listened sympathetically to Senator Ashley and I asked him how we could help. He said he would be heading to Italy in October to meet up with his daughter who was playing at the world renowned La Scala theatre in Milan.

He said his investigator may have stumbled upon a possible clue, but wouldn't say any more over the phone and wanted to meet in person to discuss it. He offered to pay for me and Winston to travel to Milan and I accepted.

We flew from London Gatwick to Milan's Malpensa Airport on a Saturday morning and met Benson in the lobby of the city's Mandarin Oriental Hotel, where Winston had reserved us a room each for our visit to Milan, just a short walk from the famous theatre. Senator Ashley was a tall man, with slightly receding grey hair and a gaunt frame. He had the look of someone who had experienced more than enough pain for one lifetime and after being in his company for only a few minutes, I felt compelled to do all I could to recover his daughter's stolen cello.

Over coffee, the Senator told us the investigator's search had led him to New York, where an unlikely conversation with a former police chief, now also a private investigator, had finally unearthed a possible lead. The ex-policeman had heard rumours from his former colleagues about some chatter being picked up on a police surveillance tape that mentioned a Stradivarius cello. The New York Police Department were routinely monitoring phone calls in and out of a social club called Gennaro's in Little Italy, known to be the operational headquarters of the Genovese crime family.

The incumbent boss of the Genovese mob was a Sicilian gangster called Marco Cannizzaro. A formidable money maker in the modern day criminal underworld, he had a reputation for being more focussed on building wealth through rigging construction contracts and white-collar crimes, like insurance fraud, rather than the darker world of prostitution and gambling, which Cannizzaro thought was outdated and carried more risk.

One of his underbosses had been overheard talking about a Stradivarius cello with an unknown person on his cell phone inside the club, which the officers listening in thought was very unusual.

Benson's investigator told him that the full extent of his potential to find the cello had been reached and, since the Senator had received an insurance pay out, the NYPD did not regard questioning the mafia about the cello as a priority. Doing so would only tip off the Genovese mob about the presence of the listening device inside the club and the police were after them for much bigger crimes than a stolen musical instrument.

When Senator Ashley had finished bringing us up to date he looked drained and I told him we were willing to try and help, if he, in turn, was prepared to pay us a fee for doing so, whether we recovered the cello or not, since I couldn't guarantee we'd be successful. He agreed, saying again he thought we might be his last chance, but he felt it was worth giving it a final shot.

He emphasised that it was not a matter of money. Benson was a very wealthy man from his former law career, he had received $500,000 from the insurance pay out and could have easily bought Christina another Stradivarius. But he wanted the actual cello his dying wife gave to their daughter. A replacement instrument wouldn't do.

I agreed a deal with him for a set fee of $50,000, plus expenses, which he would pay even if we were ultimately unsuccessful. However, if we recovered the cello, he would pay us another $50,000 on top. At the end of our meeting with Benson, he invited us to join him for that night's concert at La Scala so we could see his beloved Christina perform. I accepted and he handed me two tickets, saying Winston and I would be seated next to him and we arranged to meet in the theatre's bar at seven o'clock.

He left Winston and I in the Oriental's lobby, saying he was heading for Christina's apartment in the city. Winston then went to check us in at the front desk as I sat pondering all the information Benson has divulged about our quest to find the cello.

I took in the scene around me. The hotel's reception area was a very contemporary space, with a mix of stone tiles and wooden floors, filled with sleek Italian furniture as well as a modern glass and stone fire pit as its centrepiece.

There were lots of new arrivals checking in so Winston had to join a long line. I spotted a woman sitting alone in an armchair around twenty feet across from me. She was beautiful, with a stunning tanned face framed by long wavy dark hair. She was wearing black jeans and a black round neck top, no items of jewellery except for a bright yellow gold watch and she sat with one leg tucked underneath her, a discarded pair of shoes lying on the floor beside her chair as she leafed through a paperback looking very relaxed.

I found it difficult to gauge how old she was. She was so attractive and elegant that she could have been aged anywhere from twenty-five to forty-five and she caught me gazing at her when she paused reading to turn a page.

I smiled at her as we made eye contact and her lips turned slightly upwards at the corners of her mouth, before she shyly looked back down to her book. We exchanged a few more glances at one another, before Winston appeared at my shoulder saying our rooms were ready and he passed me an electronic key card.

I stood and picked up my overnight bag, then followed Winston's lead towards the elevator, stealing one last look at the gorgeous woman in black before entering the elevator with wistful thoughts about what might have been.

Both of our rooms were on the fourth floor, but not next to one another this time. I was at the end of a corridor while Winston was closer to the elevators in the centre of the building. My room was just as tastefully decorated as the lobby downstairs, with a large king-sized bed, flanked by a matching pair of wooden side tables and a couple of mid-brown leather chairs at the end of the bed.

Downlights in the ceiling, modern table lamps and flexible reading lights at the head of the bed provided a range of ambiance options and, through in the bathroom, there was a large stand-alone bath with a separate shower cubicle, along with grey and white marble tiles throughout.

I called down to the concierge desk to ask about hiring suitable attire for the concert and the guy I spoke to was most helpful. He made late afternoon appointments for Winston and me at a nearby gentleman's outfitters only fifteen minutes away by taxi. I then called through to Winston's room to let him know then we grabbed a light lunch together at the Mandarin's informal bistro.

I set Winston a post-lunch task of doing some digging online using one of the internet terminals available for rent in the hotel's business centre to see what he could find out about the Genovese and their boss.

Meanwhile, I decided to make a few phone calls to auction houses in the New York area to see if any of them knew anything about a Stradivarius cello for sale.

We re-grouped in the lobby a few minutes before our three o'clock taxi pick up arranged by the guy on the concierge desk. Winston, it seemed, had been much more successful with his search than I had been, since my enquiries had yielded a big fat zero. He had unearthed an online article about Cannizzaro, which he brought me up to date on as we rode in the taxi.

Winston told me that the author of the piece hadn't met with Cannizzaro herself, but had put together a flattering profile of the mob boss, centring around a passion he was rumoured to have for fine wines. Apparently, he was an avid collector of Italian reds and had an enviable cellar full of scarce vintages. I mulled over whether this information might give us a way in, but my thoughts were interrupted by our arrival at the menswear store.

We entered a very handsome boutique, which had rails of designer men's clothing for sale in the front two thirds of the store, with the rear being dedicated to formal evening wear hire.

I led the way up to the back and as we approached, a middle-aged assistant looked up towards us from behind a counter. Realising we were his three-fifteen hire appointments he grimaced immediately at the sight of the oversized ape standing behind me.

Nevertheless, he welcomed us and began a very professional appraisal of our requirements, whilst running a tape measure over some key parts of our bodies. An hour and a half later, I had been transformed into a suave, sophisticated looking aristocrat, in my opinion. I had selected a dark red velvet dinner jacket with a crisp white dress shirt, along with a pair of black tuxedo trousers, cummerbund and bow tie, finished off with a pair of shiny black patent leather shoes.

Winston, on the other hand, was dressed in a much more traditional ensemble, mostly because his sheer size limited the options. He wore an all-black tuxedo with a white shirt and black shoes.

"How do I look, boss?", he asked.

"Very sharp. Like a well-dressed Bond villain."

We changed back into our own clothes and the store assistant neatly folded our outfits into suit carriers, which Winston took hold of as I paid for our rentals and asked our host to call for a cab to take us back to the hotel.

A short while later, after a shower and a shave, followed by a room service dinner, I was again dressed like a peacock, and ready for the concert.

I met Winston by the elevator on our floor and we rode down to the lobby together, with Winston hulking over me and looking like a giant penguin. I think we both strode through the hotel's reception area feeling very proud that we'd scrubbed up so well. I know that I for one, had never been dressed up so fancy before and I felt a pang of disappointment that the dark-haired beauty I'd seen in the lobby earlier was no longer there to see me in my finery.

When we emerged from the hotel, though, I began to feel a little more ordinary, as we joined the scores of fellow concert goers heading for the theatre just yards away, resplendent in their formal evening attire.

I showed our tickets to a serious looking official at the main door of La Scala, who, in response to my request for directions to the bar, answered me curtly in Italian with only his hand gestures giving me any clue as to where we might find it. Happily, less than a minute later, we'd found the bar and spotted Senator Ashley, who, like us, was dressed like an Academy Award host.

He smiled as he saw me approaching, we greeted one another then Winston offered to get some drinks and headed off to the bar for three whiskies. I told our client what we'd read online about Cannizzaro's interest in wine and that I was working on a strategy for approaching him in New York, but mostly I was trying to let Benson know that we were already working on getting his daughter's cello back.

Winston returned with our drinks, which we each sipped slowly whilst making small talk about our regal surroundings. Benson told us how proud he was that Christina was playing at this incredible venue and mentioned more than once, how sad it was that Cindy wasn't there to see her performance.

Before long, a bell sounded from somewhere in the room and it was time to take our seats. An usher led the three of us to a private box, which was among what seemed like hundreds of similar boxes surrounding the stage over six floor levels in the shape of a horseshoe. I couldn't think of a more beautiful, or for that matter, a more intimidating setting for any young musician to perform in.

The orchestra took the stage amid rapturous applause from the excited audience and Benson was quick to point out Christina holding her reserve cello and taking a seat near the front of the assembled musicians. She looked radiant in a silver ballgown. She glanced upwards to smile at her father in the box before carefully organising the sheet music in front of her. The audience burst into applause once more as the conductor took centre stage, then the theatre fell silent, ready for the evening's entertainment to begin.

There followed, one of the most unexpected and spectacular experiences of my life. We were treated to a most sublime performance of Antonio Vivaldi's Four Seasons, uniquely arranged and extended to over three hours, excluding a short break in the middle. It was the most beautiful music I had ever heard, made even more wonderful by the acoustics and atmosphere of what was a truly magical setting.

Benson was very tearful at the end, as the entire audience rose to a standing ovation, with appreciative applause continuing long enough after the conductor had left the stage, to be rewarded with his prompt return, as is customary, which he used to acknowledge first the whole orchestra, then a few soloists. The musicians stood and bowed in turn as the final crescendo of applause marked an evening of triumph for everyone on stage.

As other members of the audience made for the exits, Senator Ashley led us back to the bar to await the arrival of his daughter. I ordered champagne, then when she burst into the room moments later, the embrace she shared with her father brought a lump to my throat.

Winston and I were introduced to Christina, we toasted her success as I made an overconfident and unwise promise to find her stolen cello and return it to her.

Benson invited us to join them and some other members of the orchestra for a post-concert dinner, but I declined his offer respectfully, saying we had to return to the hotel and get some sleep in readiness for beginning our search for the cello in earnest first thing in the morning.

After saying our goodbyes, King Kong and I left the bar area, but before exiting the theatre, my eyes were drawn to a figure standing alone off to one side. It was the dark-haired woman from back at the hotel, she was dressed in a figure hugging black sequined ball gown that shimmered in the light from the theatre foyer's chandeliers.

She noticed me and our eyes met, then she smiled at me welcomingly, so I excused myself from Winston, told him I'd see him later, and approached her as Winston disappeared.

"Good evening, did you enjoy the concert?", I asked.

"Yes, it was wonderful. I love Vivaldi, but I've never heard the Four Seasons played like that before", she replied with a heavy Italian accent, her voice smooth and velvety.

"I saw you in the Mandarin hotel this afternoon, are you staying there", I asked.

"Yes, are you?"

"Yes. I'm Bronson", I said.

"Francesca", she replied.

"Are you waiting for someone?", I asked.

"No, I came to the concert by myself. My sister's in the orchestra. She was the Principal Second Violin tonight. I saw her a minute ago. She's going out to dinner with some others, but I don't know them so I didn't want to go", she said.

Then she was very candid with me.

"I saw you in one of the boxes and thought I recognised you from earlier today. I stayed behind to see if I was right. And to ask you why you chose to wear Silvio Berlusconi's dinner jacket", she joked, and we both laughed.

"I had no choice", I protested, "it was the last one they had at the rental place. Anyway, I might ask you why you're wearing Maleficent's dress to a symphony performance", I kidded.

"Ooh, that's a good one", she said, her beautiful green eyes looking directly into mine.

"Well, since you're not waiting for anyone, may I escort you back to the hotel? So long as you promise not to prick my finger with a spindle and send me to sleep for a hundred years", I said, and she gave me a playful nudge.

"Alright. I promise I won't send you to sleep, but if you make any more jokes about my dress, then I might have to turn you into a frog or something", she replied, with a mock serious expression.

I held my arm out, offering it to her, theatrically.

"Shall we?"

"Certainly, Il Cavaliere", she replied, addressing me cheekily by Berlusconi's nickname.

She took my arm and we left the theatre, but the full length and tightness of Francesca's gown, not to mention her high heeled shoes, meant we had to walk slowly as we set off in the direction of the Oriental. The October evening air was cool, so I slipped off my dinner jacket and wrapped it around her shoulders as we walked.

"Wow, what fragrance is that you're wearing?", she asked, picking up the smell of my cologne from the collar of the jacket.

"It's a one-off scent, actually. It was made by a bespoke perfumer in London", I replied, feeling that I must have sounded so pretentious.

"It's beautiful, what's in it?", she asked.

"Sandalwood, vanilla, lemon and a couple of other ingredients. It was a gift."

"Oh, yeah? From a girlfriend?", she asked.

"No. I did some work for a guy a few years back whose sister owns the perfumery. I guess he was pleased with my services, so he arranged for his sister to make me a bespoke fragrance, as a kind of bonus payment."

"It smells divine", she said.

We had arrived at the hotel, but she wanted to continue walking for a bit, so we carried on.

"What kind of work do you do?", she asked.

"I trade things, valuable objects", I replied, not realising at first how abstract my response must have sounded.

"What kind of valuable objects?"

"All kinds of things, really. Paintings, jewellery, rare watches, scotch whisky, sometimes precious stones. Occasionally bigger things like vintage cars or antique furniture."

"I've never heard of someone doing that for a living before", she said.

"And what about you?", I asked, "Surely you don't really cast spells for a living?"

She laughed again.

"Don't be silly", she said, "I'm a vintner. My family owns a vineyard in Tuscany. We make some of the finest wines in the world. My sister, the violinist, is the only one in my family who isn't involved in the business."

"Which vineyard?", I asked, intrigued.

"Masseto."

"Masseto?", I repeated, incredulous, "the Bolgheri region vineyard where Masseto Toscana is produced?", I asked.

"Yes", she said, "we're very proud of our wine."

Wow, I thought, as we continued our stroll. We were several streets away from the hotel and it suddenly struck me that, in the darkness, it may not be wise to go much further. I said so to Francesca, admitting to her that I didn't know the city, and wasn't that familiar with where we had wandered off to.

I then heard footsteps behind us, coming at pace, getting louder. Just as I turned to see who was approaching, I caught a glimmer of a blade in the right hand of one of two shadows heading straight for us.

I quickly grabbed the dinner jacket from Francesca's shoulders and wrapped it around my arm thinking it might offer some protection against the knife. I pulled Francesca behind me, with my eyes fixed on the guy with the knife. I figured this was a mugging and readied myself to just give up my wallet and get us out of there unharmed.

Then suddenly, just before they were upon us, a hulking figure appeared from nowhere behind them and blocked what little street lighting there was like an eclipse. A pair of gigantic hands grabbed each of the two would be attackers from behind and their advance was halted violently, as if they'd collided with an invisible clothes line, each man landing with a sickening thud as their backs slammed onto the ground.

Francesca screamed and I led her by the hand across to the other side of the street, as I watched Winston bring his size twenty dress shoe down like a slab of concrete onto the hand holding the knife, then he bent down to wrestle the shiny metal blade from the guy's trapped hand.

Winston then struck the fallen thug with a savage punch to the side of the head and idiot number one was knocked out. The winded second guy tried to get to his feet, but as he rose, Winston grabbed him by the throat and flung him through the air, the back of his head smacking into the wall of a building with an awful clunk and I instantly feared the blow had killed him.

"Get back to the hotel, boss", he said, and with Francesca still gripping my hand tightly, she kicked off her high heels, grabbed them with her free hand, then lifted her dress as much as she could and we started back in the direction we had come from. She was shaking with fear.

"Who were they? Did you know them? Who was the man who saved us?", she asked.

"Probably some local muggers. They must've watched us leave the theatre and assumed we were an easy target for rich pickings. The big man is with me. He'll have been watching them, watching us. Thankfully."

"Should we contact the police?", she asked, still shaking.

"I don't think so. I'm not sure what my friend, Winston, will do with them and I wouldn't want him to get in trouble with the Carabinieri."

My heart was racing, from the shock and adrenaline as we made it safely back inside the hotel. We went straight to the bar and I ordered a couple of whiskies, straight without ice or water. We gulped them down and the barman raised his eyebrows inquisitively at me.

"I'm Scottish", I said by way of an explanation, then ordered two more. I didn't want to hang around and tell the barman what had just happened in case the thugs were seriously injured down the road, which might bring some trouble our way from the authorities.

The barman handed over our second glasses of scotch and I gave him a fifty Euro note in return.

"Let's get out of here", I said to Francesca, and we headed for the elevator with our drinks. On the way, we passed by the reception area and Francesca collected her key card from a woman behind the desk. When the elevator door opened, we stepped inside and I asked which floor her room was on.

"Three", she replied.

I pushed the button and the door closed. Then Francesca threw her shoes down onto the floor of the elevator, pulled me towards her and we kissed passionately. I'd never felt so alive, feeling a rush of warmth all over my body as we continued kissing until the elevator pinged when we reached the third floor.

She grabbed her shoes from the floor and we stepped into the hallway. Our glasses were empty and we laughed realising we must have spilt our drinks all over the elevator floor. When we reached her room, she opened the door, pulled me inside and there, in the darkness with this Tuscan goddess, I experienced the most exhilarating, adrenaline charged night of passionate love making of my entire life.

In the morning, I awoke to the sound of the shower running from the bathroom. I found a pen and notepad in a bedside drawer and scribbled a quick note to Francesca saying I would be back soon, then I put on my shirt, trousers & shoes, grabbed the rest of my clothes and slipped out of the room to head upstairs. I took a quick shower in my own room, put on some fresh clothes and went downstairs to the bistro.

Ten minutes later, I knocked gently on the door to Francesca's room and she opened it wearing only a bathrobe.

"Buongiorno Signor Berlusconi", she greeted me, with a smile.

"Good morning. I brought coffee and pastries", I said, as she opened the door wide to let me in.

We enjoyed a lazy breakfast together lying on the bed, reliving the drama of the previous night's close encounter in the street. I felt so comfortable with her and, seeing her in the daylight wearing no makeup, I was struck by how naturally beautiful she was.

I could have happily spent days with her, but realising that Winston and I had work to do, I gently broached the subject of my departure. Francesca was understanding, but told me she felt we had really connected and didn't want this to be goodbye. I said I felt the same, so we exchanged contact details and shared a long embrace before I left her room.

Before I had gone far, though, she called me back. I turned and saw her with my dinner jacket, which she was holding up to her face, enjoying a last burst of my fragrance from the collar.

"That cologne of yours is amazing", she said, which immediately jolted my brain into a flashback of almost the exact same goodbye I'd had with Max's wife outside their house in Belgravia more than five years before.

I kissed her one last time then pulled myself away and walked off in the direction of the elevator, realising without any shred of doubt in my mind that the reason Max had screwed me over at the whisky auction was because he'd recognised the smell of my cologne on Rebecca when he returned home that night, back in 2005. He must have mistakenly concluded that I had slept with his wife. The daft old fool.

My situation with Max would have to be resolved at some point, but for now I needed to get back to London and focus on the search for the cello.

I went upstairs and packed my things, then walked along to Winston's room and knocked on his door. He welcomed me inside and we played catch up on the events of the previous night. I told him I was smitten, but didn't share any details. A gentleman never tells, after all.

Likewise, he didn't tell me what he'd done with the two thugs after we left him, other than to say the streets were clean. I didn't know what that meant exactly, nor did I want to.

We left our rented formalwear with the hotel concierge who agreed to return it on our behalf and I gave him a generous tip. We then set off for the airport by taxi and flew back to London that afternoon. I tried to focus on finding the cello, but spent most of my journey home thinking about Francesca, with a growing pang of regret that I'd had to leave her behind in Italy.

EIGHTEEN

Back in London, Winston and I got to work planning our next move in the hunt for the cello. I called Senator Ashley and asked him to email me all his investigator's reports, then when they arrived, I printed them all out and we started pouring over the details.

Our focus was very much on a transcript of the taped conversation from the social club, as well as information that we used to map out the names and organisation structure of the Genovese crime family, which wasn't all that difficult, since the investigator's ex-police chief contact had provided him with plenty of information copied from the latest NYPD files.

We used a wall of the office in our apartment to pin up photos with names of each of the key players in a hierarchal layout, with Marco Cannizzaro at the top, as the undisputed boss. From what we could gather, Marco's empire seemed to operate without a Consiglieri and unusually, there was not one, but three under-bosses below him, known as Captains or Capos. One was Marco's younger brother, Antonio, and another was his brother-in-law, a guy called Savio Corradetti, who was married to Marco's sister. The third under-boss was the one we were most interested in. His name was Enzo Mannarino and he was the guy whose voice had been heard saying the words "Stradivarius" and "cello" on the surveillance recording.

Although he was caught on tape at Gennaro's Social Club on Hester Street in Manhattan's Little Italy, Enzo's territory was in Brooklyn, a borough that he rarely left. His crew ran extortion and gambling rackets, as well as a few other criminal enterprises, from a pizza restaurant called Nico's, on Twenty-First Avenue in the Bensonhurst area of Brooklyn's Community District Eleven.

The police files mentioned that Mannarino's most trusted soldier was a man called Michael Fiorella, a fully initiated mafia member, or 'made' guy, of Italian descent who ran a gang made up of around twenty junior members and associates. The strong-arm stuff, like extorsion and gambling, was left to other soldiers within Mannarino's faction. Fiorella's main business was in stolen goods and the police believed his small crew were behind scores of unsolved high-end burglaries in and around New York over the past seven years, with not one of his guys ever being convicted.

As a result, the NYPD had nicknamed Fiorella's gang of evasive thieves, the Bensonhurst Ghosts, and although the police files contained very little information about this tiny part of the Genovese crime family, it did report that Fiorella spent most of his time at an Italian cafe on Seventy-Sixth Street, between Nineteenth and Twentieth Avenues, right in the heart of Bensonhurst.

When we had finished creating our wall of crooks, Winston and I both agreed that it was going to be nearly impossible for us, a couple of mostly law-abiding, foreign civilians to penetrate the biggest crime family in New York.

Nevertheless, I thought back to Benson Ashley's face when I last saw him, sullen and alone, but full of pride for his daughter, and remained steadfast that we were going to give it a crack at least. I asked Winston to book us flights to New York and to rent an apartment for three months, somewhere close to Fiorella's Brooklyn hangout.

He went through Melinda Baker, Senator Ashley's PA in Boston, who took out a lease for us in her name, which as a US citizen, was much easier to set up quickly. Our base in Brooklyn was to be a two-bedroom, single bathroom, second floor apartment at 7301, Twentieth Avenue in Bensonhurst, just three blocks away from the café on Seventy-Sixth Street.

We left for New York's JFK airport on a Friday lunchtime flight out of London Heathrow. Winston had booked us in Business Class again for the long-haul flight and I was looking forward to getting my head down for some sleep on British Airway's lie-flat seats.

After checking in, our Business Class tickets entitled us to join a shorter, priority, line for the mandatory, but torturously slow, security checks, before we could get to the British Airways lounge near our departure gate. However, priority line or not, when we reached the security area, there were people everywhere and it later transpired that Terminal Three's computerised passenger check-in system had crashed earlier that day, resulting in mass delays and chaos throughout the whole airport.

Tensions were high throughout the security area as desperate travellers cursed the slow pace of the lines and a few complained about missing their flights to security staff who seemed unsympathetic. As Winston and I neared the front of the line, we started emptying our pockets and filling up shallow trays with all our belongings, including my watch, belt, wallet, keys and passport, as well as my shoes.

A security woman sent me to the left and Winston to the right as we were directed to place our trays onto separate conveyor belts for scanning, to keep the lines of people moving as quickly as possible.

I was beckoned to walk through a full body metal detector by an officer at the far side of it and a green light illuminated when I passed through. The same officer then ushered me forward so I could retrieve my stuff from the tray once it had been scanned.

When I spotted my tray emerge from the scanner, I hastily started grabbing my possessions like a crazed octopus. I put my watch back on, then my belt, but as I went to pick up the rest of my things, someone bumped right into me from behind. The accidental shove sent me crashing into several trays on rollers at the end of the scanner's conveyor belt, sending both the trays and their contents onto the floor, my own stuff included.

Along with a few others, I clambered over and around people to collect my sprawled-out possessions from the floor, but as I was bent over, I got jostled again by a big woman to the right of me. I lost my balance for a second time and ended up on the floor, seeing my watch skidding away from me, the clasp of which must have opened as I instinctively bent my wrists to break the fall with the palms of my hands.

It was pandemonium, with security staff trying to help people clear the debris from the floor. I picked up my watch and stuffed it into my front jeans pocket, grabbed my wallet, keys and passport from the floor with one hand, then picked up my shoes with the other and stepped away to a quieter spot to sort myself out.

Winston appeared beside me, completely oblivious to the mayhem I'd just been through. Evidently, he had endured no such trouble going through security via the other route. I spotted a sign for airport lounges and we followed its directional arrow, which took us down a series of walkways and through the Duty-Free shopping area.

I was a bit frazzled by the time we finally arrived at the entrance to our lounge, where we were greeted by an offensively polite Barbie doll. Winston showed her our boarding passes and she checked us off in a register, then pointed us towards the refreshments area, saying also that departure information screens were dotted throughout the lounge.

I snagged us a couple of unoccupied couches facing each other, with a low table in between, while Winston went to grab a couple of bottled beers from a glass fronted fridge. As I sat down, I felt the watch inside my pocket, so I stood to take it out and went to place it back on my wrist.

Then I stopped.

My own watch was already on my wrist. I'd been attempting to slip somebody else's very similar timepiece onto the same wrist.

Shit. I'd picked up someone else's watch in the melee at security. I sat back down on the sofa and glanced around the room furtively to see if anyone had seen me trying to put a second watch on my wrist.

Winston arrived with two opened bottles of Budweiser and clocked the weird expression on my face as he sat down opposite me.

"Something going on, boss?", he asked, then looked around the room as if that might give him a clue.

"Back at security, when you met me beyond the lines of scanners and metal detectors, did you notice anybody hanging around, looking like they'd lost something?", I asked him, trying to look innocent.

He thought for a second.

"No. Why?"

I told him and he looked down at the watch in my right hand. I handed it to him and he gave it a once over.

"It looks a lot like yours. Is it the same model?"

"No. My watch is a Rolex GMT Master and that one's a Rolex Sea Dweller"

He glanced at the watch on my left wrist, then looked back to the one he was holding in his hand.

"Well, they look really alike, Bronson. I can totally see why you picked it up thinking it was yours."

"What the hell should I do?", I asked.

"Don't ask me", he answered, being of no help.

I left him sitting inside the lounge with the extra watch and went out to take a wander back over to where we had exited security. I leaned against a stone pillar, about thirty feet away from racks of empty trays at the end of the security area and spent a few minutes casually watching the people, looking for anybody who seemed distraught at having misplaced a valuable watch.

Having spotted nobody obvious, I went back towards the shopping area and found an information desk. I asked a guy behind the desk if anybody had reported anything missing.

"Like what?", he asked me.

"A gents' wristwatch", I said.

"Make and model?", he asked, picking up a telephone as if he were about to check with a lost property department, or something.

"I'd rather not say. Just a man's watch", I responded.

He hung up the phone and looked at me curiously.

"Look, why don't you just make an announcement on the public-address system and see if anybody shows up", I suggested.

"Okay, I'll do that. Where will you be?", he asked.

"I'll wait over there", I said, pointing to some empty seats outside a Burger King.

I walked away, sat down and kept an eye on the information desk. Another airport official arrived to speak with the guy at the desk about something. I tensed up, fearful that she was asking him about a missing watch, but evidently, she wasn't, as neither of them looked over in my direction. The two conversed for a few minutes, presumably about some other airport issue, then the other official left the guy alone at the desk, and he started tapping away distractedly at a computer keyboard.

I waited. And watched.

It took the guy another fifteen minutes to put out the PA announcement, then immediately turned his attention back to his computer.

I waited some more, my eyes glued to the information desk, half hoping that nobody would show up and half wondering curiously if anybody would.

My mind raced, speculating.

If nobody responded to the announcement, did that mean its owner didn't know it was missing yet? I figured that was possible, bearing in mind the chaos at security and people rushing to make it to a gate in time for their flight. Maybe the owner did realise his watch was gone, but didn't care enough to miss a flight over it. That didn't seem likely. I mean, who wouldn't be bothered about a Rolex? Unless of course, it wasn't real. It could be a fake. I thought about how it felt in my hand back in the lounge. It was heavy and felt solid. I didn't think it was a fake.

I waited there for another twenty minutes and nobody showed up, so I returned to the BA lounge and re-joined Winston, relaying to him where I'd been and that nobody seemed interested in the watch.

I gulped down my beer and Winston got up to check the departure screens. He returned saying it was time to go and handed the Sea Dweller back to me. I looked at it closely and decided it was the real thing, then returned it to my front pocket and we set off to find our boarding gate.

I didn't relax about the watch until we were on the plane and I'd consumed a couple of swift gin and tonics. Then, after a movie and a delicious meal, I forgot all about it and nodded off to sleep.

A couple of hours later, I awoke to the sound of a steward announcing that we would be landing soon, so I followed the instructions to return my seat electronically to its upright position and readied myself for our arrival in New York.

We disembarked and endured the tediousness of the customs line before collecting our luggage and taking a yellow cab to Brooklyn. Our last visit to the Big Apple had been in the high summer temperatures of 2001, at the time of the apocalyptic 9/11 attacks. The climate was very different this time, with snow falling heavily and the taxi took almost an hour to reach our apartment in the wintry conditions.

We collected a set of keys from the building's Superintendent, then made our way up to our home for the next few weeks on the second floor. The apartment felt small compared to our own place back in London, but it was clean and fully furnished. I let Winston have the larger of the two bedrooms, since he had done all the work arranging it with Melinda Baker.

By the time we had unpacked our things, there was a break in the weather, so we went out for a walk around the neighbourhood to get our bearings. We headed north-east on Twentieth Avenue, then turned left onto Seventy-Sixth Street and went past Fiorella's hangout, the aptly named Café Italia, but neither of us glanced inside. We continued walking for another three blocks, then turned right and went north-east again until we came across a Mexican restaurant and bar on the corner of Sixteenth Avenue and Seventy-Second Street.

We went inside out of the cold and a young Hispanic waitress showed us to a table in the middle of the restaurant. I ordered a black bean burrito while Winston went for steak enchiladas and we both ordered bottles of Sol, Mexican beer, as we waited for the food.

Ever since we'd left London, I'd been mulling over how we could approach the mafia about the cello and thought I may have an idea, so it was time to try it out on Winston.

"So, we're not criminals and we don't know anything about stolen goods, correct?", I asked him.

"Right", he replied, firmly.

"We're also not cops, so hopefully we don't have anything about us that would make any mobsters think we were undercover NYPD, or something."

"Okay", he said, nodding.

"And if we do manage to talk to any of them, we can't let on that we know about Mannarino mentioning the cello, because that would blow the cops' surveillance at the social club in Manhattan", I continued.

Winston said nothing, just listened, presumably hoping I was going somewhere, rather than just rambling on.

"What stuff do we know all about, Winston? Who could we be that wouldn't need us to lie about it or fake it?"

"Paintings, wines, watches?", he suggested.

"Antiques", I said.

"Yeah, antiques", repeated Winston, but he wasn't catching on yet.

"We're British antique dealers, staying in New York for a couple of months and we're on the hunt for bargains to take back home so we can sell them to Russian billionaires for a healthy profit", I explained.

That was my pitch. Winston sat assimilating.

"That could work, boss", he said finally.

"If we start by visiting a few dealers around Brooklyn and hanging out regularly at Café Italia to get our faces known, we're bound to bump into Fiorella's guys sooner or later."

"Okay, say we bump into them. Then what?", he asked.

It was a fair question.

"We start by becoming familiar to the people in the café. The staff and the regular customers. We gradually nod and say hello to people we see often. We make chit-chat with the waitresses. Then, if we can spot the mobsters and do the same with them, we might eventually get accepted by them for what we are, which is a couple of dealers on a buying tour. If they start asking us about what kind of antiques we're looking for, we can tell them all sorts of things and throw in the mention of a rare musical instrument now and again, to see if it raises any interest."

"Not bad", said Winston, looking like he was warming to my idea.

Our food came and our conversation paused for a bit while we ate. We enjoyed two more beers each, then I paid the bill and we walked back to the apartment via a different route to continue our familiarisation with the area.

I went to bed early, aiming to stave off any looming jetlag due to the five-hour time difference and didn't sleep too badly. I did wake up at four o'clock the next morning though, and watched TV in the living room, switching between news and weather channels until Winston arose.

We figured there was no time like the present, so we showered and dressed, then went straight to Café Italia for some breakfast. There was about three inches of snow on the ground, but the sky was a clear blue, with no sign of any further snowfall coming any time soon. It was nice to get out in the fresh air, but it was very cold, the air temperature hovering around zero.

We entered the café just after eight and it was nearly full, with plenty of customers building up a healthy calorie intake to see them through a wintry day at work or whatever.

We were greeted by a nice looking middle-aged waitress who seated us at a table by the front windows and we both asked for coffee.

We scanned the breakfast menu and chose easily. Eggs and bacon for me, the same, but with pancakes added for Winston. The waitress returned with our coffee and took our food orders, which gave me a chance to talk to her.

"We're from London looking for antiques. Do you know if there are any dealers close by we could go and visit on foot?", I asked her.

A badge on her uniform said her name was Monica.

"Antique dealers? I don't know, let me ask around", she replied, with a heavy Brooklyn accent.

Then she bellowed out towards the counter at the back for the whole restaurant to hear.

"Hey Teresa, do you know any antique dealers around here? These guys are looking to decorate their English castle or something", which got a few smiles from the other diners.

An older man's voice responded right away, from behind Winston and we both turned to face him.

"There's a place down on the Parkway, you know the Belt Parkway? What's it called? Julie's Antiques. Yeah, I think that's the name. It's about thirty blocks south of here though, that's quite a walk. Probably be better with a cab, especially in this weather".

"Thanks a lot", I said.

"I think there's maybe a couple more places, but they're way west of here, you know? In Fort Hamilton, right over at the other side of the Gowanus Expressway, before it turns into the Verrazano Narrows Bridge to Staten Island. I can't think of any other antique places in South Brooklyn", he added helpfully.

The old guy's impromptu satellite navigation rendition brought some friendly mocking from Monica the waitress.

"Wow, Joey. What are you today, a genius savant or something, huh? Are you Rain Man?", she teased.

"No, I used to be a delivery driver, alright? I know my way around here that's all", he said, pretending to be offended, playing along.

"Oh, you know your way around, Joey? I don't see you finding your way around to the tip jar very often, huh?", she joked, and laughter erupted from around the diner.

What an entertaining place. I didn't think we were going to struggle to join in with the banter there, once we got our faces known. That first visit to Café Italia was a blast. The hilarious waiting staff and the quick-witted regulars bounced off each other the whole time we were in there.

We hadn't seen anybody with slicked back hair carrying a violin case, in a shiny silk suit with a pinkie ring though, but maybe gangsters kept late hours and wouldn't appear before noon. Either that or my pre-conceived image of who we were looking for was a bit out of date. Yeah, it could've been that.

We spent the rest of that second day taking taxis to the antique places the old guy mentioned. More to start getting our faces known with the dealers than anything else. The first place we tried though, the one on the Belt Parkway, was run by a monster of a woman, presumably Julie? When we told her we were just browsing, she went nuts and threw us out, saying she didn't want deadbeats in her store.

I made a mental note to email Bloomingdales and recommend they try adopting Julie's bedside manner to optimise sales. No browsing, people. Buy stuff or get the fuck out.

The other two dealers in Fort Hamilton were much more welcoming and we spent more than an hour in each, chatting with the owners and looking around their shops. I spotted loads of colonial furniture pieces that I wanted to buy for myself. That is, if I ever decided to build a mansion house in the country someday.

I asked both dealers if they knew of anywhere that sold antique musical instruments, like 18th or 19th century pianos or string instruments. Neither of them knew for sure, but said we should try a street in North Brooklyn called Atlantic Avenue, which was famous for having about fifteen independent antique shops within a mile of one another.

We followed their advice and visited two or three Atlantic Avenue dealers every day for the next week, until we were well and truly antiqued out.

NINETEEN

Throughout the whole of our first month in Brooklyn, we had breakfast every second or third day at Café Italia. We also ate there for lunch and dinner three or four times a week and before long we were part of the regular crowd.

All the waitresses knew us, as did most of the other diners and having spent so much time there, we soon became convinced that a small group of about eight to ten guys who we saw in their regularly, were most likely Fiorella's boys. They seemed to be a tight crew, all men, aged between twenty and fifty years old, who always sat together in the same section at the back of the restaurant.

They would be in there from about lunchtime, most days, and a few of them would take part in the banter and jokes with the waiting staff. None of them appeared to be trying to keep a low profile, but none of them behaved overtly conspicuously either.

The main reason Winston and I were sure these were our guys, was because one of them, an older man of about fifty, spent most of his time at Café Italia either sat having one-to-one conversations at a permanently reserved table at the back, or behind the closed door of a small office right next to his regular table.

Over a period of weeks, Winston and I gradually moved our table preference closer and closer to the back of the café, nearly always sitting at the same table, no matter if we were there for breakfast, lunch or dinner.

The mark of how well accepted we were at Café Italia became apparent by the amount of mocking we received from the waitresses and the owner, a burly Italian guy who ran the kitchen, but who loved venturing out front whenever there was fun to be had with the regulars.

Most of the jokes made at our expense were aimed at our Britishness, the fact we claimed to be antique dealers, which seemed to be taken as proof that we were gay, and, of course, Winston's size, which attracted comments and friendly jibes no matter what part of the world he was in.

We caught a break one day when we went to the café for lunch and Monica the waitress let us have it as soon as we came in the door.

"Oh, my. Look who just walked in. It's the Twins, Arnold Schwarzenegger and Danny DeVito", she said and got howls of laughter from the crew at the back.

"I don't look like Danny DeVito", I complained.

"Trust me, you do next to him, honey", said Monica.

I made eye contact with a couple of the gangsters as we sat down, rolling my eyes in jest at Monica's jibe. Then, for the first time, one of the more sociable guys at the back tables joined in the fun.

"Hey Scotty?", he had heard me bantering with Monica before, so he knew I was Scottish, "Are you and King Arthur there really a gay couple? I mean, how the hell does that even work? Physically I mean? If a guy that big is givin' you somethin', how come you can still walk?", he joked and all his buddies laughed along with him.

"Sorry to disappoint, but we're not actually a gay couple", I replied, "however, if Winston here did ever decide to have a go at me, I reckon it would probably feel like someone had stuck a giant caber up my arse", which brought a huge roar of laughter from the whole café.

"Winston? That's your name?", our tormentor asked and Winston nodded at him.

"And what the hell is a caber?", the same guy asked.

"Leave them alone Tommy, they're good customers. The big one helps me get the good wines from the top shelf 'cause I can't reach 'em by myself", said Monica.

I turned to address the guy she had called Tommy.

"A caber is a twenty-foot-long wooden pole, usually made from a Larch tree. It's about four inches in diameter and weighs around 175 pounds", I explained.

"And what do you do with it?", he asked.

"You mean apart from sticking it up people's asses, Tommy?", some other crew member at the back chimed in and the others laughed again.

"It's used in a test of strength at a traditional Scottish Highland Games", I started, then used actions to help me explain more fully.

"You start with your body in a crouch, the caber oriented vertically, holding the bottom end with your hands interlocked and with the other end pointing upwards, resting on your neck or shoulder. Then you propel the caber upwards and forwards so it turns end-over-end before it lands", I said.

"How do you decide who wins?", Tommy asked.

"You get higher points if the caber lands straight ahead, at the twelve o'clock position. Lower points are awarded for efforts that finish at an angle, or if the caber lands on its end then falls back towards the thrower. The distance thrown doesn't matter", they seemed to find my explanation interesting.

"What do you call the event?", asked Tommy.

"It's called tossing the caber", I replied and everyone fell about in raucous laughter at my inadvertent reference to jerking off.

Winston joined in the laughter, but said nothing.

Then the office door at the back of the café opened and the older guy stepped into the dining area.

"What's goin' on?" he asked, directing his question towards Tommy, "You guys know I'm workin', right? You mind keepin' it down a little, huh?", he said.

"We're sorry, boss", said Tommy, then as the older man began turning away he called after him, "Hey Michael, did you ever see a guy this big before?", he asked, pointing at Winston who was sitting down.

"Hey, Winston, right? Go ahead and stand up a second will you. Let my boss here see how close your head is to touching the ceiling", said Tommy.

Winston stood up, revealing his full height to an amused audience. Tommy's boss, Michael, looked him up and down.

"Jesus Christ, my house is smaller than you", then he turned and went back to the office as his friendly wisecrack towards Winston landed well with everyone in the place.

We sat back down and Monica took our lunch order as the guys at the back settled down. I thought we'd made a good impression, taking the jokes in the friendly manner they were intended and learning a couple of the guys' names.

We enjoyed a light lunch of club sandwiches with cola and left the place an hour later, with Tommy at the back sending us on our way with a polite farewell.

"Take care, boys. Watch out for splinters when you're tossing each other's cabers tonight, huh?"

I flicked my middle finger up at Tommy through the window as we walked away from the café on the street outside and saw him howling with laughter just before he went out of view, so I figured he'd taken my visual retort in good fun.

We left it a couple of days before making a return to Café Italia for dinner on a Friday night. When we arrived, Teresa the other waitress, led us to our usual table and left a couple of menus with us. We asked for cold beers to drink and she went off to fetch them.

The tables at the rear were all empty when we arrived, so we enjoyed a nice meal at a leisurely pace and waited to see if Tommy, Michael or any of their buddies showed up.

Around nine o'clock, we heard the door open, then a familiar voice hailing us loudly from the front of the restaurant.

"Hey, it's Braveheart and the King of England. How you doin' boys?", it was Tommy and he patted Winston gently on the back as he led his troops to the back of the diner. His buddies all sat down, but Tommy put his jacket on the back of a chair then wandered back over to our table.

"So, what are we havin' tonight fellas?", he asked, all friendly.

"We just finished eating", I replied, "Winston had steak and I had a chilli dog. Wasn't bad".

"How was your steak, big man?", he asked Winston.

"Good", Winston replied with a nod.

"Alright, I'm going to have a steak too. If it's good enough for the big guy, it's good enough for me", he said, then returned to his buddies at the back tables.

Winston and I stayed put, drinking cold beers and chatting. We also enjoyed the atmosphere of the evening crowd, with the waitresses doing their best to insult all the customers, who lapped it up.

At ten-thirty, I was thinking about heading back to the apartment, when Tommy appeared at my shoulder once again. He and his crew had finished eating and a few of them had left. The café had thinned out, with many of the night's customers presumably having moved on to enjoy a Friday night out, and others perhaps just heading home before the place closed at eleven.

"Monica told me you guys are antique dealers, right?", Tommy asked, looking at me.

"Yeah", I replied, "We buy low, sell high, you know?"

"What kind of things do you buy?", asked.

"A wide range of things", I answered, "mostly very high value stuff like works of art by old masters, vintage cars, jewellery, furniture. Anything from, say, $100,000 upwards. The rarer, the better. That's usually what brings the best price. Condition and provenance are very important, obviously", Tommy slid into the seat opposite me, next to Winston, as I was talking.

"And what are you looking to buy here in Brooklyn?", he asked.

"We're open to pretty much anything that's selling here for a good price, that we think could sell for significantly more back in London. There's a lot of rich people in London nowadays, with big houses that need filled up with stuff", I said.

"I bet he does all the heavy liftin' though, right?"

"No. Winston's my close friend and business associate, but his primary responsibility is to protect us and the things we handle. When we do deals with people for very high value items, we sometimes attract assholes who try to screw us over. Winston helps make sure that doesn't happen", I said plainly.

"Is all your stuff legit?", asked Tommy.

I stared at him, pretending that his question had put my guard up.

"What do you mean?", I responded and he thought for a moment.

"Let me put it another way", he said, "Does everything you buy come with a fully traceable history?"

"You mean provenance?"

"Yeah, provenance."

"Most of the time, yes. However, when you're dealing with, for example, an ancient manuscript that's more than four hundred years old, authenticating its provenance can be somewhat arbitrary and might need to involve educated guesswork."

We noticed the staff were tidying up around us, getting ready to close, so I asked Teresa for our bill.

"Your business sounds interesting guys", said Tommy as we all stood, ready to leave.

He looked at me.

"You're the boss though, huh? What's your name?"

"Yeah, I'm the boss. My name's Bronson."

"Tommy."

We shook hands.

"Well, it was good to meet you, boys", he said as Winston and I made to leave, "see you around" said Tommy, with no mention of cabers this time.

"Sure. Goodnight, man", I said and we left for the cold walk back to our apartment.

We left it a couple more days before going back to the café again on Monday afternoon, but this time, we brought a prop with us.

Winston and I went to our usual table and ordered coffee. Tommy was already in there and nodded a 'hello' of acknowledgement in our direction when we sat down.

Winston pulled out a map of Brooklyn and spread it out on our table. We'd been marking the locations of antique shops we'd been to and were using our 'coffee break' to update the map with some scribbled notes about a place we'd claim to have been to that morning.

We made a point of talking loud enough for Tommy to overhear us making a fuss over a failed negotiation with an antique dealer that he would assume we had just returned from, but which never happened at all.

It wasn't long before his curiosity got the better of him and he left his friends to come over to our table.

"What the hell are you two doin', looking for buried treasure or somethin'?", he joked, then sat down next to me.

"Just trying to figure out our next move, man. What are you up to today?", I asked him.

"This and that", was his evasive reply, "one of our Brooklyn antique dealers trying to take you for a ride?", he asked.

"Maybe", I replied cagily, "we might've stumbled on something that might be worth doing a deal on", I lied.

"Hey, good for you two. What have you found?", he asked, looking genuinely intrigued.

"We were in a place this morning, in Central Brooklyn, where Winston spotted a violin. When we showed some interest in it, the dealer said it was a genuine Stradivarius", I explained.

"A Stradi-what?", he replied, a funny look on his face.

Our espressos arrived and Tommy ordered one for himself.

"Stradivarius", I repeated, "it's the Latin name for the Stradivari family who made what most people believe to be the finest string instruments ever, back in the seventeenth and eighteenth centuries. Their violins, violas and cellos, particularly those made by Anthony Stradivari, are said to have a unique sound with an incredible clarity. Many makers have tried to copy his designs, but nobody has been able to recreate the same sound quality."

"Are they worth a lot of money?", he asked.

"Yeah, the real ones are worth a fortune. His violins reach the top prices, several hundred thousand dollars, minimum. A few of his violins have sold for several million, but even genuine cellos go for big money."

Tommy let out a short wolf whistle, impressed by the numbers.

"So, was it a real one you saw this morning?", he asked.

"I'm as certain as I can be that it wasn't", I replied.

"How can you tell?"

Teresa reappeared with Tommy's coffee, also an espresso, which he downed in one gulp.

I explained to Tommy that original Stradivari instruments had the Latin words 'Antonius Stradivarius Cremonensis Faciebat Anno' inscribed on their label, indicating the maker, Antonio Stradivari; where it was made, Cremona, Italy; and the Latin words for "made in the year", followed by a four-digit year date, which on the label of a genuine Stradivarius would normally have the first digit as a printed numeral, a '1', for example, with the remaining three digits of the year written in by hand.

I ordered another round of espresso for all three of us.

"The violin you saw today didn't have all that on its label?", asked Tommy.

"Actually, it did. The problem was the year, 1745."

"How's that a problem?"

"Antonio Stradivari died in 1737, meaning the one we saw this morning was a copy."

"Huh. So, it isn't worth shit? Is that what's got you all hot and bothered?"

I sighed for a moment, before I answered.

"No. Our problem, is whether we should still make an offer for it. Good copies that are genuinely from the 18th century, which are in beautiful condition and produce a great sound, can sell at auction for big money too, even without being a Stradivarius. Trouble is, we'd be taking a gamble buying it, because the market for copies blows hot and cold, so its profitability would be impossible to predict."

The coffee arrived and we each drank in silence for a minute.

"Sounds like you've got a dilemma. What if it had been the real thing?", he asked.

"It would have been perfect. I'd buy it, probably along with a few other things we've seen here, then me and Winston could go home. But instead, I'm stuck in limbo on the violin, I've got a Rolex I need to fence or sell to a pawn shop and we're burning expense money like crazy", I said scratching my head, deliberately looking irritated.

"Wait, wait, go back a step. You got a Rolex you need to fence?", he asked with surprise.

"Yeah."

"Is it hot? You know, stolen?"

"Of course not. Well, not really. I found it", I said, as if that explained everything.

"Uh huh?", he said mocking me.

I told him the story of how I picked up the Sea Dweller from the floor at Heathrow Airport by accident, then tried to find its owner, but nobody showed up. He loved it, especially the part where I was spread-eagled on the floor with all my stuff scattered everywhere.

"That's hilarious, man. I would have loved to have seen your face when you tried to put that second watch on your wrist. What's the Sea Dweller thing you picked up worth?", he asked.

"On its own, without any spare bracelet links, a box or papers, probably around $10,000. If I could get a box and the other stuff though, maybe $14,000 or $15,000."

Tommy's expression turned serious for a moment.

"What if I said I could help you out?", he said.

"With what? The watch?"

"Yeah. Let's say I could get you a genuine Rolex box, the links you need and some papers. Well, the papers would probably not be genuine, but say I got those things for you and my help meant the watch sold for an extra $4,000 or $5,000. What kind of cut would I get?", he asked.

"I'd say I would probably split the difference with you. $2,000 or $2,500?", I answered.

"Okay deal", he said, and didn't seem to be kidding.

"Deal?", I repeated.

"Yeah. Gimme a couple of days, Bronson. Meet me back here at eight-thirty on Thursday night, okay?"

"Okay, sure. Thanks, Tommy", I said trying to look bewildered and grateful.

I paid our coffee bill, leaving a good tip for Teresa, then Winston and I left the café and went back to the apartment, elated that my half-baked plan had worked.

TWENTY

Thursday evening arrived and we went to the café early so we could eat before we met up with Tommy at eight-thirty. The tables at the back were all empty when we arrived. We enjoyed a nice dinner at our usual table and enjoyed a couple of bottles of beer afterwards. Then we waited.

Just before eight-thirty, Tommy entered Café Italia, accompanied by his boss, Michael. As he passed our table, Tommy motioned for us to join them in the back with a nod of his head. We followed them into the office, which was sparsely decorated. The only furniture in the room was a big rectangular desk with a telephone on it and a few chairs. We all sat down, then Tommy's boss took charge.

"I'm Michael Fiorella", he said.

"I'm Bronson, this is Winston", I responded.

Michael nodded at us.

"Tommy tells me you guys are a couple of antique dealers, right?", he asked.

"Yeah", I answered.

"He said you were lookin' to buy a violin the other day", he said, looking at me.

"Yes. I'm still thinking about it."

"Tommy says you're an expert, that you can tell what's real and what's not."

"Most things, yeah. If I couldn't, then I wouldn't still be in the antiques business, I guess."

He looked at me for a long moment, sizing me up.

"Tell me about the watch", said Fiorella, changing the subject.

"Yeah, Bronson. Tell him about you in the airport. This is great Michael, you'll love this", said Tommy.

So, I retold the story of my Keystone Kops moment of absolute buffoonery at Heathrow, followed by my attempt to find the Rolex's owner, then my decision to just keep it and sell it on.

By the end of my tale, Michael was smiling, amused.

"Do you have the watch with you?", he asked.

I took the Sea Dweller out of my pocket and handed it to him. He carefully looked it over.

"This is a nice watch", he said, then he looked up at Tommy. A signal for him to speak.

"I couldn't get you a set of links, Bronson. Not in two days. I got a Rolex box and some bogus papers, but I'd need more time to get the links", he said.

I suspected there was more coming.

"But, me and Michael, we came up with another idea", here we go, I thought.

"How 'bout you sell the watch to us, as it is, no box or nothin', then we sell it on ourselves, once we find a set of links. We got plenty of contacts and we'll have no problem moving it. What do you say?", asked Tommy.

"How much?", I replied.

"You said it would be worth at least $14,000 with the box and stuff. $10,000 without, right?", asked Tommy.

"Yeah, about that", I answered.

Silence. Michael and Tommy looked at each other, non-committal.

"Could you give us a minute, fellas?", Fiorella asked and we left the room without saying anything.

Tommy closed the office door behind us, remaining inside to talk to his boss, so Winston and I went back to our table and finished off our beers.

A minute or two later, the office door opened again and Tommy beckoned us to re-join them inside.

When we were back in the room and seated, Michael made me an offer for the watch.

"It's a nice watch, but it doesn't have any papers or a box or any of those link things, right?", he asked.

"Right", I repeated.

"And you two will struggle to find those things here yourselves, so you'd probably end up takin' the watch back to England, then try to get the other stuff over there, or you might move it on back home without any of the stuff", he said.

I waited.

"Or, we could give you $8,000 cash for the watch right now, and you make out pretty good for something that you found on the floor for free", then he sat back, both he and Tommy watching my reaction.

"I estimated its value at $10,000 minimum for just the watch on its own, and I know the watch market", I said.

"But it doesn't belong to you, does it, Bronson? If you try to sell this back home with no receipt or box or any of that other crap, you might struggle to find a buyer who doesn't think its stolen.

"Then you'll get impatient, the watch is hanging around, and you'll end up selling it to a used watch dealer for less than I'm offering you now", said Michael. He was good at this. A bird in the hand and all that.

I paused, taking in what he'd said. I looked at Winston who didn't offer anything at all. Thanks, mate, I thought.

"Nine", I said, a counteroffer.

"Eight and a half", came Michael's reply.

"Done", I said and we shook on it.

Everybody smiled. Tommy and Winston had enjoyed our little pissing contest.

Fiorella pulled out an enormous wad of hundred-dollar bills from his pocket, counted out eight-five of them on the table, then picked up the $8,500 and handed it to me.

"Now, remember, Bronson. In taking this watch off your hands, I did you a favour, alright? Why don't you and the Yeti go outside and take a walk with Tommy, we got a favour we want to ask from you in return", he said.

That made me slightly nervous. Was I in organise crime now?

I paid our bill for dinner, then Winston and I left Café Italia with Tommy. We walked south-east along Seventy-Sixth Street for a few blocks, Tommy and I side-by-side, with Winston walking behind us.

"Okay, so, here's the thing, Bronson", Tommy began, "A few months ago, Michael's boss gets a phone call out of the blue from this guy in New Jersey. Now, this guy is in the same kind of business that we're in, but we come from different sides of the track, you know what I mean?", he asked, looking at me.

I nodded, I got it.

"This guy tells Michael's boss that he's got a problem. Some guys that work for him, bought somethin' from another bunch of guys they do business with up in Boston, but it's somethin' the boys in Jersey are not that familiar with and they haven't been able to move it.

"So, they've been stuck with this thing for a while now and this guy asks Michael's boss if we want to buy it from his guys in Jersey, so we can take a shot at movin' it ourselves", he said.

"What is it?", I asked.

"It's a cello. This guy tells Michael's boss it's a Stradivarius", he said, then waited to see my reaction.

I laughed.

"Okay, is it stolen?", I asked.

"I don't know. I guess maybe the guys in Boston found somethin' that didn't belong to them, just like you and that watch, huh?", he said, smiling at me.

"Where do me and Winston come into this?", I asked, knowing full well what favour he was about to ask.

"The word around the camp fire is the guys in Boston didn't know what it was and sold it to the boys from Jersey for $5,000. One of the guys in Jersey took it to an antique dealer who told him he thought it might be an original Stradivarius, because of its label, but wasn't sure", said Tommy.

"And?", I asked.

"And, hearin' it might be an authentic Stradivarius, possibly stolen, nobody the Jersey guys contacted wanted anything to do with it. Too high profile, too much risk.

"Then you and I had a conversation about a violin the other day, which I relayed to Michael and he, in turn, mentioned to his boss, the guy who got the call from Jersey about the cello a few months back", he paused as we turned the corner onto Twenty-First Avenue, heading south-west.

"Then Michael's boss comes up with this idea that maybe we meet with the guys from Jersey, check the cello out and make them believe it's a fake, but we buy it from them anyway for a knock-down price. Then we sell it to you and everybody wins. Well, except for the guys in Boston and Jersey", he said.

"And tell me, Tommy. Who gets the job of authenticating the cello as being a real Stradivarius or not?", I asked, knowing the answer.

"Come on, Bronson. Where's your sense of adventure. You're an expert, right? You're in Brooklyn to buy high value things, huh?", he chuckled as he saw my fear at being in the middle of a mob transaction.

"What do you think, Winston?", I called over my shoulder and turned to face him, whilst continuing to walk, backwards.

"It would mean we could go home soon, boss", he said.

I feigned a sigh of defeat.

"Ah, fuck it, we'll do it. What's the plan?", I said, and Tommy slapped me hard on the back.

"Atta boy, Bronson", he said, then explained the plan to us.

"This Saturday night, you and the Hulk go for dinner at Café Italia and I'll pick you up in a car around nine o'clock. Then we go to the house of one of our guys, where we meet up with some guys from Jersey with the cello. You inspect it, tell them it's a copy, then leave our guys to make the Jersey guys an offer, and that's it", he tried to make it sound easy, which I knew it wouldn't be.

"Okay", I said.

A car that I had no idea had been following us, drew up to the kerb side and Tommy hopped in, then the car drove off leaving Winston and I on the freezing cold street.

TWENTY-ONE

Saturday night came and I was as nervous as hell. Winston seemed more amused than anything, mostly by my unease. We went to the café at seven-thirty for dinner, but I barely touched my burger. Winston horsed down a steak sandwich, then finished off my leftovers.

We paid for dinner then waited outside. At nine o'clock, a dark saloon car slowed to a stop beside us and Winston approached the driver's window, which buzzed down revealing Tommy at the wheel.

"Hey, hop in guys", he said.

We got in the back, where Michael Fiorella was already sitting.

"Good evening, Your Highnesses", he kidded.

"Hey", I replied.

We drove south-west for about half an hour to a house on Langham Street, in the Manhattan Beach area of South Brooklyn. Tommy babbling all the way and making jokes, probably trying to relax me.

It was a two-storey detached house, with a red brick exterior, a stylish arched portico at the front door and white window frames. The front garden looked immaculately kept and there was a wrought iron fence painted black and gold surrounding the property.

The four of us were welcomed inside by a middle-aged lady who offered to take our coats before ushering us through to a large den at the back of the house. Four other men were already in the room and I spotted a large black cello case in a back corner as Michael began introductions and those who had been sitting, stood up to meet us.

"Bronson, Winston, I'd like you to meet my boss, Enzo Mannarino", said Michael.

He was a squat guy who had short dark hair and who looked about the same age as Michael. Then Mannarino took over to introduce us to an older man who had risen from behind a desk, which made me think it was his house we were in.

"This is our boss, Marco Cannizzaro", he said.

I think I almost shit my pants as I realised I was in the presence of the head of the Genovese crime family. I mean, who was I going to meet next, God?

"Good to meet you Bronson, Winston", the older guy said.

Then he introduced us to the other two people in the room.

"These are two friends of ours from New Jersey. Vincent Calabrese and Joey Zarella", he said.

The lady returned to the room with a tray full of glasses and a bottle of scotch. Tommy poured a couple of fingers into each glass, then handed one to everyone in the room.

Calabrese collected the big case from the corner, brought it into the middle of the room, set it down flat on the floor, then opened it to reveal the cello inside.

"Go ahead, Bronson, why don't you check out the cello and tell us what you think", instructed Fiorella.

Winston helped me lift the cello out of its case and stand it upright with its endpin resting on the floor. He held the instrument by its neck as I looked all around it carefully. The maple back, ribs and neck of the main body were in excellent condition, with only a few tiny marks on the back edges.

The colour looked right and the varnish was also in good order. There were a few small marks on the back of the scroll at the top of the neck, no doubt from being laid against a hard surface. Stradivarius or not, for a piece that had been made three centuries ago it was in very fine condition.

Now for the moment of truth, I thought, as I turned on the small torch on my iPhone and used it to peek inside the 'F' holes to look at the all-important label on the inside surface of the back. I asked Winston for a second opinion of the label inside and we swapped positions so he could look with the torch.

He nodded, then we returned the cello to its case on the floor. Winston and I had been checking to confirm it was Christine Ashley's missing cello. All the information on the inside label matched the police reports from the burglary in Boston, so I was more than happy. I could feel the tension in the room, as they all waited for my next words.

"It's beautiful Michael, the finest musical instrument I've ever laid eyes on, or touched with my hands for that matter. Everything about its design, construction, materials and age are correct for the Stradivarius era", I said, seeing the faces of the two guys from Jersey flush slightly with optimism before I continued.

"Condition-wise, I'd say with a high degree of confidence, that it's Near Mint, which is the third highest condition rating out of the eight rating levels on the recognised scale, behind New and Mint. Overall, I think it's an exceptional example."

I paused for a moment, then carried on.

"The label attached to the inside surface of the back contains all the expected information about its origins. It says it was made by Anthony Stradivari, in Cremona, Italy, and states the year of manufacture as 1709", I said, finishing my appraisal.

Calabrese couldn't contain his excitement.

"So, it's an original Stradivarius then, right? Antonio Stradivari made these things in Cermona until he died in 1737, correct?", he asked me.

He'd obviously been doing some research on the internet. I prayed his research wouldn't contradict what I was about to say in a moment or two.

"Yes, that's correct. He did", I said and Calabrese let out an exclamation of triumph, towards his boss.

Then I kicked him in the nuts, figuratively speaking.

"But Antonio Stradivari didn't make this cello though", I said plainly, with confidence, but being respectful towards Calabrese, who's jaw dropped.

"What?", he said, his eyes burning into the front of my skull.

"There's a problem with the year", I said.

"What fuckin' problem?", said Calabrese, his temper rising.

"Cool it Vinny", said Zarella, who then asked me to explain.

"There are two issues", I said, "Firstly, the '17' in the '1709' has both digits printed, with the '09' written by hand. No genuine Stradivarius label has ever had the first two digits of the year in printed format. Never. An authentic Stradivarius would only have the first digit, the '1', printed, and the remaining three digits would be written by hand."

Silence in the room as I paused.

"And the other issue?", Zarella asked.

Calabrese next to him began to look deflated.

"A plague epidemic took hold across Europe in 1709, following the Great Northern War. The Stradivari family closed its workshops for eighteen months to try and incubate themselves. As a result, not a single instrument produced by Antonio Stradivari bears the year mark of 1709. This cello is probably an attempted copy, but it is an exceptional one and was certainly produced by a very talented maker in the early 1700s. It's still worth a lot of money, just not as much as a genuine Stradivarius", I said.

I held my breath and hoped nobody killed me.

There was a moment of silence as everyone thought through what I'd said. Then came the killer question.

"How much would you say this cello would sell for at auction, Bronson?", Marco Cannizzaro asked.

"I think, on a good day, it might fetch as much as $200,000, based on its condition", I announced, which seemed to bring everyone's spirits up a little.

"Okay, thanks a lot, Bronson", said Cannizzaro, "Enzo, why don't you take Vinny and our other guests into the living room, so Joey and I can talk."

And with that all but the two mob bosses left the room, with me trying to keep as far away from Vincent Calabrese as possible, making sure Winston was between me and Vinny as we walked through to the front room.

A minute later, the nice lady, who I assumed was Cannizzaro's wife, came through with another round of drinks and my fears subsided a little when Enzo and Vinny took turns breaking Tommy's balls.

Although the humour lifted Vinny's mood, I remained on edge and kept my mouth shut, praying that the Jersey guys would leave soon. I could see that Winston was keeping an eye on everybody, which gave me a little comfort, but not much. These guys were career criminals and were very likely heavily armed.

Five minutes later, Joey Zarella appeared at the doorway of the living room, his meeting in the den with Cannizzaro was evidently over.

"Come on, Vinny. Let's go. Goodnight guys, thanks", he said, then the two Jersey mobsters left the house and drove off down the street.

Marco Cannizzaro then appeared in the doorway, with a stern expression on his face, scanning the room until he spotted me, then fixed his eyes on mine.

I felt my legs starting to shake.

Marco's expression then changed slowly to a huge wide grin and the others, recognising the signs of victory, started laughing and patting each other on the back.

I nearly threw up.

A smiling Cannizzaro then asked me to join him back in the den by myself, so I followed his lead, leaving Winston with the others. We sat down and I saw the cello still lying on the floor, inside its open case, which made me assume he'd just bought it from the guys from Jersey.

"How much did you pay for it?", I asked.

He ignored my question.

"So, Bronson, is that thing really a copy?", he asked pointing at the cello on the floor.

"Hell no. It's as real as a fucking heart attack", I replied and he started chuckling as I breathed out a sigh of relief.

"What about all that stuff with the year number and the plague?", he asked.

"Bullshit. I made it up."

He looked at me as if he thought I had balls of steel.

"So, there's no doubt in your mind that this cello is an authentic Stradivarius?"

"None whatsoever, it's a hundred percent genuine, no question."

"Great", he said, "you want to buy it?"

Hell yes, I thought.

"From you? Right now?"

"Yeah, why not. I got no use for a cello, none of my kids ever had an aptitude for music. There's no official paperwork with it, no verifiable provenance documentation. Who the hell else am I going to sell a stolen Stradivarius to, if not a civilian antique dealer who'll be on his way back to London within a week?"

I thought for a minute, feeling that success was so close, but desperate not to blow it at this stage.

"How much would you want for it? Bearing in mind the things you rightly said about how difficult it could be to sell. I'd face those issues myself, if I bought it from you", I said.

"What would be a fair price, Bronson? Make me an offer. A realistic one mind."

I breathed deeply, then went for it.

"I could pay you $400,000 for it. That would be fair in my opinion and would allow me some room for a modest profit, even if the lack of documentation means I end up having to sell at a low-end price."

He mulled this over patiently.

"How about, $450,000?", he asked.

I feigned anguish, then ventured a final offer.

"I could go to $425,000, but not a penny more."

Marco rose from his seat to shake my hand.

"Deal", he said, then he called through for the others to come back into the den.

"We happy, boss?", Enzo asked as he led the guys back into the room.

"We just made a quarter of a million bucks in less than ten minutes. So yes, Enzo, we are very happy indeed."

Now that we had agreed a deal, Marco no longer minded that I heard their profit amount, which meant I could work out how much he'd paid the other mob boss for it.

Enzo, Michael and Tommy shook their boss's hand in congratulations, while Winston sidled over to me.

"You alright, boss?"

I nodded.

The Genovese capo, the soldier and the junior-member congratulated me, then we all had a good laugh as Tommy entertained us with a humorous summation of the previous half an hour.

"I thought Vinny was going to rip your head off when you said it wasn't a Stradivarius, Bronson. Your crazy. If everybody in London has a poker face like yours, then I'm never fuckin' going there. No way."

His delivery was really funny.

Cannizzaro then brought us back down to earth, with some instructions for Tommy to bring me and Winston back there, to his house, on Monday so we could do the exchange. Marco gave me a card with some bank details on it so I could arrange the $425,000 transfer first thing on Monday morning.

We said goodnight and thanks as we left Marco in his den and went out to the street for the ride back to Bensonhurst. Tommy was all talk again, throughout the whole journey back and I felt exhausted when Winston and I were eventually dropped off outside Café Italia, which was closed for the night.

We walked back to the apartment and I fell into bed, exhausted from the stress, but thrilled that we were now very close to getting the cello back to Senator Ashley and his daughter.

I called Benson first thing on Sunday morning and told him the good news. I hadn't checked in with him since we left London, but although there was plenty to catch up on, I didn't really want to share too much about our mafia deal with a United States Senator, so I focussed on the funds transfer, which he said he would take care of personally.

I thought I detected emotion in his voice as we ended our conversation and felt pleased that we'd managed to come through for him.

At ten-thirty on Monday morning, Winston and I were picked up outside the café by Tommy, alone in his car. I'd already confirmed with Senator Ashley that the money had been sent to Cannizzaro's account and was satisfied that everything was in order.

Half an hour later, we arrived at Marco's house in Manhattan Beach, which looked even prettier and much grander in daylight. Very classy, I thought.

His wife welcomed us indoors and led us through to the den where Marco was waiting, seated behind his desk. Cannizzaro greeted us all warmly and told me that he too had checked the status of the money transfer and his bank had confirmed all was good.

He offered each of us a glass of red wine, which he poured into big round glasses from a crystal decanter. We all clinked our glasses and took a sip.

It tasted amazing. Marco, detecting my instant delight, picked up the empty bottle it had come from and handed it to me. The label said 'Giacomo Conterno Monfortino, Barolo Riserva DOCG, Italy', and had been bottled in 1990.

"This is superb Marco. What a smooth and rich flavour."

I swirled it in my glass and gave it a quick nose.

"Dark fruits, very concentrated", I said.

"I get cherries and liquorice", he said, after he'd nosed his glass, then he took a sip.

The two Neanderthals in the room drank theirs too and seemed to enjoy it, but had no real appreciation for what they were drinking.

"Yeah, this is great stuff, boss", said Tommy.

For once, he seemed out of his comfort zone.

"Do you know about wines, Bronson?", asked Marco.

"I know a little about lots of nice things, I suppose. I love drinking good wine, like this. I try to appreciate it."

"Come with me, I want to show you something."

Marco led me out of the den, along a hallway to a door that took the two of us down a set of steps to a cellar underneath the house. Tommy and Winston stayed behind.

He opened a door at the bottom of the steps and switched on a light to reveal a huge thousand bottle wine cellar, with floor to ceiling racks covering all three of the cellar walls facing us as we entered through the door at one end. There was an oxblood coloured Chesterfield leather couch in the centre of the room, an antique mahogany table sitting in front of it.

I felt like I was in Aladdin's cave and Cannizzaro was the genie. I was bowled over by the scale of his collection. He took me on a little tour around each of the three walls of racks filled with bottles, talking passionately about the wines he had, all of them Italian. He knew the names, vineyard and region of every bottle in there, and told me a couple of funny stories about how he'd acquired some of them.

I asked him if he had any Masseto Toscana, from Francesca's vineyard in Tuscany, but he said he didn't, and I made a mental note to send him some one day. I was very impressed and complemented him on having such a wonderful collection. We turned to leave, with Marco leading the way back toward the cellar door, when I stopped cold.

The stone wall to the right-hand side of the cellar door didn't have a rack full of wine bottles against it. Instead, it had a glass fronted cabinet built into it, so that the glass front was flush with the stone wall surrounding it.

Behind the glass, six unopened bottles of wine stood upright inside the cabinet, spaced equidistant from one another, in semi-darkness.

Marco, having seen me stop, flicked another light switch and the cabinet was instantly illuminated by tiny spotlights inside, angled towards the bottles, which were now bathed in light. I stepped closer. None of the bottles had a label. Each one had a black wax seal at the top and each one had the letters "Th.J." etched into the glass.

I felt like I'd been hit by a thunderbolt. Marco spotted my recognition.

"Do you know what these are?", he asked.

I couldn't speak, which seemed to amuse him.

I looked even closer and saw more markings on each bottle. The first one was a 1775 sherry, then next to it was a Chateau Laffite 1787. I looked along at the others spread out inside the cabinet. Two bottles of white wine, both Chateau d'Yquem, a 1787 and a 1784, followed by a Mouton and finally a Margaux.

"The lost Jefferson collection", I blurted out, completely stunned.

"That's right. Jesus, you know your shit, Bronson. You're the only person I've ever brought down here who knows what they are", he said.

"Where did they come from?", I asked.

"Well, they're French, obviously", he started, but I interrupted him.

"No, I mean, how did they get here, in this cabinet, inside your house? How did you get a hold of them?"

"Oh, right. A French guy. Louis Morel was his name."

"Morel", I repeated, remembering the name.

I thought back to what Max had said about a recluse called Louis Morel, who Max reckoned may have taken them out of France with him when he went off to live in the American mountains somewhere.

"Yeah", said Marco, "That guy was a first-class prick. I don't know, maybe all French guys are like that. Anyway, a few years back, we had part of our crew doing some business in upstate New York.

"This guy Morel had a kid who fell in with the wrong crowd, got into drugs, then became an addict and built up a colossal debt with his dealer up there. It turned out the kid didn't have any money, so the dealer went after the kid's father."

Then he paused, watching me, perhaps gauging how much he was willing to trust me with. I desperately wanted to know what happened next, but also feared for what he might tell me.

He carried on.

"This Louis Morel guy, he lived in a fucking fortress halfway up the Adirondack Mountains, in Lake George. I mean this guy's place was like Fort Knox. The drug dealer and his crew couldn't get near the place, so they contacted our boys up there and asked for some help. I gave the okay and we helped those guys out."

"And?"

"And, a few boys stormed Morel's house one night, they found him inside and made him pay off his kid's debt. They persuaded him to open his safe and took what they were due in cash.

"Turns out though, that as well as taking a cut, my guys also relieved Morel of six bottles of wine they found in his safe. My crew passed the wine up to me as a tribute and here they are."

"What will you do with them?", I asked.

"Well, I'm not going to drink them. They're French and I don't like French wine. But, I know they belonged to Thomas Jefferson and they'd be worth a hell of a lot of money if I needed to sell them some day."

I felt that gave me an opening.

"Marco. If you ever need to sell this collection, please let me be your first call. I know a guy back in London who's been looking for these six bottles for twenty years. He's rich and he'll pay you more than anybody else for them."

"Alright, Bronson. I'll bear that in mind."

I stole one last look at the wines behind the glass before we went back upstairs. I shook hands warmly with Marco, thanked him for the wine and reminded him about calling me if he ever had to sell the six Jefferson wines, then handed him my contact details on a card before saying goodbye.

Winston was already in the car, the cello inside its case on his knees across the back seat. I joined Tommy in the front and we set off back in the direction of Bensonhurst.

A half hour later, we pulled up outside Café Italia, which looked busy with the lunchtime crowd. Tommy slowed the car to a halt, then I got out, closed the door and he buzzed the window down so we could say goodbye, as Winston clambered out of the back seat with the cello.

"See you later, alligator", he said, a cheeky smile on his face, "You two should get yourselves into Manhattan and see if you can get your cabers polished by a couple of beauties in the city", he suggested.

I thanked him and poked my head and shoulders in through the front passenger window to shake his hand, but before our hands touched, I heard Winston's voice call out from behind me.

"Get down, boss", he shouted.

I hit the ground.

I then heard the crack of gun shots and felt the whiz of bullets flying over me. Tommy had spotted movement down the street and was already getting out of his car in a crouch, a semi-automatic pistol in his hand, ready to return fire.

Winston was on the ground with the upper half of his body on top of me, holding my head to the ground and his bottom half covering the cello case. Then there was silence, as Tommy and Winston took turns peaking down towards the other end of the street where the shots had come from.

I'd lost count of the amount of times I'd nearly shit myself in the past week and made a mental note to book us an easier gig next time.

A long minute later, Winston picked me up off the ground and Tommy joined us round at the kerb side of the car. Everybody was alright and Tommy was convinced the gunmen had escaped in a white pick-up truck that sped off in the opposite direction.

"Who was it?", I asked.

"Probably a couple of assholes from New Jersey or Boston", Tommy replied, "they'll have figured out they got played by us on the cello deal and wanted to try and save face a little."

He offered us a ride to our apartment, which, under the circumstances, seemed like a better plan than a couple of marks walking around the neighbourhood giving the gunmen a much easier second chance.

He dropped us off near enough to our apartment on Twentieth Avenue. I didn't want him to know exactly which building was ours. Tommy then took off, along with our best wishes, as we dived inside the apartment block and darted upstairs to the second floor.

I decided we were leaving New York immediately, so I asked Winston to call an airport car rental company and hire us a minivan, while I called Senator Ashley up in Boston to tell him we were heading up there to see him right away.

Winston managed to get a van delivered to our apartment and three hours after being shot at, we were travelling north to Boston on the Interstate 95, with the cello case secured in the back alongside our bags and with New York, for now, fifty miles behind us.

It took us another two and a half hours to reach the greater Boston area, then we followed the mini-van's satellite navigation route guidance for a further forty-five until we arrived outside Senator Ashley's house in the upper-class neighbourhood of Jamaica Plain.

He lived in a beautiful Victorian house on Eliot Street, with white painted outer walls and a light grey roof. The whole tree-lined street looked stunning in the fading daylight. When we arrived, Benson was standing on his porch and waved when we pulled up at the kerb side.

Winston carried the cello inside while Benson hugged me and shed tears of gratitude as we returned his late wife Cindy's parting gift to their daughter to its rightful home.

We had a great night in Benson's home. He called Christine in Milan to tell her the good news, with neither one of them caring that it was the middle of the night in Italy. He had Chinese food delivered for the three of us and gave Winston and I a bedroom each for the night.

In the morning, I calculated our total expenses on a sheet of paper, which amounted to just under $40,000 and passed it to Benson, along with the keys to our rented apartment in Brooklyn, which I'd forgotten to give to the Superintendent, since we left in such a hurry. He said his assistant, Melinda, would take care of all that.

He called his bank and immediately transferred $140,000 to my account, then Winston and I thanked him for his hospitality and we all said goodbye.

We set off back to New York in the mini-van with Winston driving, while I used my smartphone to book us on the next available flight back to London.

Six hours later, we took off from JFK at dusk and, after a nice dinner onboard, I thought about how relieved I was to be leaving gangsters and gunshots far behind, as I fell into a deep dreamless sleep.

TWENTY-TWO

Los Angeles, California
April 2014

Since our successful trip to New York, Winston and I continued to chase after high value trades, while somehow managing to stay away from guns, mobsters and ball-busting waitresses. Maybe because I banned us from doing business in New York ever again.

In 2012, I arranged for a case of Masseto Toscana to be sent to Marco Cannizzaro in Brooklyn through Francesca at her vineyard in Tuscany. I'd kept in touch with her over the phone and via emails since Milan and hoped that one day we might see each other again.

I wanted to reiterate my request for Marco to contact me first if he ever chose to sell the Jefferson wines, so my gift of the Masseto was intended as a sweetener to make sure he didn't forget about me. He emailed a thank you to me, saying he had tried Francesca's wine and thought it was wonderful.

Winston and I kept well away from New York ourselves, but we did however, return to North America, to the West Coast this time, in pursuit of a lost Pablo Picasso masterpiece, his 'Seated Woman with Red Hat'.

The painting had been gifted to the Evansville Museum in Indiana back in 1963, but went missing for the next fifty years after being misidentified. When it was donated, despite having Picasso's signature on it, the museum attributed the painting to an unknown artist, named Gemmaux, by mistake, since the word 'gemmaux' appeared several times on the artwork's accompanying documentation. As a result, it was put into storage in the Evansville's basement and never put on show.

As it turned out though, gemmaux wasn't the name of an artist, or even a person for that matter, but the plural of the word 'gemmail', which is an artist's technique of layering glass while adding a clear liquid enamel across the surface before firing it. Picasso hadn't used this technique often, with only fifty or so of his works known to have been created by this method.

In 2012, an expert from Guernsey's auction house in New York was researching Picasso's gemmaux works and came across a listing of a gemmail piece in a catalogue from the Evansville Museum. He went to Indiana to see it, recognized it as a lost Picasso masterpiece then with the Evansville's agreement, arranged for it to be transported back to New York so it could be officially authenticated.

Then came an unexpected turn of events, which meant the painting never made it to New York. Armed thieves stopped the truck carrying the painting, just south of Pittsburgh, and made off with Picasso's 'Seated Woman with

Red Hat', along with several other works that were supposed to be auctioned at Guernsey's. The authorities searched far and wide, but found no trace of the stolen paintings. The thieves had covered their tracks well.

Two years later, in early 2014, I received a cryptic email from Michael Fiorella in Brooklyn telling me he'd heard something from a Genovese ally in California about a painting he thought would be of interest to me. He didn't want to give away any more by email or talk about it over the phone, and gave me contact details for someone in Los Angeles he said I should call instead. I replied thanking him for the tip and dialled the number.

"Hello?", said a voice through the speakerphone in the office of my London apartment.

"Hello", I answered, "My name's Bronson Larkin. I'm an art dealer in London, England. A mutual acquaintance said I should call you", I said.

"Hold on", said the voice, then he gave me another phone number to call instead.

I called the second number and got a different voice.

"Daniel Rossi", said the voice.

"Bronson Larkin", I responded, "I was asked to call you?"

"Yeah, thanks. Look, a friend of mine in Brooklyn told me you can tell if something's real or not", he said.

"Possibly. It depends on what it is."

"Well, me and my friends here in LA have stumbled upon something, a painting. But we don't know if it's the real thing or not."

"Okay, how can I help?", I asked.

"I thought, maybe you could take a trip to California and check it out. For a fee, of course, plus I'd pay for your flights and a hotel room. What do you think?"

"Sounds interesting. Yeah, I could manage that. There'd be two of us, though, and my fee would be $1,000."

"No problem. Do you want one hotel room or two?"

"Two. Give me your email address and my man Winston can sort out the details and timing with you. We could be in LA within a couple of days if its urgent", I said, then we ended the call.

I was intrigued and, with the March weather in London being cold and miserable, I figured the West Coast of the States would be a nice place to hang out for a while. I initially didn't mind not knowing what I would be going there to look at. With this guy happy to cover our travel and accommodation costs up front, then pay me a nice little fee on top, I figured there wasn't much for us to lose.

Daniel transferred $3,000 to my bank account and, once it cleared, Winston booked our flights then made reservations for a couple of hotel rooms in LA. We took a direct flight from London Heathrow to LAX Airport on a Monday morning and the sixteen-hour journey passed a lot quicker than I expected. We took a taxi from the airport to the Hilton Hotel in Hollywood.

After checking in, we put our luggage up to our rooms, changed clothes and went for a walk to check out the neighbourhood. It felt great to be in shorts and a t-shirt, knowing it was near freezing back in London. There was a cloudless blue sky and the streets were lined with palm trees. We passed numerous high-end boutiques and strolled along the 'Walk of Fame' on Hollywood Boulevard, picking out the names of movie star legends on the five-pointed terrazzo and brass stars embedded in the street.

In the evening, we enjoyed a nice dinner at a Thai restaurant a few blocks north of where we were staying. Winston had arranged with Rossi for us to be collected at ten o'clock the following morning outside our hotel.

The next morning, we ate a light breakfast then hung around the hotel lobby and waited.

Just after ten o'clock, a car drew up outside and Winston went to see if it was our ride. He signalled over to me with a 'thumbs up', then I walked out to join him in the back of the light blue saloon and the car drove off.

Daniel Rossi was in the front passenger seat. He turned to face me in the back as he introduced himself. He looked about forty-five with dark hair and sharp facial features. He had a crooked nose that looked like it had been broken more than once and there was a noticeable scar above his left eyebrow.

Both these features served as a stark reminder to me that we were in the company of professional criminals, maybe even murderers. I swallowed hard and made a mental note to keep my wits about me. Winston, sitting next to me, looked completely nonplussed.

We made benign small talk about the contrasting weather between London and California and Daniel pointed out a few sights as we travelled west through Beverly Hills before we arrived outside a stunning villa on South Bentley Avenue.

Winston, Rossi and I got out of the car and the driver remained inside. We were then welcomed into the house by our host, a guy called Jimmy De Luca, who Daniel introduced to us as a friend of theirs, meaning De Luca was a 'made' member of the mafia, just as I took Daniel to be.

Recalling a previous visit to a mobster's home, when my appraisal of the Stradivarius cello In Brooklyn seemed to upset Vincent Calabrese, I felt butterflies in my stomach as we stepped over the threshold and the front door closed ominously behind us. De Luca led us along a hallway into a large open parlour at the end, which was filled with beautiful French antique furnishings and a polished marble floor.

In the middle of the room, there were two large couches facing one another and De Luca motioned for us to take a seat. I noticed a wooden easel set up with a framed painting resting on it in the far corner and assumed that was what I was there to inspect. I didn't know if these guys wanted me to declare the painting to be real or fake, which suddenly made me feel anxious. What would they do if I gave them the wrong answer?

De Luca instructed a housekeeper to make us some coffee and Daniel invited me to check out the painting. I stood up and walked over to the easel with my legs feeling slightly weak. I stopped a short distance away from the painting and began my appraisal.

It was a three-foot-high portrait of a seated woman wearing a red hat. At first glance, I thought it looked an almost rudimentary piece, but the more I studied the colours and raised texture, which gave the painting a kind of three-dimensional effect, I sensed it was something much more remarkable.

In the top right corner, it had the unmistakable signature of Pablo Picasso in black and, after another ten minutes spent examining the artwork closely, I was convinced it was the original Picasso gemmail artwork that had been stolen on route to New York in 2012.

I hastily searched online using my iPhone to see if there were any photos of the painting and found just two images, both taken right before it left the Evansville museum on its fateful journey east. I compared the pictures on my phone with the painting right in front of me, and became even more certain.

Daniel and Jimmy looked mildly agitated, as if they were growing impatient and wanted to hear my opinion.

"What do you say, Bronson?" asked Daniel.

I was hesitant for a moment. Despite being in an air-conditioned room, I felt a bead of sweat run down my back under my shirt and prayed the answer I was about to give was the one they wanted. I glanced at Winston who also seemed tense. I took a deep breath and tried to be confident.

"Well Daniel, Jimmy. I believe this to be a genuine Pablo Picasso. A very famous piece called 'Seated Woman with Red Hat', which was misidentified by a museum in Indiana and put away in storage for half a century, then stolen shortly after its rediscovery two years ago.

"The seated woman is reported to be Marie-Thérèse Walter, Picasso's mistress, and the unusual texture of the painting is the result of a seldom used technique called gemmail, where the artist builds up the picture in thin layers of glass while adding a clear liquid enamel across the surface before firing it to set."

I looked at Rossi and De Luca, trying to judge whether they took what I'd said as good news or bad. Winston seemed to be watching for their reaction too. De Luca turned to Rossi and gave him a satisfied nod, then Daniel Rossi looked at me.

A broad grin slowly appeared on his face as he looked at me like I was his new best friend. I breathed a huge sigh of relief and wiped sweat from my temple. Coffee arrived and was served by the housekeeper, then after she'd left the parlour, Jimmy De Luca asked me what I thought the Picasso was worth.

I thought for a moment.

"In the tens of millions of dollars", I said, "but that's what it would likely sell for at a legitimate auction. I'm not sure how much a stolen Picasso would go for, nor am I familiar with any market for such an item. The Russians might be interested, possibly. Maybe the Chinese. It's hard to say."

"What about the guys who owned it before it got stolen?", asked Daniel.

"The museum in Indiana?", I asked, "They might be an option, sure. I think I read somewhere they got a substandard pay out from their insurers because the painting had never been officially authenticated, but there was enough circumstantial evidence from artworld experts to validate a claim. Therefore, the insurance company wouldn't have paid out as much as the painting's true value, but the museum probably still got several million from the claim."

They both looked rather pleased with themselves, then hit me with a request.

"Would you and the big guy here be interested in some work while you're out in LA?", asked Rossi.

"What kind of work? I stay on the right side of the line. I've got a lot to lose, so I don't want to make a bad decision and get involved in something I shouldn't", I replied, looking at Winston, who remained expressionless.

"We know a guy. Someone we've used before as an intermediary. Maybe, through him, we use a middle man to contact the museum in Indiana about selling them back their painting", said Daniel.

"What middle man?", I asked.

"Someone completely independent, but who's knowledgeable about the artworld and can talk the same language as museum experts", he said, then paused briefly before hammering it home, "You know? You?"

He smiled.

"Me? As the middle man between your intermediary and the people from Evansville? I thought I was just here to inspect the painting."

"You two are off the grid out here. All our regular guys are well-known to the authorities. You guys are perfect for this."

I looked at Winston who shrugged ambivalently. He was clearly unsure, uneasy perhaps.

"What would we have to do, exactly?", I asked.

"First of all, you contact the museum and convince them you've seen the real painting. Then you persuade them to buy it back from us, for a fair price. If they go for it, we give you the painting and you hand it over to the museum once they've made the payment", said Daniel.

"And, what would our end be?", I asked.

"One percent", said De Luca.

I thought about it, looked at Winston and did some sums in my head. If the museum bought the piece for $5,000,000, we'd earn $50,000. That was a lot of money, but the risks were high. This was criminal activity.

"Make it two percent and we'll do it", I found myself saying, immediately worrying I'd regret it later. I didn't dare look at Winston.

"Great", said De Luca.

We shook on it, then Daniel led Winston and I to the front door and left with us in the same blue saloon that had brought us there.

A day later, Daniel emailed me the intermediary's contact details, an accountant in Chicago we would never meet. In my room at the hotel, Winston and I pulled our heads together to try and work out a plan that would bring us success without going to prison.

We left the hotel and I bought a pre-paid cell phone from a random electrical store nearby. I used it to call the Evansville museum in Indiana from a quiet side street away from the crowds on Hollywood Boulevard. After being put through to the curator, I told her I was calling on behalf of some guys that had the stolen Picasso and asked if the museum would be interested in buying it back.

I told her I was a British art dealer visiting Los Angeles, that I'd appraised the painting myself and was one hundred percent certain it was the real thing. I described the gemmail technique and all other aspects of the painting in detail. She listened carefully and seemed to accept that I was being genuine. She needed to discuss the proposal with the museum's board of directors, so I told her I'd call her again the next day and hung up.

I gave the cell phone to Winston who immediately crushed it under his foot and discarded the pieces in various trash cans on the street as we walked back to the hotel.

The next morning, I bought another burner phone from a different retailer and called the museum curator in Evansville from a quiet booth inside a breakfast diner.

She told me the directors were uneasy about dealing with criminals, but I told her it was simply a yes or no thing. Did they want the painting back or not? I also said there was interest from Chinese and Russian collectors if the Evansville decided to pass. This was obviously a lie, but I had to try and convince her somehow.

She asked for more time to discuss it further with the directors before coming to a decision. I gave her one hour. We left the diner and I was a nervous wreck, anxiously checking my watch every five minutes.

 I called her again using the same cell phone and she said the museum would do it, offering $7,500,000 to get the painting back. Thankfully for my sake, the deal was on.

I'd been told not to have any further contact with Daniel Rossi and that I was to go through the accountant in Chicago, who had full decision-making responsibility. I called the guy, who told me his name was Tony, which I figured was in no way truthful, and he said the seven and a half million bucks the museum had offered was acceptable, no haggling required.

I then had to somehow convince the museum to transfer the money to a bank account in the Cayman Islands, which Tony the accountant gave me the details for. He said his guys would deliver the painting to us in the parking lot of our hotel once the money had been received. We would then have to hand it over to the museum in Indiana ourselves.

I tried not to think what the mafia guys might do if we screwed this up. I felt pressure building up inside as I prepared for my next conversation with the curator.

I called her using yet another pre-paid phone and gave her the sort code and account number of the bank in Grand Cayman. She still seemed slightly hesitant and I tried hard not to sound too desperate or panicky. I covered the mouthpiece with my hand so she wouldn't hear me taking a deep breath, then I reminded her that the guys who had the painting didn't care who they sold it to and if the Evansville didn't make the payment, they would sell it to someone else and the museum would never see it again.

She finally said she'd arrange the payment, then I told her I'd call back in three days with the Picasso's location, once I'd received word that the money had been received.

The next day, I called Chicago and the accountant said the money had arrived in Grand Cayman, and that it had then been immediately transferred through a series of subsequent banks to eliminate any chance of leaving a trail. He then told me the plan for getting the painting to us.

The next morning, I watched from my hotel room window as Winston collected a large wooden box from a couple of unknown guys down in the parking lot and realised at that moment, that we were way past the point of no return.

That afternoon, Winston rented a car and we drove all the way from Los Angeles to Indiana, with the boxed painting on the back seat. The journey took two days and we stopped for a night at a roadside motel halfway there. We registered with bogus names and paid for all our meals, accommodation and fuel with cash to avoid leaving a trail.

When we arrived in Indiana, we drove to a storage rental facility on the outskirts of Evansville. We figured I had a less conspicuous appearance compared with King Kong. Therefore, wearing a baseball cap and a pair of sunglasses, I entered an office and pre-paid for a week's container rental in cash, scribbling the name 'Al Capone' illegibly on a registration form, along with a made-up address.

An attendant showed me the container's location on a site map and handed me an instruction booklet for how to lock it with a six-digit code number of my choosing. I thanked him, then joined Winston back out in the car and we drove to our container.

We put the painting inside and locked it up. I chose Pablo Picasso's date of birth, 25-10-81, as the six-digit electronic access code. Then we left the storage facility and headed south for a hundred miles or so, before I called the museum curator from a safe distance.

I told her the where the painting was, who's name the container was registered under and the access code. I then thanked her, said goodbye, hung up and tossed my final burner cell phone out the window, watching it smash into smithereens on the road behind us in the car's rear view mirror.

The deal was complete, which was a huge relief and left me with mixed feelings. We'd earned $150,000 for a week's work, which on paper sounded amazing. However, we'd broken the law in the process.

Our two percent was transferred into my bank account the same day and I transferred Winston's cut to his account online using my iPhone. We would never meet or hear from Daniel Rossi or Jimmy De Luca ever again.

During the drive back to Los Angeles, I thought through what we'd done and started to rationalise. Sure, we'd crossed the line of legality, but nobody got hurt, physically. The museum got its painting back and probably had sufficient funds from its 2012 insurance pay out to cover the $7,500,000 anyway. I felt we'd covered our tracks well enough that our involvement would never be detected. In the end, I decided the reward had been worth the risk and resolved not to beat myself up about breaking the law.

.

TWENTY-THREE

Back in LA, Winston and I checked out of the Hilton and decided to extend our stay in California. We needed a car so we could travel from place to place as we pleased, but I didn't want to drive some plain rental vehicle, preferring to buy something cool instead. I figured if I bought something desirable and used it for just a short time, it would be easy enough to sell on before we returned to the UK.

Winston found a nearby car dealer online that specialised in European classics, so we took a cab out to the place in North Hollywood and found an absolute gem. The owner had around forty classic sportscars from the 1960s onwards, including several Ferraris, Mercedes and an Aston Martin.

He had a red 1968 E-Type Jaguar, left-hand drive, with a 4.2 litre engine and an automatic gearbox, which I immediately fell in love with. But unfortunately, the dealership's owner said it was his own collector's item and wasn't for sale.

We searched his lot thoroughly and eventually found a winner. A 1978 Porsche 911 cabriolet, in Guards red with a black convertible roof, black wheels and a black leather interior. It had done only 17,000 miles, was in immaculate condition and came with a full history. I took it for a test drive and loved it instantly. The sound it made was awesome. I haggled the guy down from his sticker price of $56,500 and we shook hands on a deal at $49,200.

The engine in Porsche's 911 model is at the rear of the car and the small boot compartment at the front only had room for one of our bags, so Winston had to store his on the miniscule back seats. After doing some paperwork and transferring the money, I drove off in my very own vintage sportscar.

I had to pull over less than a mile after leaving the dealership though, to put the convertible roof down because Winston's mammoth head was protruding up into the fabric roof and ruining the car's aerodynamics.

Once we had the top down, the ape had ample headroom and the ride seemed so much better with the sun on our faces and the wind in our hair as we sped off along the highway.

We went on tour for a couple for weeks, enjoying California's amazing scenery and the early Spring sunshine. I felt a million miles away from chilly old London. We stayed in motels, quite happy to leave five-star luxury and fine dining for another time. We met scores of terrific, friendly people everywhere and even managed to visit a couple of vineyards along the way.

We'd journeyed north-west from Los Angeles, through Bakersfield, enjoying the drive with the top down. I felt so free and unencumbered as we spent the first week hopping from town to town without a care in the world, the stress of the Picasso deal soon forgotten.

At a restaurant in Fresno, we met a couple from Manchester, England, who were on a wine-tasting holiday. They talked excitedly about a vineyard they'd visited that was just a forty-minute drive to the north, up near the Yosemite National Park. They said the owners were great and the wines were exceptional, so Winston and I decided to pay it a visit.

After calling to make an appointment, we set off the next morning and arrived at Westbrook Wine Farm shortly before mid-day. Our hosts, Ray and Tammy greeted us warmly and started us off with a tour around the production facilities where they carried out the fermentation, blending and bottling operations.

Tammy talked us through the whole wine making process before she and Ray served up a first-class lunch of smoky barbecued chicken wings, along with their flagship Claret, named 'Fait accompli', which was superb.

After lunch, we enjoyed a couple of hours of tasting, which covered all the wines produced at Westbrook. By the middle of the afternoon, I felt slightly buzzed, even though I'd only been tasting the wines and not swallowing, rinsing with water between tastes.

Fresh air seemed like a good idea, so Ray set Winston and I up with a motorised bicycle each and a guide map of the vineyard, which had several different routes for us to follow, so we could explore the vast estate by ourselves. Although Winston's bike was a little undersized for his massive body, our tour of the growing areas began well enough.

Since the bikes were motorised, we breezed around the vines effortlessly, stopping every now and then to read up about the grape varieties around us. After about half an hour, with me leading the way in single file along one of the routes marked on the map, I glanced back and saw no sign of Winston on the trail behind me.

I stopped my bike, got off and walked back a short distance before noticing the spinning front wheel of Winston's bike, which was over on its side, protruding from some foliage at the edge of the trail. As I got closer, I found a spread-eagled gorilla lying next to the fallen bike.

"Are you alright?"

"Yeah. Took my eye off the trail for a second. I'm fine."

He got to his feet and righted the bike, which seemed to be undamaged. He looked a little woozy and his eyes were a bit hazy, but he said he was okay, so we carried on.

When we reached the far end of the vineyard, the route we were following turned back towards where we'd started from. Most of the way back was slightly downhill, which made the ride even easier and I found myself having to feather the brakes to keep from going too fast.

Around half a mile from the winery buildings, the trail became slightly wider and steeper so I slowed right down to maintain control of the bike. As I did so, Winston flew past me like a ballistic missile and I watched in horror as his bike veered off the trail a hundred yards ahead of me.

He went over the bike's handlebars when its front wheel hit a rock, sending Godzilla spiralling through the air and into a small pond at the edge of the trail.

When I arrived at the scene, I found him back on his feet, wading clumsily through the knee-high pond water towards the trail. His seemingly indestructible bike lay among some plants nearby, yet again showing no obvious signs of damage.

I sat down on the rock that Winston's bike had collided with and he trudged over to join me, soaking from head to toe. He checked out his body and appeared to be miraculously uninjured.

Neither of us spoke while we sat for a moment.

"Winston?"

"Yes."

"Are you drunk?"

"I think I might be, yes."

"When we did the tasting, were you swallowing the wine?"

"Yes."

"You weren't using the spit bucket and rinsing between tastes?"

"Nope."

"Huh."

We sat in silence again for another moment or two. Then I caught a whiff of the putrid smell of pond water coming from his wet clothes.

"That's disgusting", I said.

"Sorry."

"It's a good job the car's a convertible. I wouldn't want to be cooped up next to that smell all the way back to Fresno", I teased.

Poor Winston.

"Come on, let's head back and you can get cleaned up."

Ray and Tammy were remarkably nice about the state Winston returned in. They said it wasn't the first time a guest had fallen off one of their bikes and were glad he wasn't hurt.

We lay down in the late afternoon sunshine for a while so Winston could dry off. I didn't want him to wet as well as smelly during our return car journey.

We thanked our hosts graciously before getting into the car, roof down, and heading south towards Fresno, with Winston looking forward to taking a long hot shower back at the motel.

TWENTY-FOUR

After being out of the city for a fortnight, we made our way back to Los Angeles for a final few days before we went home to England. Winston booked us a couple of rooms at the ultra-luxurious Sofitel Los Angeles in Beverly Hills. It was one of the finest hotels I'd ever seen and my room had a stunning view of the iconic Hollywood Hills to the north.

After a fortnight living in cheap motels we enjoyed an indulgent first night at the Sofitel, sampling the wonderful food and exquisite local wines in the hotel restaurant. The next morning, after a light breakfast, I did a quick search online using my smartphone and found an interesting looking antique shop on Wiltshire Boulevard.

We decided to pay it a visit, but it was too far to walk and parking looked limited, so we took a taxi from the hotel and left the Porsche behind. What a find it turned out to be; a wonderful emporium of high end antiques.

It had everything from furniture to paintings, bronze figurines to rare books. There were beautiful vintage lamps, some magnificent porcelains and an impressive collection of antique clocks. I quickly became immersed in all the beautiful objects around us, fascinated by the finest array of collectables I'd ever seen.

The owner was a very attractive blonde-haired woman of about forty, with blue eyes and a knockout smile. She seemed to take an instant shine to Winston from the moment we entered. She was very friendly and I saw her gazing at Winston unmistakeably as we browsed around.

After a short time, she introduced herself to Winston and they started chatting. Her name was Jan and the two talked away together as I continued exploring.

They must've hit it off, because when I finally joined them at the front of the shop, Winston told me she'd invited us to join her at a party the following night. It was being held at the home of one of her best furniture clients who lived in Bell Air.

She wrote down her full name, cell phone number and the address for the party. We agreed to meet her there around eight o'clock.

We spent the next day lazing around the hotel, reading magazines and snacking at the bar. At seven-thirty in the early evening, I drove the two of us in my car to the address in Bell Air. When we arrived, we both looked at one another in disbelief, then checked the address Jan had written down to make sure we were at the right house.

A giant pair of metal gates at the front of the property were open, beyond which we could see a gigantic mansion house in the distance. A young parking valet approached my window.

"Good evening, sir. May I have your names please?", he asked, but before I could answer, I heard Winston's voice.

"Oh my God, Bronson."

I looked straight ahead out of the front windscreen and saw Jan, arm in arm with Hugh Hefner, strolling casually on the driveway heading in our direction. The party was being held at the fucking Playboy Mansion!

Jan called out to the valet that we were with her and she waved at Winston next to me. He got out of the passenger seat and met Jan with a kiss on both cheeks, then shook hands with Hef, as I stumbled out of the car awkwardly, struck by nerves at the sight of the world-famous magazine founder.

Hugh approached the car as I sorted myself out.

"Wow, that's beautiful, man. Is she yours?" he asked me.

"Yeah. I bought it a couple of weeks ago. Me and Winston just finished a little tour around California in her. We had a great trip."

"I'm Hugh", he said.

"I know", I replied smiling, "have you ever met anyone in the last forty years who didn't know who you are?", I said rhetorically, which made him laugh, "I'm Bronson."

"Where are you from? You sound English", he said.

"No. I'm Scottish, but I live in London."

"Come on in and enjoy the party", he said and I handed my keys to the valet, then the four of us walked towards the house. Hugh looked back towards the driveway gates when he heard the valet start up the Porsche. He gave me an appreciating nod at the raspy sound of the car's engine.

Jan soon linked arms with Winston and led him away to get drinks and mingle with the crowd. There were people everywhere, having a good time, with music playing loudly and the mansion all lit up spectacularly. Hugh gave me a tour of the house, telling me all about the antique furniture inside, saying that Jan had an exceptional eye and that he'd bought most of his collection from her.

When we entered the dining room, he showed me a wonderful antique dining table, made of mahogany, which had quite a history. He shared all the details with me about the table being an original Thomas Chippendale commissioned by John Hancock in 1776. It was a beautiful piece with ornate carved legs and matched carving all the way around the edges of the top.

"It's magnificent", I said, "how come the chairs don't match?", I asked.

"You don't miss a thing, do you?", he replied smiling.

"Nobody knows what happened to the original Chippendale dining chairs. Maybe they were chopped up in desperation during a harsh winter and Hancock didn't have any money to pay for firewood", he joked.

"It's extraordinary", I said, "would you ever sell it?"

"You serious?"

"Yeah, sure."

"What are you going to do with that red Porsche outside when you fly back to London? Are you going to get it shipped over there? It's left hand drive, remember. Wrong side of the car for you Brits, huh?", he asked.

"I was going to sell it here before going back in a few days. You interested in a swap for the table?"

"I don't know. What's the car worth?", he asked.

"I paid $49,200 for it two weeks ago."

"I'm not sure my dining table is worth that much."

I disagreed with him, but said nothing.

"How about I leave the Porsche with you when I fly back home, and you keep the table for me until I have a dining room big enough to put it in, then I'll arrange to have it shipped?"

He looked pensive for a moment. I think he was imagining how much fun it would be to have one of his girlfriends drive him around Bell Air in the bright red sportscar with the top down.

"Alright, deal", he said and grabbed my hand to shake on it before either of us changed our minds.

I was thrilled. I was going to have to sell the car in a day or so anyway and, for me, the table was a much better investment.

Hugh took me outside and introduced me to scores of other party guests, many of whom, he himself was meeting for the very first time. I remember thinking what a legend this guy was, as dozens of young bikini clad beauties paraded around him, showing what seemed to me to be genuine affection for the eighty-eight-year-old.

I spied Winston and Jan sitting comfortably in each other's arms on a huge bean bag in the garden. There were also a few bunnies playing water polo in the pool nearby. Their ball bounced towards me from the pool after someone's wayward goal attempt, so I picked it up and walked over to give it back, but suddenly felt Winston grab me from behind. He picked me up with ease and launched me into the water fully clothed, much to everyone's approval, including Hef who I saw bent over laughing.

I climbed out of the pool and sprinted towards Jan and Winston, then dived on top of them, causing Jan to shriek. After sharing a very cold and wet group hug with the ape and his new girlfriend, Hugh came to my rescue by asking one of his house staff to take me inside so I could dry off.

She led me to a shower room in the house, where I stripped off my wet clothes and dried myself with a towel. The girl returned a few minutes later with a white robe and slippers for me, then she took my clothes away to have them dried.

I emerged from the house to rapturous applause when everyone noticed I'd not only slipped on the robe and slippers, but was also now wearing Hugh's trademark white sailor's cap, which he'd handed to me as I approached the crowd.

The party was an absolute hoot and I couldn't recall the last time I'd had such a good time sober. An hour later, I was back in my dry clothes and ready to drive back to the hotel.

Jan told me Winston would be spending the night at her place, so I kissed her on the cheek and said goodnight to them both, then thanked Hugh for his hospitality, reminding him about our deal, before walking to the front gate to get my car.

I loved the drive back along the clear night-time streets of Los Angeles, in what would end up being my final blast in the high-performance Porsche.

I slept well, maybe due to the lack of alcohol, then rose early the next morning and went for a swim before opting for a healthy room service breakfast of pink grapefruit and scrambled eggs with spinach. Winston appeared around eleven having had a brilliant night with Jan. He told me he really liked her and she'd given him Hugh's contact details to pass on to me.

It was time to go home though, so I asked him to book us a flight back to London, while I filled in some paperwork to transfer ownership of the car to Hugh. Jan appeared in the hotel lobby as we were checking out, to say goodbye.

I gave her the keys and documentation for the car, which she promised to pass on to Hugh. I told her where the car was parked in the hotel lot, then went to the concierge desk and organised a cab to the airport, leaving Jan and Winston to say farewell to one another.

We rode to the airport in silence having had an amazing and very lucrative trip to California. Four and a half hours later, we were soaring above the coastline of Florida on a return flight to London that felt much longer than the outbound one had.

TWENTY-FIVE

A year after our trip to California, in early May of 2015, I bought a bigger safe for the apartment, which had become a necessity as our collective piles of cash and other valuables outgrew the previous one. And, it was while transferring items from the old safe to the new, that I came across something I hadn't seen, or thought about, for many years, but which, upon rediscovering it, would ultimately lead to the biggest deal of my life.

I had not set eyes on the Patek Philippe 1518 wristwatch I'd bought from Michael Barker since 2001. I'd stashed it away inside the safe upon our return from New York and hadn't looked at it since, even when Winston mentioned to me how buoyant the rare watch market was a few years later.

I took it out of its box and looked at it. It really was a beautiful watch and it was still in mint condition. I realised, of course, that it was bound to be, since I'd never worn it and Barker had claimed that he hadn't either.

This made me think about its maker though, who surely wouldn't have wanted this magnificent piece of engineering to be stuck in a dark box, never to be seen or worn. Maybe it was time to sell it on to someone who would wear it as its maker intended.

I asked Winston to have a look at the watch market on the Internet and see if he could estimate the 1518's current value. He duly obliged and searched on his laptop for a couple of hours, then got back to me with an answer I wasn't expecting.

"Well, how much?", I asked.

"Who knows?", said Winston, throwing his hands up in the air, frustrated.

"What do you mean?" I asked, puzzled.

"It could be worth anything from around the half a million dollars you bought it for in 2001, right up to three or four times that", he said.

"Why such a wide range?"

"Two reasons. One, there are so few left in existence that no examples have been seen at auction since 2000, and that was the very occasion when you yourself attempted to buy Barker's one at Sotheby's in London. Meaning, there is no recent sales history to base a current estimate on", he explained.

"Hmm. And two?", I asked.

"Reason two is, the rare watch market has gone bonkers over the past twelve months. The number of wealthy individuals with an interest in fine timepieces has soared. As a result, there are more buyers than ever for the rarest watches and it's almost impossible to predict how much the wealthiest collectors might be prepared to spend to outbid their competition at an auction", said Winston.

"Interesting", was my response. Then Winston had a suggestion.

"Why don't I phone around the auction houses that focus solely on rare watches and see if they have any idea about its current value?", he said.

"Good plan", I said.

I left him to get on with it, while I made a fourth attempt to reconcile a troublesome stack of £50 notes, that I'd previously counted out to equal ninety-nine, ninety-eight and one-hundred-and-one, when there should, in fact, have been a nice round, one hundred of them. I swore that stack was messing with me.

By the time Winston joined me in the lounge with an update, I'd finished sorting out the new safe and sat on the couch with my feet up.

"I've called Sotheby's, Christie's, Bonhams, Antiquorum and Fellows. They've all checked inhouse, as well as consulting with their other branches worldwide and, so far, none of them is prepared to even take a guess at the current value of your 1518 over the telephone. Unsurprisingly, however, every single one of them wants you to choose their house to auction your watch", he said.

"Typical", I said, "Everyone's an expert in valuations after the fact, but nobody wants to stick their neck out beforehand."

I thought for a minute.

"Do you think you could put together some data on past results for Patek Philippe models sold at auctions worldwide over the past five years?", I asked.

"Yeah, all the houses have that information on their websites now. It'll take a bit of time, a couple of days maybe, but sure, I can do that, boss", he responded.

"Perfect. Let's see which auction house has been the most successful at achieving the highest prices. Get on it first thing tomorrow", I said.

"You don't want me to start right now?", he asked.

"No. Right now we're going to the pub. My head's burst from counting out all those stacks of banknotes, without much competence as it turned out, and I need a pint", I said and off we went.

The next morning, Winston hid in the office with his laptop while I went off to browse around some antique shops in Covent Garden. The weather was warm and sunny so I chose to walk, picking up a takeaway coffee before heading east past Kensington Gardens and Hyde Park on Bayswater Road. It took about an hour to reach the chic marketplace, but I was glad of the fresh air and needed the exercise.

I went into a shop that sold nautical collectables and paraphernalia, but the items were all brand new and commercially produced. Not what I was after. The next place I tried was a small independent jeweller selling hand-made rings, necklaces and bracelets. Again, nothing in there for me, but it was a cool place with loads of beautiful, unique items. I saw a gorgeous white gold pendant in the shape of a butterfly, which prompted a wave of nostalgia as I thought back to Coco Chanel's butterfly brooch.

I moved on and popped inside the Covent Garden Market Building, where I came across a place that looked a lot more promising. It was a more traditional antique shop with a huge variety of items for me to search through. There were old books, coins, stamps and furniture. I saw vintage clothing and personal items like Victorian hand mirrors, smoking pipes and even old chamber pots. Yuck.

I spent a good forty minutes in there and was about to leave, but as I approached the door, the owner came bustling in holding a large cardboard box, followed by an assistant, also carrying a box. New stock, I wondered? I decided to stick around for a bit.

They set the boxes down beside one another on a table next to an open door that looked like it led to a back office, then the owner went back out leaving the young assistant in the shop by herself. She soon became preoccupied with her smartphone.

I sidled up to the new boxes and peeked inside. The larger of the two boxes was filled with old toys and children's books. I glanced at the assistant, who was texting on her phone, before looking inside the smaller box.

There were a couple of big old leather tomes with a stack of paper items underneath. I picked up the large books to see what the papers beneath them were.

"Is it okay for me to lift these out to have a look?", I asked the assistant.

"Yeah", she replied, still looking at her phone.

Just then, the main door opened and the owner returned with yet another box. He smiled as he set it down on the table next to the others.

"Come on, Justine, there are still boxes to come in", he said to the young girl, then looked at me.

"Sorry, Sir. Can I help you with anything?", he asked.

"I'm good thanks. Just having a look at the stuff in here if that's alright?", I asked.

"Yes, yes. Please, take your time. Sorry we're so disorganised this morning. If you find anything of interest, let me know and I'll give you a price. Everything's for sale", he said, then left the shop again, followed by his assistant.

I glanced at the titles of the two large volumes, but they were both encyclopaedias, of no interest to me, so I laid them down on the table, then lifted the stack of papers out of the box. I leafed through them one at a time starting at the top, turning them over as I went.

There were some early 20th century theatre programmes, some of which looked like they had been autographed and could be collectable, so I laid them to one side on the table. Then I came across some old sheet music that seemed to be from the same era. There were some handwritten notes and dates in the margins, which I thought could mean they were authentic music sheets used during live performances so I put them on the table too.

I shuffled through the remaining papers, but found nothing else, so I put those back in the box, then looked again through the pile of programmes and sheet music I'd set aside.

I thought one of the music sheets looked out of place. It was in much poorer condition than the others, with a black ring mark on the front page and a few tears along the edges. It also had worn fold marks and was badly discoloured.

I looked at some faint text written by hand at the top of the page, which read, '3.3.12 to W.H.H. Play this for me, Mother'. The printed title of the music on the sheet was 'On the beautiful Blue Danube', the famous waltz composed by Johann Strauss II.

This sheet intrigued me, but it would need further investigation, so I placed it in the middle of the stack of programmes and other music sheets, which I kept to one side then I returned the two encyclopaedias to their cardboard box.

The owner and his assistant came in the front door with more boxes and put them on the table next to the others. He looked as if he was about to head back out, so I got his attention.

"How much for these?", I asked.

I handed him the stack of old papers. He flicked through them quickly, paused slightly on one of the programmes, then handed them all back to me.

"Make me an offer?", he said, smiling.

"Twenty quid?", I asked.

"Done", he said.

I pulled out a £20 note from my wallet and handed it to him, then left the shop with the papers in my hand.

I went to a small bistro in Covent Garden and ate a sandwich while looking through the sheets again. I had a contact at Bonhams in Knightsbridge who I thought might be willing to check out the stack of papers. She was an expert in ancient manuscripts and rare books, so I figured she would be worth a try. It was on my way home anyway, so after I'd eaten, I took a taxi to Montpelier Street, just south of Hyde Park.

I entered Bonhams' distinctive dark grey building and Gloria greeted me warmly, kissing me on both cheeks.

"Long time no see, Bronson", she said.

"Good to see you", I responded, "do you have a minute?"

"Yes, of course, follow me", she said and led me along a hallway to a small room, where we sat and after a few catch up pleasantries, I handed her the papers.

"What do you make of these?", I asked.

She skipped through them all, then went back to the start to go through them again and, like me, she paused at the damaged 'Danube' music sheet.

"This looks interesting", she said, "what can you tell me about this one?", she asked, holding up the sheet.

"Not a thing", I replied.

"Oh, come on, Bronson. Really?"

"I just bought them all an hour ago from an antique dealer in the Convent Garden Market Building. They were in a box that had just arrived. I don't think the owner had even set eyes on them himself, before I stepped in and bought these for twenty quid", I explained.

She stared at the front of the sheet.

"The hand-written text at the top might be something. The W.H.H. looks like someone's initials, don't you think?", she asked.

"Yeah, I thought that too. I figured it was maybe a sheet given to a musician by his or her mother. You know, saying, 'play this piece for me', or whatever. What do you think?", I asked.

"Could be", she said, turning it over to look at the back, then turned it over to the front again, "the 3.3.12 looks like a date. 1912 do you think? It looks pretty old", she said.

"Yeah, I think it's 1912, assuming it's a date. It can't be 1812 or earlier. Strauss didn't compose 'The Blue Danube' until 1886", I said.

"I'm not sure. Can you leave it with me for a while? We have technicians here who can do carbon dating, which might give us a ballpark age for the paper. It probably won't be that accurate though. I also have a colleague who's a handwriting expert. Maybe the style is consistent with a specific period", she said.

"No problem. Here's my contact details", I handed her a card, "call me if you come up with anything", I said and stood up.

"Will do. Good seeing you, Bronson", she said then I thanked her and left.

The early afternoon was bright and hot when I left Bonhams, so I took my jacket off and carried it over my shoulder during a leisurely walk back home to Phillimore Gardens.

TWENTY-SIX

Geneva, Switzerland
June 2015

A day or so later, Winston had finished his mini project compiling pricing data from past watch auctions and called me through to the office.

He showed me a spreadsheet he'd created on his laptop and talked me through it. Winston had converted all sales currencies into US dollars, using average exchange rates on the day of sale, to help us compare like with like.

The first thing I noticed was that prices had been rising over the past five years. Patek Philippe models of a similar age, specification, materials of construction and colour combination had sold for increasing amounts all over the world, year-on-year. Just as he'd concluded earlier that week, there were no recorded sales of any 1518 models.

Another interesting observation was that the volume of annual auction sales for the brand had been diminishing year-on-year. Did that mean there were fewer and fewer good examples available, or fewer buyers?

Winston and I poured over the data he'd collected for over an hour then agreed on a couple of firm conclusions. Firstly, that increasing prices combined with decreasing volumes was indicative of a seller's market, so it could be a great time to put my 1518 up for sale.

And secondly, that without a doubt, the best house to auction my watch would be Phillips in Geneva, Switzerland. Their auctions had consistently achieved the highest prices for rare Patek Philippe timepieces since 2010, and they were reputed to be the world's foremost Patek Philippe experts, with the auction house and the celebrated watchmaker both being based in the same city.

I made initial contact with Phillips via email, explaining what I had to sell, and attached some photos I'd taken with my iPhone, showing the watch from different angles, as well as its original box and documentation. I signed off by saying I looked forward to hearing back from them and left my mobile phone number, including the International dialling code, so that they would know I was in the UK.

I hit send, then went to put the kettle on for a cup of tea while I waited for a response. The kettle hadn't even boiled when, within a minute or so, my phone rang, with the screen showing a long number indicating the call was from overseas.

"Bronson Larkin", I answered.

"Hello, Mr. Larkin. This is Sofía Basso, calling from Phillips in Geneva, Switzerland. How are you today?", she asked.

"Great, thanks. You?"

"Very well, thank you", she said, "I got your email just now and wanted to see how we could help you sell your wristwatch. Is now a convenient time to talk?", she asked, politely.

"Yes, now is perfect", I said, and we were off and running.

She asked me to provide every conceivable detail about my 1518, which I did as best I could over a fifteen-minute phone conversation. There were one or two questions she asked that I couldn't answer, not having owned the watch since new myself, but she said this was okay and that Phillips might be able to provide any missing information themselves, once their experts had inspected the watch in person.

She outlined the auction house's fee structure, terms and conditions, which I was fine with, then we discussed a possible auction date. Sofía told me that Phillips had already scheduled a rare watches auction for Thursday, 18 June 2015, at its sales room in Geneva. That was only four weeks away, which she said would be more than enough time to get my 1518 added to the online catalogue. She also said Phillips would put the word out among known collectors that my ultra-rare example would be coming up for sale.

I asked her for some guidance on price, but she said they would need to inspect the watch before adding an estimated range into the catalogue. We agreed to meet at Phillips' premises in Geneva at two o'clock on the afternoon of Monday, 15 June, three days before the auction, then our call ended and I shared the plan with Winston.

A few days later, I got a call from Gloria at Bonhams in Knightsbridge. She said her team had finished its analysis of the 'Blue Danube' sheet music and invited me to pop back in for a discussion.

Winston joined me this time, as we walked over to Montpelier Street in the late afternoon, with the intention of heading out for a nice dinner afterwards. Gloria hadn't seen Winston for some time so she greeted him with a big hug, which made me slightly envious.

Gloria led us through to a room like the one I'd been in a few days earlier, where we were joined by one of her colleagues. We did quick introductions and made some pleasant some small-talk, before Gloria laid the Danube sheet on the table and her colleague, Andrew, told us what he thought.

"The carbon dating that we did was kind of a waste of time. The age range it gave us was very wide, 1890 to 1940 in fact. We agree with you that the '3.3.12' text is a date and our expert says the handwriting at the top is consistent with the most prevalent style of the early 1900s. The font used in the printed title of the music is also from the same period. Therefore, we're happy to declare that the handwriting at least is from around 1912."

Andrew paused and looked up, maybe to check we were following him okay. We nodded and he continued.

"Okay so, that's the when. Now comes the what. The paper's origins are impossible to confirm, but the discolouration and the black ring mark are evidence of water damage, so despite its apparent poor condition, based on its age and the fact it's been in water, the sheet's in pretty good condition."

I then saw a smirk growing on Gloria's face, in anticipation of what Andrew was about to reveal next. I couldn't tell whether her expression was one of amused mocking because I'd found absolutely nothing at all, or excitement because the sheet I'd discovered was, in fact, something noteworthy.

I could see Winston was getting bored, as was I, so Gloria prompted Andrew to press on.

"We think that the who", he said, "makes what you've found, very special indeed."

I perked up and gave Winston a nudge.

"We think the W.H.H. are the initials of Wallace Henry Hartley, an English violinist from Lancashire", said Andrew.

He watched for my reaction, which probably underwhelmed him.

"Never heard of him", I said, "Was he a world-famous violinist, whose old sheet music is worth hundreds more than the twenty quid I paid for it?", I asked and Winston seemed amused by my sarcasm, which Andrew ignored and carried on.

"He wasn't famous while he was alive, no. But he became so upon his death. Hartley started his working life at a local bank, then moved to Bridlington in 1903 to join an orchestra. In 1909, he joined the Cunard Line as a musician and served on the ocean liners RMS Lucania, RMS Lusitania and RMS Mauretania.

"Cunard then changed the employment terms of all its musicians to that of temporary workers, with Hartley's new employer, a music agency called Blacks, supplying musicians back to the Cunard Line, as well as the White Star Line, on a short term, per-voyage basis", said Andrew.

I thought I saw Winston trying to stifle a yawn, then came Andrew's dramatic bombshell.

"In April 1912, Wallace Henry Hartley was appointed the bandleader on the RMS Titanic for its maiden voyage from Southampton to New York. He died on 15 April 1912, when the vessel sank after being hit by an iceberg. There's no way of checking to be certain, Mr. Larkin, but all our experts believe that the sheet music you found, belonged to Hartley and that he most probably played 'Blue Danube' on the Titanic using this very sheet of music, containing a note from his mother scribbled on the top."

"Holy shit", I said, which got a smile from Gloria. Andrew went on.

"Hartley died in the disaster. His body was recovered almost two weeks after the sinking, fully dressed, with his music case strapped to his body. We think the relatively good condition of the sheet you found is due to it being inside his music case when the Titanic sank", Andrew had finally finished talking and I sat there dumbfounded.

Then Gloria weighed in.

"We have a museum interested in buying the sheet music from you, Bronson. Would you like to know how much they're offering?", she asked.

Hell yes. I nodded.

"£78,000", she said.

"Fuck me", I exclaimed, "I paid £20 for it, for God's sake".

"Happy days, boss", said Winston.

"Yeah. Happy days", I repeated, awestruck.

I left the 'Danube' sheet with Bonhams then took Winston, Gloria and Andrew out for dinner and drinks to celebrate. We had a brilliant time and parted company around midnight to head home.

The next morning, Gloria called to say the auction house would charge me £800 for its authentication services and that the museum would pay Bonhams a percentage for handling the sale. She said she would arrange an electronic bank transfer for £77,200, so I gave her my account details and she took care of the rest.

A couple of weeks later, Winston and I were on a plane bound for Geneva, with my 1943 Patek Philippe locked securely in Winston's cabin luggage.

After landing at Geneva's Cointrin Airport, we took a taxi straight to Phillips' Swiss headquarters on Rue de la Confédération in Central Geneva, just a block from the south bank of Le Rhône river, where it feeds into Lake Geneva.

We were met in a reception area by Sofía who welcomed us with champagne then escorted us to the boardroom where she introduced us to a few of her senior colleagues. A preamble of meaningless small talk must have been a mandatory business practice in Switzerland, so Winston and I endured it whilst smiling politely.

I then asked Winston for my watch, which he removed from his bag and handed to me. I opened the lid of its box and laid it on the boardroom table, then sat down to let the experts take charge.

I looked on with interest as several people in the room put on white gloves to inspect my watch as it was passed around. A couple of guys held it up in the light to look for scratches through a jeweller's magnifier.

They also inspected the box and the documentation, then held a brief discussion in French, which neither Winston nor I understood. Winston's understanding of the French language, it seemed, only extended to ordering vintage red wine whenever I was picking up the bill.

It was a pity they hadn't chosen to converse in German, as Winston would probably have understood every word, following his time in Berlin working for Thomas Richter.

No matter, the room soon fell silent as the Phillips Managing Partner, a man called Jost Amacker, took over and addressed me with a valuation.

"Mr. Larkin, you have an exceptional watch here. We can find no fault whatsoever with its provenance or condition. May I ask, when did you buy it and how much did you pay for it, sir?", he asked.

"I bought it from a banker in New York, on 11 September 2001. The guy I bought it from told me he bought it in 1988 from a guy who had owned it from new. I paid $490,000 for it", I said. Full disclosure.

"Less than half a million dollars? You paid a very good price, Mr. Larkin. Your watch's value has appreciated considerably over the last fourteen years", said Amacker.

I had bought it back then thinking it's value could double over ten years, but if truth be told, I really had no idea what it would be worth at that moment. He looked around the room, consulted in French with a couple of other guys, then looked back at me.

"We think your watch should fetch between eight and nine and that's what we recommend is entered as an estimate range in the sale catalogue", he said.

Winston looked at me to see if the number pleased me or not.

"$800,000 to $900,000. Is that a conservative estimate?", I asked.

Everybody in the room looked at Amacker, who was looking straight at me.

"Are you making a joke, Mr. Larkin? Is this the British sense of humour?", he said smiling broadly.

"What do you mean?", I asked him, seriously.

"I mean millions, Mr. Larkin. Eight to nine million dollars is our estimate for your watch", he said.

Winston lurched forward in his chair as if he hadn't heard him properly.

"Could you repeat that please?", he asked.

"Eight to nine million US dollars", Amacker repeated, "that's an eight or a nine, with six zeros after it, in United States currency", he turned to his closest colleague, "am I saying the number right in English?", he asked and his colleague nodded, slightly bemused.

"Wow", I said, "that's fantastic. I'm delighted."

I mean, what else could I have said? What word in the English language could possibly do justice to how I felt at that moment. I was absolutely elated and rose from my seat to hug Winston. This eased the tension in the room as the Phillips guys all starting smiling, then their boss was ready to move on.

"What would you like to set the reserve at, sir, for Thursday's auction?", he asked me.

"What would you recommend?", I asked, happy for the experts to guide me.

"We've made a number of enquiries with serious collectors and I can tell you that there is genuine interest in your watch from all over the world. I think we should set the reserve at $8,000,000 and I will be very surprised if the early bidding does not blow that figure out of the water, Mr. Larkin", he said.

"That's fine with me. Eight million is good", I was in dreamland.

Amacker stood up and came around to our side of the table, then we shook hands, before he left the boardroom, which signalled that the meeting was over. Winston then finalised some arrangements with Sofía for our attendance at the auction in three days' time, as I handed my watch to one of her colleagues who took it away, hopefully to store it in an impenetrable, ten-inch-thick, cast iron, bomb-proof safe.

Sofía escorted us back to the reception area and arranged for a private car to take us to our hotel. Winston had made reservations for us at Le Richemond, the legendary five-star luxury hotel on Jardin Brunswick's Rue Adhemar-Fabri, on the north side of the river.

We were giddy in the back of the black limousine as it glided through Geneva's busy streets, crossing over Le Rhône on Rue Des Moulins towards the hotel.

The majestic white exterior of Le Richemond was bathed in sunshine on that late Monday afternoon when the car pulled up outside. The driver lifted out our bags from the boot and placed them onto a bronze arched bellboy trolley in front of the building. I thanked him and handed over a tip of ten francs, before looking up to take in this beautiful old building.

It was eight storeys high, with red awnings on the ground floor and red painted balcony railings on each of the floors above, contrasting with the bright white walls as the building rose to a grey stone penthouse at the top. Looking up from street level, I could just make out a perimeter of glass around the outdoor terrace areas on the top floor, and thought the panoramic views of the city and Lake Geneva must be amazing from up there.

Winston checked us in at the reception desk, while I took a stroll around the public areas on the ground floor. He met me in the lobby soon after and handed me a key card, then we took the elevator up to our rooms, which were a few doors apart on the sixth floor.

We each had a one bedroomed Junior Suite and I was surprised by how eclectic the décor was. My room had antique walnut bedside tables and period furniture, alongside contemporary lighting and a state of the art bed, but it all seemed to work beautifully. My room also had a spectacular view of Lake Geneva.

We enjoyed a dinner of sublime French cuisine and Winston ordered the most expensive white wine on the list, a bottle of Domaine Ramonet Montrachet Grand Cru Chardonnay, which cost me a staggering 1,350 CHF.

I didn't care though. It was time to celebrate our greatest deal ever and we spent most of the evening swapping fanciful ideas about what to do with the money.

I went to bed that night continuing to fantasize about what I could do with $8,000,000. I'd long thought about maybe moving back to Scotland and building a mansion in the country one day. I drifted off to sleep with visions of a Palladian style stone portico and a grand internal staircase.

In the morning, over breakfast, I suggested to Winston that we cool the money talk for a while. After all, the watch hadn't even been sold yet. We had some time to kill before the auction on Thursday, so I picked up a tourist map in the hotel foyer and we ventured out to explore the city in the warmth of the bright Geneva sunshine.

We spent the next couple of days sight-seeing, including a visit to the Patek Philippe Museum, which had an incredible array of watches, musical automata and ancient portraits, as well as a horology library.

It was fascinating to learn the company's history as well as the intricate art of watchmaking through a variety of exhibits dating all the way back to the 16th century.

We also visited the Art and History Museum, where we spent almost an entire day strolling around the most magnificent collection of archaeological discoveries, antiquities, artworks, furniture, arms and musical instruments, spanning some 15,000 years of history.

On the night before the auction, I started to feel nervous. So, after dinner we walked round to the Hotel d'Angleterre, a few streets away from our own hotel. We stepped into its Leopard Bar and discovered it had some of the finest cognacs and scotch whiskies in the world.

I noticed a rather decadent looking curved glass bottle on a shelf behind the barman and asked him what it was.

"That's a fifty-year-old Macallan single malt whisky from Scotland, sir", came the reply.

I smiled.

Unbelievably, despite my lifelong appreciation of fine malt whiskies, as well as my attempt to buy a Macallan Lalique Fifty at auction back in 2007, which was foiled by Max, I had yet to try my most coveted of drams.

Time to change that, I thought.

"What's the price for a single measure?", I asked.

"250 francs per serving, sir", he replied.

"Great, give me two doubles please, no ice?"

"Certainly", he said, and began to prepare our drinks.

"You know you just spent the equivalent of $1,000 on our first round of drinks, right?", asked Winston, at my shoulder.

"Of course. Go and find us a pair of comfortable chairs", I replied, shooing him away.

The barman smiled.

"Hey, what's the story with the fancy bottle?", I asked him.

"The whisky was put into its cask in 1949, then bottled in 1999, as a special edition to celebrate the new Millennium. The decanter's an official Macallan Baccarat Crystal design with a copper-lined stopper. It's beautiful, no?", he asked.

"Yes, stunning", I couldn't agree more.

"Do you sell much of it? At 250 francs a measure?", I asked.

"You'd be surprised", he replied, "there's a lot of wealthy whisky drinkers in this town. Then, of course, there's all the rich tourists we get too. The hotel's policy is to always present the empty decanter as a souvenir to the customer who finishes it", he said.

"That sounds cool", I responded.

"Go ahead and take a seat with your companion and I'll bring your scotch right over", he offered.

The bottle looked about a third full. I thanked him, then went and joined Winston at a table with two big leather chairs. I relayed the story about the decanter to him. The barman arrived a minute later and set our drinks down on silver coasters, then left a small jug of water on the table.

"Would you like to pay now, or shall I start a tab for you, sir?", the barman asked.

"Tab please", I said and handed him my credit card, which he took with him to the bar, scanned it, then returned it to me a moment later.

I swirled the liquid gently around in my glass then gave it a nose. All my senses were filled with wonderful warming aromas of honey and lemon. It was slightly woody too with just a hint of peat.

Winston and I clinked glasses and each took a sip.

I rolled the whisky around in my mouth, letting it touch all my taste buds, slowly moving it over my tongue in different directions, several times, savouring the slightly fruity, spicy and smoky flavour for nearly a whole minute before swallowing gently and enjoying its slightly citrusy and peaty finish.

"Wow. That was sensational. This is going to be worth every penny, Winston", I said.

"Best I've ever tasted", he agreed.

I took my time, savouring my first ever glass of the famous fifty-year-old over the next forty-five minutes. Winston finished his glass long before I did, saying he thought it was incredible.

I ordered the same again and we indulged ourselves for another hour with this amazing drink, then the barman told us the hotel had a cigar lounge, so we went through for a look.

I picked out a couple of Monte Cristo cigars and we took a seat at a table. Only one other table was occupied when we arrived in the cigar lounge. We lit up our cigars and continued to savour the Macallan, with me thinking I'd died and gone to heaven.

Then an arsehole showed up.

Just as the barman left the room through a door at the rear, a tall middle-aged guy walked into the lounge accompanied by a smaller man and in the loudest, rudest voice, started barking orders.

"Hello? We need service. Someone get me whisky", he called out loudly.

He looked slightly inebriated and spoke with a German sounding accent, but who knows where he was from. In Switzerland, they spoke three national languages: German, French and Italian, plus he may have been a foreign visitor like us. I could tell he hadn't made a good impression with Winston, who glanced at me and rolled his eyes.

"Hello? Come on we're waiting", he bellowed out again.

He paced the room impatiently, which got on my nerves.

"This is a cigar lounge, sir. Perhaps you should try the bar next door", I suggested to him.

"This isn't the bar? They told me this was the bar. Idiots", he exclaimed and departed from the room with the other guy following behind.

"You're welcome", I said sarcastically after he left the room.

The subsequent peace and quiet didn't last long when the two guys returned to the lounge with drinks a few minutes later. The barman came in too and helped them select a couple of cigars, then he left.

The men chose a table in the corner away from the other occupied ones, but the tall guy talked very loudly, his voice filling the room. Even the people at the other table started glancing at him with looks of irritation.

Within around five minutes, he and his companion were ready for another round and he started yelling out again from his seat this time. The barman reappeared, looking professionally indifferent to the guy's jarring manner. He demanded another round of the same drink they'd just finished, but told the barman to make them doubles.

A few moments later, I watched the barman return with the bottle of Macallan fifty-year-old and poured double measures into each of the other men's glasses, then left again.

I felt really irked by the tall guy. Not only by how rude I thought he was, but also by how fast he'd drained his first serving of such a special whisky with little sign of any appreciation for it.

I had hoped that Winston and I would have the remains of the Macallan all to ourselves, then I could take the decanter home as a souvenir, but it seemed we weren't going to be the only ones drinking it that evening.

I went back to enjoying my cigar and sipping my dram, trying to ignore the noisy man. Then, twenty minutes later when our glasses were empty, I asked Winston to go through to the bar and order another round of doubles. I also asked him to check how much was left in the bottle. He returned saying there looked to be about eight to ten measures left, but once the barman served our latest round there would only be a few servings remaining.

The barman came through with the Macallan once again, and replenished both our glasses. I thought Winston had been right. The bottle looked nearly empty when the barman took it back through to the bar.

I went to use the men's room, thinking maybe the tall guy didn't know about the last customer being gifted the empty decanter. I returned to my seat in the lounge feeling nice and relaxed, courtesy of a nice dinner, a good cigar and my dream scotch. My nervousness about the auction all but gone.

"You're trying to beat me to the bottle, eh?", said a voice from the corner table. The loud guy was addressing me.

I turned in my chair slightly, to face him.

"I'm just enjoying my drink", I said then raised my glass to him and said, "cheers".

It was almost midnight by the time my glass was empty again. The guys in the corner had switched to drinking cognac an hour earlier so I figured we could enjoy one final round of to finish off the Macallan, before I took the empty decanter away with me.

Our cigars had been smoked long ago, so we left the lounge and walked through to the bar to order one final dram. When we approached the bar though, the decanter was gone from its place on the shelf.

Winston and I looked at one another, confused. I feared that the tall guy had beaten me to it. Then the barman appeared in the hallway between the bar and the lounge, holding the empty decanter and my fears dissipated.

He must have been looking for me since I'd left my seat in the cigar lounge, so I walked towards him to accept the decanter.

But as I neared the hallway, the tall guy came into view, his hands outstretched taking the bottle from the barman.

I was horrified. They both noticed my disappointment.

"Ha, ha. I win, and you lose", said the tall man, gloating at me.

What a prick I thought, but said nothing and returned to Winston through in the bar.

"Where's the bottle?", he asked.

"The tall guy has it. He must've finished the Macallan before we came through here. The barman just gave it to him in the hallway."

"That's too bad. Want me to go and take it from him?", asked Winston, always happy to assist me by force when required.

The barman came back and looked very apologetic as I asked to settle my tab. I saw the asshole walk past outside the windows, peering in at me, a big grin on his face as he held up the empty bottle triumphantly.

The barman handed me the bill, which I checked before adding a generous tip, then returned it to him along with my credit card.

Just then, we all heard a loud crash from outside.

Winston darted to one of the windows and started howling with laughter. I joined him at the window and saw that the tall man had dropped the bottle, which had smashed on the ground into a thousand pieces, all glinting in the light from the street lamps.

Serves him right, I thought, smiling to myself. It felt almost worth not getting the decanter myself to see that pompous arsehole drop it, but not quite.

I signed a credit card slip and retrieved my card, then we walked back to Le Richemond and went to our beds.

In the morning, I got up early and went for a swim, then met Winston in the restaurant for breakfast at eight. I was feeling good about the auction as we enjoyed some banter mocking the guy who dropped the whisky bottle the night before.

We packed our things, then left our luggage at the bell stand and checked out of the hotel. We planned to collect our bags after the auction and fly back to London in the early evening.

We enjoyed a leisurely walk from the hotel to the auction house in the warm sunshine, arriving just after one-thirty.

Sofía welcomed us inside and showed us to a lounge that was separate from the sale room, which had a large flat screen TV so we could watch live coverage of the auction. We sat on comfortable arm chairs and watched the screen to see if we recognised anyone, but neither of us spotted a familiar face.

The auctioneer for the watch sale was Jost Amacker, Phillips' Managing Partner, and the room was packed full when he got the auction underway.

The first twenty lots, a variety of brands from Rolex to Omega, all sold around their estimates, then before too long came a series of Patek Philippe models, which also sold well.

After an hour and a half, it was time for my 1518, which Amacker announced as the star lot of the auction, then opened the bidding at 6,000,000 CHF, just under $6,500,000. Several bidder paddles were raised in the room, along with interest from telephone bidders, so the auctioneer had a choice of people from whom to accept an opening bid.

Within a few minutes, the bidding rose to over 9,000,000 CHF, surpassing both the reserve and upper limit of Phillips' pre-auction estimate. I was getting more and more excited as things continued unabated and gladly accepted a cold glass of champagne from Winston as I sat on the edge of my armchair.

Moments later, the price was up to 10,500,000 CHF, with only two bidders remaining, both at the auction in person. They continued raising their paddles, one after the other, two mega-rich collectors battling it out for my watch. Adrenaline surged through me and my heart pounded with excitement at the sheer magnitude of the bids.

Finally, the pace slowed down and with bids being heralded in smaller increments, I reckoned Amacker's hammer would come down soon. After a few moments of indecision and tense pauses in the bidding, the hammer eventually came down with a loud crack.

My watch had sold for a staggering 14,750,000 CHF!

This equated to more than $15,000,000 and, based on the day's exchange rate, over £11,000,000. I was rich and, based on our prevailing arrangement, so was Winston.

We bounced around the viewing lounge screaming and whooping at the tops of our voices, hugging one another and slapping each other on the back. I grabbed a bottle and sprayed champagne everywhere in celebration.

Phillips' staff greeted us with big smiles and hearty handshakes of congratulations. The auction house had made out very well with the sale, earning big commissions for themselves, so they brought yet more chilled champagne and we all enjoyed a glass or two.

An hour later, once I'd calmed down, the auctioneer's financial director told me the buyer had arranged an electronic bank transfer and asked me to check if the payment had arrived in my account. After a few quick taps on my iPhone, I confirmed to him that it had, then I showed Winston the balance on the screen and he hugged me again, elated.

Half an hour after that, Winston and I were again being chauffer driven back to Le Richemond in a black Mercedes limousine arranged by Phillips to collect our luggage. We were then taken to the airport and three hours later we were onboard a plane bound for London.

What a week, I thought. Stumbling on a genuine page of sheet music owned by the Titanic's bandleader, then making a killing in Geneva with the best trade of my life. Incredible.

Before going to bed that night, back in Kensington, I called Francesca in Tuscany. We'd spoken over the phone at least a couple of times a year since Milan and she seemed thrilled for me when I told her all about the previous fortnight. I still thought about her often and felt a longing to be with her again, as I drifted off to sleep.

TWENTY-SEVEN

A few days after our return from Geneva, I transferred a third of the windfall to Winston's account as usual, but felt that I wanted to do something extra special to celebrate how well we'd done.

I booked appointments for the two of us at Savile Row's legendary bespoke suit maker, Anderson & Sheppard. As an extra treat, I also organised a chauffeur driven Rolls Royce to take us there. Winston was ecstatic when we pulled up outside the tailor's premises on Old Burlington Street.

We enjoyed a superb experience getting measured for custom made three-piece suits, which took an entire day, since it was our first ever fitting. We had to make countless decisions on style, fit, fabric and colour, for which I was glad to have the professionals on hand to guide me.

For Winston, the opportunity to have something made to fit his gigantic frame properly made it even more special.

There was a seemingly endless selection of details to choose from, like the number of buttons on the cuffs of the jacket, or the placement of a pocket on the waistcoat. By the end of the day, I was exhausted, but we'd had loads of fun and I had no doubt whatsoever that the hours we'd spent at the tailor would prove invaluable, when we put on our finished suits around sixteen weeks later.

We went to the Savoy Grill restaurant that night, where we enjoyed a world-class dinner along with delicious wine. Over coffee at the end of our meal, I decided it was time to broach a subject with Winston, which I'd been mulling over for the past few months, but had only made a firm decision on after we made our millions in Geneva. I felt apprehensive and had no idea how he would react.

"I'm leaving London, Winston", I blurted out.

He seemed to freeze, shocked by what I'd said.

"I'm going to buy some land up in North-East Scotland and build my dream home", I explained.

He smiled, instantly understanding me.

"We've lived in the apartment and travelled around the world together for twenty-five years. You're my best friend and you always will be. You've helped me immeasurably and we've had some amazing adventures, along with some close calls."

"But?", he said.

"There isn't necessarily a 'but', Winston. Yes, I've decided to move to Scotland, but I've no intention of giving up trading. You've been so loyal and dependable in everything we've done, but you're a multi-millionaire in your own right now and you don't need to work anymore, if you don't want to.

"I'm not saying I don't want you to join me up in Scotland. I would absolutely love that. One hundred percent. I'm just saying, if you want to go off and do your own thing, mate, then this is probably the right time. I'm offering you your freedom, Winston."

He stayed silent for a long time, thinking about everything I'd said, before he replied.

"Bronson", he started, "you've never felt like my boss, even though I call you that all the time. You're more like the big brother I never had. I think we have a great bond between the two of us and I honestly can't think of anything else I would rather do than head to Scotland with you and carry on playing the game", he said.

"You sure?"

"Positive", he said without any hesitation.

"Alright then", I said, "we're going to Scotland", I smiled and stood to shake his hand.

I ordered champagne and toasted our decision, then we left to hit a West End nightclub until the early hours. We arrived home around three in the morning, both worse for wear. What a day we'd had.

The very next day, I started work on my next project: to find suitable land up in Aberdeenshire for building my country mansion. Despite a hangover, I felt inspired and searched online all day, but it was another fortnight before something promising came up.

Around fifteen miles north-west of Aberdeen, in the countryside a few miles north of the bustling market town of Inverurie, a thirty-five-acre piece of land was being sold by a retiring farmer. The area was a mix of fields and woodland, which had stunning views and an enviable collection of mature trees.

Winston and I flew up to Aberdeen to view the land and decided it was perfect. After making a good offer, which was accepted, I made a second journey north a month later to sign missives and transfer the money through a local solicitor, which concluded the purchase. I was now a land owner.

My parents recommended a renowned local architect to me, Taylor Design Services, which had designed several prominent new country houses in Aberdeenshire. After three or four initial meetings, I awarded TDS the job and worked with them closely to design my dream house.

After gaining outline planning permission, then full detailed planning approval once the design was finalised, I awarded the build to a local contractor, recommended by the architect. A month later, the build started and I made fortnightly trips to Scotland to monitor progress.

The house took nearly twelve months to complete, slower than planned due to a particularly long Aberdeenshire winter. When it was finally ready for us to move in, I put the Kensington apartment up for sale, which fetched an incredible £2,750,000 from a young Russian buyer.

Winston and I both then sold our rental properties, which gave me another £2,500,000. I assume Winston did just as well from selling his.

We held a going away party with all our London friends before moving all our belongings north to Scotland. As agreed, I contacted Hugh Hefner in Los Angeles and organised the shipment of the dining table.

We settled in quickly and I instantly loved being back home. I took up hillwalking and rediscovered Aberdeenshire's spectacular scenery. I played golf, visited castles and enjoyed eating out at great local restaurants. Aberdeenshire has an abundance of some of the world's finest produce, from North Sea fish to Aberdeen Angus steaks, wild venison, game and some terrific craft beers.

In early Spring 2017, I was enjoying my morning coffee in the library with the Times weekend newspaper, when I came across a story about a New York crime boss being indicted on charges of insurance fraud and racketeering.

It mentioned Marco Cannizzaro by name and said the case against the Genovese family's leader looked very strong for New York's District Attorney. Later that day, in the early afternoon, I got a call from New York.

"Hi Bronson, it's Marco."

"Hi Marco. I just read about you in today's paper. How does it look?", I asked.

"Not too good. Looks like I'll be going away for a while. Hence, the reason I called."

"I'm sorry to hear that. How can I help?"

"You still interested in the Jefferson collection?"

"Yes, of course."

"I need to put some money away for my wife Veronica and our kids in case I'm out of the picture for a long time. If you buy the six bottles from me at a good price, I should be able to set aside enough money for them to be taken care of."

"Okay. How much?", I asked.

"You're the expert. What's your best offer?

"How about $1,400,000?", I ventured.

"Come on, Bronson. You can do better than that."

"Alright, I could maybe go to $1,600,000", I said.

"Make it $1,750,000 and I'll ship them to you for free."

I thought about it, but it was really a no brainer.

"Alright, deal", I said.

"Great. I'll email you the account details, then I'll ship the bottles as soon as the money clears. Email me your address, and I'll let you know when they've left the States", said Marco.

"Will do", I said, "Listen, Marco. I really hope things don't turn out as bad as you fear. I mean it. Good luck, man"

"Thanks a lot, Bronson. You're a good guy. Take care of yourself. And that gorilla of yours."

"You too", I said, then our call ended.

Poor Marco, I thought. Still. If you play with fire, you'll probably get burned at some point. I told Winston about my deal to buy the Jefferson Collection and he asked if I was going to call Max to straighten things out.

Not just yet, I told him.

I transferred the money to Marco's account within a day or so, then a week later, he emailed me saying the wines were on their way to Scotland. He gave me the vessel name and manifest information, then within another ten days, I finally had my hands on them. The lost Jefferson wine collection. Six wine bottles over two hundred years old.

I took some photos of them and emailed them to Francesca, knowing she would get a kick out of what they were and the fact I'd managed to acquire them.

In her reply, she said she loved the story behind the wines and hoped I'd make a good profit from selling them on. Then she wrote something that surprised me. She wanted to meet up.

It had been five and a half years since we'd met in Milan. I always assumed she would meet someone back home in Tuscany and live happily ever after, but she said she was single and asked me to go out and see her in Italy.

I jumped at the chance and said 'yes'. I was almost fifty-four years old, had never married and had no children. I thought, why the hell shouldn't I go and spend time with the one woman I'd met in my adult life that made me feel the way she had.

Winston came into the office.

"How would you like to do your own thing for a couple of weeks?", I asked him.

"What's up?", he replied.

"I'm going to go and see Francesca in Tuscany."

He laughed.

"It's about time, boss. You've been pining for that woman for years" he said.

"Have I?"

"You want me to book your flights and accommodation?"

"Yeah, that would be great. Thanks."

I printed off Francesca's latest email with her vineyard's location, along with the dates we'd agreed for me to head over there, and handed the sheet to Winston so he could make the travel arrangements for me.

I then went to try on my bespoke Anderson & Shepherd suit to make sure it still fit me as well as when I'd collected it nine months before.

It fit like a glove. They say that's what you get when you buy custom made. It was the best £4,500 I'd ever spent. Looking at my reflection in a full-length mirror, I felt like a movie star. I took it off and packed it in my luggage so I could wear it in Tuscany.

A week later, I was on my way to Italy. The only real downside of being in North East Scotland is that to fly anywhere other than within the UK, Scandinavia or a few other European countries close by, like France, Holland, Germany, Spain or Portugal, you had to take two flights to get there.

Winston had booked me return flights from Aberdeen to Pisa, via London, which took me about seven hours in all. When I landed in Pisa I rented a car and drove south along the coast into the Bolgheri region of Tuscany.

I was booked into a wonderful bed & breakfast just along the road from the entrance to the Masseto vineyard. I arrived there late at night, exhausted and fell in to bed.

In the morning, after breakfast, I walked along the entrance road into the vineyard on a warm, sunny day at the end of April. I wondered how she would look and how we would be with one another. We'd only spent one night together, over five years before, so I felt a little apprehensive, but also excited as I approached the main house.

Then, there she was. Waiting for me in an open doorway at the front of her family home. She was dressed casually in jeans with a simple Breton striped t-shirt, her hair was slightly longer than I remembered, tied up in a ponytail, but her beautiful face was just as captivating as when we'd first met.

I smiled and she ran towards me. We embraced and hugged one another tightly for almost a full minute. When we let go, she had tears in her eyes. She hadn't changed a bit. I pulled her in close and kissed her passionately, and it felt like we were back in the hotel elevator in Milan sharing our first kiss once again.

She introduced me to her mother and father who had come out of the house to join us. I then met her younger brother, as well as an uncle and his wife. They invited me inside and we enjoyed some grappa, before Francesca and I ventured out to the groves where she led me on a tour around the vast expanse of land that yielded one of the finest red wines in the world.

The chemistry from when we had first met was rekindled instantly and I found myself completely besotted. She told me I'd made her feel happy and alive that night in Milan. We laughed about how close we had come to getting mugged. I joked that the two thugs had been lucky Winston got to them before I did, otherwise it could've been very bad for them.

She enjoyed my sense of humour and throughout the whole of that day together I felt we had such a connection that I wish I hadn't waited so long before making the journey to see her.

We spent a magical fortnight together in Tuscany. Francesca showed me how their wines are produced, which I found fascinating. In the evenings we had wonderful home cooked dinners with her family, then enjoyed long walks together around the Bolgheri countryside until dusk.

We spent almost every night together, and the passion we'd felt that first night was still there. It was the most wonderful two weeks I'd ever had. No amount of money in the world could ever feel as good as how I felt when I was with her.

When it was time for me to go, she was tearful and I felt bad for leaving, but we made plans for Francesca to come to Scotland at the end of the year.

We walked hand in hand to my car and parted with a long passionate kiss. I drove back to Pisa and made the return journey back to Aberdeenshire with a heavy heart. I couldn't keep my mind off her throughout, but when I arrived back home I turned my attention to another matter. It was time for me to address the situation with Max van Aanholt.

A day after returning from Tuscany, I called Max's phone number in London and he answered after a couple of rings.

"Hello, Max speaking", he said, a voice I hadn't heard in ten years.

"Good evening Max. It's been a long time", I said.

"Bronson?"

"You sound surprised."

"I am."

"It's time for us to put what happened at the whisky auction behind us", I said.

"And why must we do that?"

"Two reasons. Firstly, because I didn't sleep with your wife."

He was silent.

"That's why you did it, isn't it? You came home from your boys' night out after I'd taken Rebecca home and you smelled my fragrance all over her clothes, right?"

"Yes."

"And, you put two and two together and assumed we had slept together while you were out."

He sighed.

"Yes, Bronson, I did. Are you telling me you and she didn't get up to anything?"

"Of course, we didn't. You were my friend, Max, you daft old fool. Didn't you ever ask Rebecca what happened that night?"

"Yes, but she told me she was a bit tipsy and she bumped into you in a pub, then you escorted her home."

"And?"

"Well, I didn't quite believe her. I wanted to, but I thought she was lying. We argued about it, naturally, but she maintained you never even set foot in our house. I just couldn't believe that you and she, both inebriated, wouldn't, you know, have a fling while I wasn't around."

"Jesus, Max. You have a warped sense of what friendship is. I didn't lay a finger on your wife and I never would."

"But she smelled of you, Bronson. All her clothes smelled of that scent of yours."

"I put my coat around her for the journey home because she was cold."

"Oh."

Then, an uncomfortable silence.

"You knew how much I wanted that Macallan Lalique Fifty, Max. That was you dishing out my punishment?"

"Oh God, I'm sorry, Bronson, really I am. I've screwed everything up, haven't I? I've ruined our friendship and I made sure you didn't get that whisky, out of jealousy and spite. I'm an idiot", he said, then, after a pause, "can you forgive me, Bronson?"

"Do you believe me when I say nothing happened between me and Rebecca?"

"Yes, I believe you. I've been such a fool."

"Okay then. Yes, I forgive you."

He breathed a heavy sigh. Maybe he was relieved that this had been resolved.

"Where have you been, Bronson? Nobody has seen you in London for months."

"Winston and I moved to North East Scotland at the end of last year."

"Wow. Do you like it up there? How is King Kong, anyway?"

"He's just fine and yes, I'm loving it up here."

"I'm so glad you called. This has been eating me up for years. Why don't we get together? I could come and see you up in Scotland", he suggested.

"Well, Max. That's actually the other reason I called you."

"Yes?"

"I've found your wines", I said.

"My wines? I'm not following you, my boy."

"The six lost Jefferson wines. You know, the holy grail you've been searching for, for twenty-five years?"

"Are you serious?", he asked.

"They're here in my house, Max."

"Oh my God."

"What will you trade me for them?", I asked, holding all the cards.

"What would you like?"

"No, Max. That would be too easy. I want you to find something to trade me. Something really special and unique."

"Value?", he asked.

"$2,000,000."

"Okay, I will. Is there a time limit on this?"

"Nope. Just find me something beautiful, something that nobody else has."

"Alright. It really is good to hear from you, Bronson. I'm so happy you called."

"It's good to speak with you too Max. Give me a ring on this number when you're ready to bring me something awesome."

I ended the call and felt relieved that we'd put the bad blood behind us. I looked forward to seeing what Max came up with and wondered how long it would take him to find something worthy.

TWENTY-EIGHT

Braemar, Scottish Highlands
September 2017

In July, an invitation for my cousin Carol's wedding arrived at the house. The daughter of my dad's brother, she was to marry her long-term boyfriend Hamish, on 2 September 2017 at a privately-owned castle estate near the village of Braemar, on the banks of the River Dee in the Scottish Highlands. The couple had chosen Castle Melville as their wedding venue after seeing an article about it in Brides magazine, then visiting the estate in person in the summer of 2016.

Carol fell in love with the place immediately. Among some 350 acres of stunning countryside, the impressive fifty-five-bedroom baronial castle was the majestic centrepiece of the estate.

The owner was Lord Craig Melville, who inherited the estate upon his father's death in 1995. The prestigious property had been in the hands of the Melville family for over 400 years and as the eldest of two sons, the title of Lord was passed on to the forty-year-old Craig, along with the unenviable responsibility of looking after the estate for the next generation.

He lived in the castle with his wife Lady Katherine, a very attractive brunette, ten years his junior. The couple had two grown up children: Edward, a twenty-eight-year-old barrister who lived in Edinburgh and Alison, a twenty-six-year-old vet who ran a private veterinary practice with her husband Donald in the village of Oldmeldrum just north of Aberdeen.

A couple of years after their children left home, Lord and Lady Melville decided to offer the castle and its beautiful grounds as a wedding venue to boost the estate's revenues and offset some of its running costs, which were considerable.

My cousin and her fiancé booked it for the whole of their wedding weekend, so on the afternoon of Friday 1 September, Winston and I set off from our house on the forty-minute drive to Braemar.

I'd never been to the castle before and was struck by how picturesque the whole estate was when we arrived in the late afternoon sunshine. The castle's silvery stone walls shimmered in the sunlight and high above a turret at one end, I saw the unmistakeable gold and red Lion Rampant flag of Scotland fluttering gently at the top of a flagpole.

After parking our SUV, Winston and I were met with the warmest of welcomes outside the front entrance of the castle by Carol and Hamish, as well as other members of both families. We also met Lord and Lady Melville who seemed very nice and I complimented them on what a truly magical setting their home would be for my cousin's wedding.

A couple of staff members showed Winston and I to the bedrooms we'd been allocated for the weekend, which were in different wings of the castle. I was shown up to my third-floor room, which had a terrific view of the nearby River Dee as it meandered around the north side of the estate just a few hundred yards from my window. The mountainous hills beyond were topped with purple heather and I could see a herd of deer roaming in the distance.

I left my bag in the room and went back downstairs to join all the wedding guests. I found my parents and the rest of my family enjoying champagne in a large marquis tent set up in one of the estate's formal gardens. It was good to catch up with them all and we had a great first evening. A catering company set up barbeque stands and cooked all kinds of local meats, including venison, beef and pork.

I left the crowd to go up to bed around eleven, but on my way to the grand staircase I spotted Winston in a drawing room on the ground floor. He was cornered at the far end of the room with Lady Melville pressed hard up against him and he was unable to escape.

I entered the room to see if Winston needed help. He gave me a pleading look when he saw me.

"There you are, Winston. I've been looking for you everywhere. Come and meet my nephew, he wants to join the armed forces and needs your advice", I lied.

At the sound of my voice, Lady Melville suddenly stepped back from him and turned to leave. She looked a little tipsy and gave Winston a funny little wave on her way out of the room.

"Thanks", he said.

"What was that all about?"

"I think she's had a little too much champagne. She's been pinching my arse all evening when her husband's not around. She keeps eyeing me up and down, asking if all my body parts are in proportion", he said.

"You've found a girlfriend. How lovely."

We were about to leave, when I saw an old sporting gun mounted on the wall above a large stone fireplace. We both stepped towards it to take a closer look. It was a twelve-bore Woodward style over-and-under shotgun, in Damascus steel, with 'J. PURDEY & SONS LONDON' engraved on the upper barrel.

"It belonged to my father", said a voice.

We turned to see Lord Melville standing in the doorway. He came in and joined us near the fireplace.

"It was a gift from His Royal Highness Prince Philip, the Duke of Edinburgh. We've hosted shoots here on the estate for the Royal Family since the 1980s", he said.

He reached above the fireplace and brought down the antique weapon. He opened it, checked the chambers and barrels to make sure they were empty then handed the gun to Winston by the stock.

Winston took the gun and performed the same visual checks before closing it. He then felt its weight in his hands and brought it up to his shoulder in a mock shooting position, looking along the barrel as he pointed it towards an imaginary target on the far wall.

"It's beautiful", he said, handing it to me.

"It still fires, you know. I took it out last October when Prince Andrew came here to open the Pheasant season. It shot perfectly true. Not bad for a gun made in 1928. It's a real gem."

I thought it weighed a tonne and couldn't imagine how anyone could shoot accurately with such a cumbersome thing.

"Are you joining us tomorrow morning?", asked Melville.

"What's happening tomorrow morning?", I asked.

"I'm taking the groom and a few others out for a shoot at nine o'clock. You two should join us."

"What will we be shooting at? Birds?", I asked.

"No. Just clays. The bride didn't want us killing anything on the morning of her wedding."

We laughed.

I handed him back the shotgun and he remounted it above the fireplace, then we bid him goodnight and left the room.

When Winston and I were safely out of earshot, I suggested that he might want to keep a safe distance from Lady Melville for the remainder of the weekend. He gave me a look of exasperation and said he'd done nothing to encourage her, but promised to try his best to avoid her all the same. He trudged off towards the opposite wing then I climbed the grand staircase and retired to bed.

Around sixty guests stayed in the castle that night and in the morning, we all assembled in a large ballroom, which was set up for a buffet style breakfast. I grabbed a bacon roll and some coffee then went outside to find the shooting party.

The clear skies of the previous day had given way to an overcast morning. It had been raining through the night, which meant conditions were damp underfoot. I found

Hamish and his best man outside the front of the hotel talking to Winston, alongside half a dozen bleary eyed others who looked hungover and who probably shouldn't have been heading out to play around with a loaded shotgun.

Lord Melville arrived in a four-wheel drive Land Rover Defender, followed by another younger chap in a similar vehicle, who was later introduced to us all as one of the estate's ghillies. The best man quickly rounded up a few stragglers and around ten of us were driven off to a clay shooting range on another part of the grounds.

We exited the cramped vehicles and were led in single file along a pathway through some fir trees towards the shooting area. The ground was very muddy and I almost ended up on my backside as we arrived at the edge of a clearing beyond the trees.

I joined Hamish and Lord Melville outside a small wooden hut in the clearing, while we waited for the others to make it through the woods.

Then there was a sudden burst of laughter and some ironic cheers from over by the trees, as the rest of our group parted to applaud the arrival of Big Foot into the clearing. Winston was completely caked in dirt from head to toe. He must have lost his footing on the path and fallen flat on his face in the mud.

He raised his muddy hands up in self-deprecating triumph to everyone's amusement, which got another loud cheer. His beaming smile made him look even more ridiculous as his shiny white teeth stood out against the black dirt all over his face. I tried not to say anything, but couldn't help myself.

"Winston", I called over to him, "what's with the camouflage face paint? The clays aren't going to shoot back."

The guys found this hilarious and Winston just shrugged. He didn't care in the slightest and took it all in good fun. A short while later, he would have the last laugh anyway, when the others saw what he could do with a shotgun.

After a five-minute safety briefing we all put on ear defenders and Lord Melville loaded a shotgun with two cartridges. He readied himself in a well-practiced stance, then called out 'pull' to the ghillie operating the throwing machines, who activated a crossing clay from left to right around fifty yards away.

Melville tracked its movement with the gun barrel aimed slightly ahead of the target and fired when the clay had reached the top of its trajectory, smashing it to pieces as the loud crack of the gunshot resonated around the clearing. He then demonstrated a straight-away shot, which he also hit first time.

We each took turns shooting at three different trajectories over the next hour and it was terrific fun. The only one in our group not to miss a single clay was Winston. This seemed to intrigue Lord Melville who attempted to compete with him on a series of more difficult shots.

The rest of us looked on in amazement as Melville and Winston traded shot after shot for the next ten minutes, with clays speeding through the air, sometimes two at a time. Some rising away, others dropping and even two clays crossing in opposite directions.

Eventually, Lord Melville started missing, then he himself stood back and joined the rest of us looking on in admiration at Winston's skill with the shotgun. The ghillie tested him with some near impossible shots, yet Winston still did not miss, receiving raucous applause with each hit.

During a pause while the ghillie re-loaded the machines, I handed Winston some coffee in a Styrofoam cup. He drank some, then once the throwers were ready again, he called 'pull' for a crossing shot and just for the hell of it fired the gun one-handed with the cup in his other hand, and still smashed the clay first time without spilling any coffee.

The boys loved it and cheered every shot. Lord Melville looked somewhat indifferent though, he was probably not used to being upstaged by a guest. When the show was over, the groom and the best man badgered Winston to tell them what he did for a living. He simply said he used to be in the army, but hadn't picked up a weapon in decades. This only brought him more admiration from the group, many of whom complemented him excitedly during the short ride back to the castle.

As everyone dispersed, Winston and I went back to the drawing room for another look at the Purdey over-and-under gun on the wall. When we were alone, I prodded a little.

"So, truthfully, when did you last fire a shotgun?", I asked.

"Last weekend", he replied smirking, then he winked at me and added, "I didn't want to spoil their excitement."

We left the drawing room and climbed the grand staircase, which was carpeted with a green and black tartan. The walls were adorned with numerous shooting trophies, stuffed heads of deer, elk, oryx and impala.

When we reached the third floor, we went our separate ways to get dressed for the wedding. I'd purchased my own traditional Scottish outfit a year ago, but this would be my first time wearing it.

My family name originated in Ireland, so there wasn't a Scottish tartan associated with Larkin. Bizarrely though, Winston's Murchison family name was affiliated with Scotland's McDonald clan. Hence, I'd chosen to buy a kilt in the McDonald tartan, along with a sporran, black long socks and Ghillie brogue shoes, which I paired with a white formal shirt, a tartan tie and a dark grey waistcoat with matching Argyle jacket.

Winston had rented an outfit that was virtually identical to the one I'd bought, albeit a supersized version, and I thought we looked fantastic as we gathered with everyone for the wedding in the estate's chapel.

Carol and Hamish's wedding ceremony was both romantic and lively, with the bride and groom reciting personally written vows to one another and everyone belting out the two hymns they'd chosen with great gusto.

Afterwards, the bridal party disappeared to one of the estate's formal gardens for professional photographs, while the rest of us went to the bar inside the castle.

The newlyweds re-joined everyone an hour later as we cheered them into the ballroom for a glorious dinner, along with a mix of both heartfelt and witty speeches, and copious amounts of wine.

An hour or two later, a band called the 'Red Hot Chilli Pipers' arrived and kicked off a momentous evening of traditional Scottish ceilidh dancing, featuring bagpipes and fiddles, interspersed with modern hits and rock 'n' roll classics, rounding off a sensational wedding day for Carol and Hamish.

There were many sore heads the next morning as we assembled in the ballroom again for breakfast, before buses arrived to take everyone along the road to continue the celebrations at the most famous and best highland games in the world: The Braemar Gathering.

The annual games event included sporting contests like tug of war, caber tossing and track races, along with competitions in bagpipe playing and traditional Highland dancing. There was tartan everywhere, along with an almost constant skirl of bagpipe music in the background throughout the day.

Once Winston had downed a few pints of ale, I managed to persuade him to take part in the caber toss. He watched a few of the others first, before deciding on a technique, then when it was his turn, failed miserably with his first two attempts, but the entire wedding party cheered him on regardless.

In the end, his final toss was a complete fluke, which nearly slipped out of his hands during his throw before landing on the grass perfectly perpendicular to his body earning him an unbelievable third place.

The winner was a muscly Glaswegian, called Derek Brannan, who combined his impressive strength with a near perfect technique that resulted in all three of his throws landing squarely perpendicular each time.

A little while later, I spotted Brannan generously gifting his winner's prize, a bottle of scotch whisky, to a young bagpiper. I reckoned the recipient must have spent the rest of the afternoon drinking the whole bottle with a friend, since our group passed by two semi-conscious young pipers lying face down on the grass on the way to the bus park, with both their kilts hiked up revealing their bare arses for all to see.

At least they'd both honoured the tradition of being true Scotsmen, by wearing no underwear beneath their kilts.

We all had a brilliant time at the games and sang our drunken hearts out during the short bus ride back to Castle Melville. Most importantly though, it looked like Carol and Hamish had the time of their lives and I felt very happy for them.

When we arrived back at the castle, Lord and Lady Melville laid on an evening supper of stovies, a traditional Scottish dish of meat mixed together with onion, potatoes, beef stock and gravy, which was served with oatcake biscuits and plenty of wine.

Late in the evening, I found myself alone in the drawing room with Lord Melville, both of us well inebriated, with me trying to trade my Matisse painting for his Purdey shotgun mounted above the fireplace.

I had no recollection of going to bed that night, but woke up with a reasonably firm notion that I'd failed in my bid to persuade Melville to part with his prized possession.

I texted Winston a suggested departure time of nine o'clock, to which he responded with a 'thumbs up' emoji. I then packed up my things and went downstairs to say goodbye to everyone and to wish my cousin and Hamish all the very best before we left.

Just before nine, I put my belongings in the boot of my SUV then drove it round to the front of the castle. I parked it facing the direction of the exit, slightly off to the side so as not to block anyone else's departure.

I sat in the driver's seat for a moment or two waiting for Winston, then got out of the vehicle impatiently and headed back towards the castle to hurry him along.

Before I made it to the front door though, I heard a woman scream, then a man's voice yelling angrily from somewhere inside. I stopped in my tracks and saw a half-naked Winston sprinting out of the castle towards me, clutching his belongings.

"Time to go, boss" he called to me.

"Why? What the hell's going…", I started.

Then I heard an almighty boom.

We both turned towards the deafening sound and saw Lord Melville, who must have emerged from a side door of the castle, striding towards us, shotgun in hand.

"I'll tell you later", said Winston, "just get us out of here."

I jumped back inside the SUV and Winston got in the passenger side just as a second round boomed loudly, with shot fizzing across the roof of my vehicle. I started the engine in a panic and sped off down the driveway before Melville reloaded his weapon, then spied the half-naked figure of Lady Melville peeking out from a first-floor window of the castle in my rear-view mirror.

"You didn't?", I asked Winston.

"I couldn't help it. I was drunk, she was drunk, everyone was drunk. She threw herself at me."

What a rascal I thought, even though I'd warned him, he still couldn't behave himself.

Once we were a safe distance from the castle, we had a good laugh about how ironic it would have been for us to avoid getting whacked by New York mobsters on the other side of the world, only to end up getting shot over Winston's fling with Lady Melville right in our own back yard.

TWENTY-NINE

Aberdeenshire, North East Scotland
November 2017

"What a story, Bronson. Truly amazing", said Max, puffing away on a second cigar in my library.

"It's been a long journey for both of us Max, but in the end, I think we've made out rather well, wouldn't you say?"

"Yes, undoubtedly, my boy. It's been tremendous fun. Oh, by the way I have a gift for you out in the car", he said.

We stood and walked out to the front of the house, passing Winston and Archie who were seated on the front steps, looking like they were having a little catch up of their own.

Max opened the back seat of the 'Marilyn' Rolls and to my complete astonishment, brought out the bottle of Macallan Lalique Fifty he'd outbid me for at the auction in London ten years ago.

I was stunned when he handed it to me.

"No hard feelings, my boy?", he said.

I hugged him and thanked him. Our reunion was complete. He and Archie went into the house to collect the wines, then reappeared a moment later. Max handed me the keys to the Rolls Royce and Archie put the Jefferson wines into their Mercedes.

As I looked in awe all around the magnificent car, Max shared with me it's incredible history, from Marilyn having it customised for her husband, its discovery in an outbuilding after his death, the restoration and sale to the Detroit car museum, then its disappearance after the fire.

Max told me several cars that were thought to have been lost in the fire were found hidden away on one of the Detroit museum owner's properties. The 2012 fire turned out to be an insurance scam and the owner had removed the most valuable cars from the museum before setting it alight himself.

The scam only came to light last year when the museum owner passed away and the executors of his estate found several of the missing cars at his house, which they auctioned off quietly to people in the know.

Max just happened to be in the right place at the right time. He was having dinner a couple of months ago with a close friend, one of London's most revered and respected Bentley and Rolls Royce dealers, who received a phone call from America about the 'Marilyn' Rolls during their meal.

With the car's slightly murky rediscovery being the result of an insurance scam, the dealer passed on the chance to buy it and that's when Max stepped in to acquire it for me.

It was a truly stunning car, a real automotive work of art and I told Max he'd absolutely nailed it by coming up with the Rolls in exchange for the wines.

All four of us shook hands then Max and Archie got in the Mercedes and left. Max had told me earlier they would be heading to Edinburgh for an overnight stop, on their way back to London.

I waved them off then went back inside the house and returned to the library. I went into the hidden room and looked at the now empty table, where the wine bottles had been. I turned and went back through to the library, closing the secret door behind me.

I then walked over to a wall of books at the rear of the library and pushed gently on a different secret door. When it sprung open, I pulled it open wide and walked into another small anteroom, similar in size to the one I'd been in with Max earlier.

The automatic light came on and I took a seat at a round table in the middle of the room. Standing upright on the table, were the real six Jefferson wine bottles that Marco had shipped to me from New York.

Winston appeared at the door.

"What on earth was in those bottles you just gave to Max?", he asked.

"Who knows? Whatever Francesca filled them with. Even if Max is true to his word and drinks them all, there's no way he'll be able to tell they're fake."

"What will you do with these?"

"I'll keep them here and wait. Maybe someday I'll let the world know they've been found. When the time's right."

I got up and left the small room, closing the secret door behind me. Then I stepped over to the rear window of the library as Winston left the room.

I gazed out across my rear garden and took in the magnificent view beyond. The rolling hills in the distance formed a dramatic silhouette in the fading light and the clouds were streaked with a blazing red colour as the sun began to set.

A roe deer caught my eye, grazing in the field beyond the garden. She had two of her young nearby. My movement at the window seemed to startle her and she looked up. Our eyes met and the connection made me smile.

In that moment I felt grateful for the life I'd lived so far, but seeing the deer with her young outside made me think about family, and Francesca. She'd be coming to see me in a month and I wasn't sure I'd ever want her to leave.

Perhaps it was time for me to give up trading and settle down. Get married and start a family. With Francesca perhaps, if she'd have me. Maybe I was done flying all around the world, chasing deal after deal.

I heard the house phone ring somewhere, then it went quiet. Winston appeared in the doorway of the library a moment later with the phone in his hand.

"Boss, there's a guy on the phone who wants to talk to you. He says he's an antique dealer in Hong Kong. He wants to know if you're interested in Ming Dynasty porcelain."

Here we go again, I thought.

"Take his details and tell him I'll call him back", I replied, then I sat back down in my armchair by the fire and savoured the last few drops of liquid gold in my glass.

ACKNOWLEDGEMENTS

I'm very grateful for the help I received from my wife, Fiona, checking my spelling and grammar, as well as some great imaginative content she provided when I was stuck.

Many thanks to my close friend, Mike Barr, for his help with creative content.

Thanks to Claire Ross-Munro for proof reading.

Thanks to my mum, Pauline, for saying she thought it was a good story.

Finally, I'd really like to thank my good friend, Norman Thompson, for guiding me through the writing process. Without Norman's experienced advice, this novel would never have been published.